G000160321

193
1993

3

1993
993

1993

MATTHEWS, PATRICIA
THE NIGHT VISITOR. PATRICIA
MATTHEWS.
F 23-627906

0727815628 1 001

by

PATRICIA MATTHEWS

ESSEX COUNTY LIBRARY
F

This title first published in Great Britain 1988 by
SEVERN HOUSE PUBLISHERS LTD of
40–42 William IV Street, London WC2N 4DF

Copyright © 1979 by Pyewacket Corporation

British Library Cataloguing in Publication Data
Matthews, Patricia
The night visitor.
I. Title
813′.54 [F] PS3563.A853
ISBN 0–7278–1562–8

Hang thy windows with vervain,
Bar the door and light the light,
Pray that God will keep thee from,
The Visitor that comes by night!
—*Ancient Witches Rhyme*

Printed and bound in Great Britain

FF 26828

PROLOGUE

The locked front doors of the Barkley Plaza opened silently, and something entered the pleasant foyer. No footsteps flattened the thick carpet, and no image registered on the watchful eye of the television screen; but something moved across the open space, and began mounting the stairway, its passage causing no more than a slight movement of air.

It had come a long way—such a long way—following the call, which had grown faint with distance; across the water and across the land; searching, hungry, full of desire. And now the call was near, so near. On the first landing there was a door. It pressed close to the carved wood, feeling for the presence of the people inside.

ONE

They were a lovely family.

Those were the exact words that Sal Bartolo, the superintendent of the Barkley Plaza, used to describe the new family, the Gerards, to his wife, Ursula, as she was serving him his usual ample dinner.

"Yep, real nice people, babe," he went on, helping himself generously to the steaming manicotti. "You know, desirable."

Ursula nodded. She did indeed know. Desirable, in this context, meant "good for the building." It meant that the family was "right" for the Barkley.

She sat down opposite him, pushed the fresh Italian bread toward him, then helped herself to the manicotti and the salad.

Sal watched her approvingly. Her plump arms shone in the soft light from the chandelier over the table—eighty-six shimmering, pure crystal prisms. Sal had installed the dimmer himself. The sight of her soft, pretty face and gentle, ample curves made him feel good all over. Maybe she wasn't a kid anymore—neither was he—but she was still a wonderful-looking woman.

Ursula read the message in his eyes, and smiled contentedly. If only the whole world could be as happy as she and Sal . . . there would be no more fighting, no more muggings in the streets, no wars; everyone would be happy just to stay home, do their work, and love each other.

He was a fine figure of a man, still. Just look at him sitting there, enjoying the food she had prepared for him. Look at those shoulders and arms. Look at that smile. The hair was going, but the high forehead only made him look distinguished.

She pushed the plate of melon slices toward him. "So what are they like, the Gerards? What do they look like?"

Sal wiped his mouth with his napkin—real cloth, Ursula really knew how to do things right. "Well, the man, Mr. Gerard, he's vice president of some big corporation, just been transferred here to New York. He's a big guy, taller than me, but not so big through the shoulders. Looks to be about forty. Good-looking, you know, distinguished. Got those white streaks at the temples."

Ursula reached across the table and put her hand on his arm. "I think you look distinguished, too, Sal."

He grinned. "Yeah, he's got more hair, but maybe that's cause he don't go rubbing it off against the headboard of the bed, like I do. Course, he don't have a sexy wife like I do, either."

Ursula giggled, and pinched his arm. "Go on now! What's *she* like, the wife?"

Sal shrugged, and took a hearty swallow of his red wine. "Classy. You know, like Jackie Kennedy classy. Not pretty though. Him being so good-looking, I thought he'd have a real stunner for a wife. Not that she's ugly or anything. She has a kind of style. Oh, hell, you know what I mean, right?"

Ursula nodded. "And the girl, the little girl. What's she like?"

Sal leaned back and stroked his full belly. "A nice, quiet little kid. Pretty, sort of like a little doll. Something old-fashioned about her . . ." He snapped his fingers, and grinned. "Got it! The kid was wearing a dress, and her hair was all neat, with one of those little clips in it."

"A barrette," said Ursula.

"Yeah, a barrette." Sal shook his head. "You know, I don't remember how long it's been since I seen a little girl in a real dress like that. All the kids now wear jeans and T-shirts. She really looked like a little lady."

Ursula rose and started clearing off the table. "Well, she has a pretty important papa. I mean, if Mr. Berando broke his own rule about letting families with children into the Barkley, the man has got to have some kind of influence, right?"

"Right." Sal burped. "Hey, you want to watch 'Kojak' or 'Columbo' tonight?"

" 'Kojak,' " said Ursula. "Tonight's supposed to be a real good one. I read all about it in the paper this morning." She suddenly began rubbing her full upper arms with her hands. "You know, I think there's a draft coming in under that front door."

Sal raised his eyebrows. "Nah! Can't be. I weather-stripped it just last week. Come on, babe. I'll keep you warm."

Arm in arm, they went into the living room.

It moved away from the door. These were not the people it sought. It must find the place. The place from which the call came. Slowly it moved up the stairs. A small speck of dust was caught by the movement and lifted from the floor to float for a second in space, before dropping to the stair. On the next landing was another door.

Tracy Cummings and Elva Miller had just finished clearing away the last of the dinner dishes.

The apartment throbbed gently with the quadraphonic vibrations of a Diana Ross tape. The music suited the funky-chic decor of the apartment—all jewel-toned, pillow-soft seating units, and soft, directed beams of light, illuminating art work and plants. There were a lot of plants. A polished crystal ball glimmered atop a small, carved East Indian table.

Tracy stretched her long, beautifully articulated

arms, and Elva watched approvingly as the thin T-shirt pulled taut over Tracy's surprisingly opulent breasts and lifted to expose a narrow strip of satin brown belly.

Elva shook her head. "You really are too much, girl," she said. "You are a beautiful thing."

Tracy lowered her arms, and laughed lightly. "Well, you ain't too shabby yourself, blondie. For a paddy type, that is."

Elva tossed back her waist-length silver hair. She knew that she was beautiful; just as she knew that her eyes were blue, and that she stood five-ten in her stocking feet. It was a fact of her existence. However, Tracy's beauty was a source of ever-present wonderment to her, and Elva would always be grateful for the course of events that had thrown them together. She often thought that she had never known what love really was until she met Tracy.

"What do you want to do tonight?" she asked. "There's a good film up the street. It's that new thing of Bergman's."

Tracy ran her long fingers through the fluff of soft, black curls that framed her piquant features. "I don't know, baby. I feel kind of spooky tonight. What do you say we get out the old Ouija board and fool around? I feel like 'someone's walking.' "

Elva hesitated. She hated the Ouija board, and the things it stood for, although she had never confessed this to Tracy. She also hated it when Tracy got "spooky," as she put it. For days, weeks at at time, Tracy could get preoccupied with that occult stuff. She'd drag out those books, and those damned tarot cards. When she got that way, she withdrew into some dark, unknown place, where Elva could not follow.

But she smiled, put her arm around Tracy's shoulders, and said, "Sure. I'll put on the drum record. You get out the board."

Elva was continually amazed at herself. She was so good at saying "no," had been all her life, except with

Tracy. To Tracy, it seemed, she could only say "yes."

Tracy opened the board and put it on top of the low, glass-topped, free-form coffee table. She seated herself on a plump, plum purple velvet pillow, and placed slender brown fingers on the planchette. Elva, choosing a deep blue pillow, sat down opposite her.

The soft, thrumming throb of the drums began to fill the room. Elva, with a faint moue of distaste, which she hid from Tracy, placed her fingers opposite Tracy's on the board.

For a few minutes, the pair sat silently, with eyes closed, as the beat of the drums began to swell. Soon, the room was alive with the sound—a sound as primal as a heartbeat.

Tracy started to speak softly, "Is anybody here? Minka, are you here? Come to us, Minka, and advise us."

Slowly, almost imperceptibly, the planchette began to move. At first its movements were erratic, then it started to move in a slow, circular motion. Both women now opened their eyes, and fixed them on the board. Tracy's eyes had a faint glaze.

"I am . . . ," the planchette spelled out, then stopped. "Yes?" Tracy said eagerly. "I am what? Who are you?"

Abruptly, the planchette jumped away from the letter L, darting first from one side of the board, then to the other. Both women watched it in amazement, as their arms were pulled back and forth. Then the planchette went still, for just a moment, before it started, briskly, and in an orderly fashion, to spell out: "This is Minka. What do you wish to know?"

Tracy glanced at Elva. They both realized that tonight Minka, Tracy's regular spirit guide, had competition. Another spirit, another force, was trying to come through.

Tracy smiled faintly. "Minka," she said softly, "who was the other, the one who was trying to get through to us?"

"Up to no good," spelled out the planchette. "Bad. You stay with me."

Elva smiled also at this touch of apparent jealousy.

"Minka, is the other presence a male or a female?" Tracy asked.

The planchette immediately began to jerk back and forth again. It almost seemed as if two beings were struggling for possession. Quickly, it spelled out several words, then slid from under their fingers to fly across the room.

Tracy's eyes were wide, and Elva's face was white, as they looked at the small, triangular piece of wood lying across the room near the stereo.

"What did it say?" Elva asked. "It went so fast. . . ."

Tracy's voice was very soft. "It said, 'I am Legion.' "

It moved regretfully away from the door of Apartment 2. There had been a call, and it had answered, but it was not the *call, not the call which it was following. Still, there was a strong pull, here. There could be pleasure here. It would return. On the third level, it knew at once that it must go on, but something inside drew it, caused it to reach invisibly inside.*

Dr. Ernest Kauffman peered around his copy of the *New York Times* at his daughter, Helga.

The girl was sitting in her usual place, on the couch, in front of the television set, but she was acting distinctly odd.

Normally, she sat with eyes glued to the picture on the tube, unmoving and ox-stolid. And normally, he paid her no more attention than he would have paid the couch itself. The girl, to Ernest Kauffman, was like a piece of furniture in the apartment, although not as useful.

Sometimes, thinking about Helga, he wondered if

he should not experience some guilt about his feelings—or, he should say, lack of feelings—toward his daughter. He knew he was considered a cold man. He knew this because others, particularly his wife, Gertrude, had told him so. He, however, preferred to think of himself as a man of logic, a practical man.

He could not help Helga. She had been to the best schools for the mentally retarded, and she had been taught all that her limited mentality would encompass. She was able to dress herself, feed herself, go to the bathroom, and to perform small, undemanding chores around the apartment. That was all that she would ever be able to do. No, he could not help Helga, but he could help others, and that was where his interest lay.

If there had been only himself to consider, he would have long since placed her in a home, but Gertrude doted on the girl. Kauffman had never been able to eradicate the guilt Gertrude felt toward Helga, but wasn't that the way it always was? The mechanic with the faulty car; the hairdresser with sloppy hair. He could cure other people, help them with their psychological problems; but he could make no headway with his own wife.

Now, for the first time in months, he really looked at his daughter, his attention snagged by her curious behavior. She was squirming. The movement brought to mind the motions a puppy makes when it approaches a person who speaks kindly to it. And she was smiling. Not her usual, rather foolish grin, but a strange sort of smile. He watched her in fascination. Her eyes were not on the TV screen, but turned toward the front door and the entryway. It was almost as if she saw something there.

As Kauffman watched, Helga arose, and stretched her arms toward the closed door, making the guttural "uh, uh, uh," sounds that she used to communicate the fact that she wanted something, then she began kneading her breasts with her stubby fingers, and thrusting her hips in a grotesque parody of a burlesque bump and grind.

Kauffman made no attempt to stop her, but watched her performance with clinical interest. He knew that the girl had normal sex urges, and he knew that she masturbated, alone in her room. This fact did not disgust him. He realized that she had to have some outlet for her sexuality. However, Gertrude had, with considerable firmness, made it clear to the girl that such behavior would *not* be tolerated in public, and Kauffman was at a loss to explain this sudden exhibition of sexual behavior.

At that moment Gertrude came into the room, carrying a plate of cookies and a glass of milk for Helga. She stopped short in the doorway, her face flaming red. "Helga!" she said sharply. "Stop that at once!"

She avoided meeting Kauffman's eyes. Moving with a brisk trot to the coffee table, she put down the food and turned to the girl, who was still going through her peculiar gyrations.

She put her small arm around Helga's beefy shoulders, and pushed the girl's hands away from her breasts. "Helga! Stop; stop it at once!"

The mother's voice finally seemed to penetrate the dim reaches of Helga's mind. She stopped what she was doing, panting, still staring at the door.

Kauffman withdrew behind his paper. Well, whatever it was, was spoiled now. Gertrude would calm the girl, and stuff her with food, until she was even bigger than she was now. He felt a mild irritation at Gertrude's interference. After all, this little episode was the only interesting thing the girl had done in years.

It felt anticipation. What a rich place this was; rich with promises of pleasure. Although there was no one there to smell it, the stairway filled with a lush scent reminiscent of musk and ripe oranges. It moved upward, still searching.

Halley McGuire pulled away from her husband's arms, as they lay sprawled in a nest of cushions before the fireplace.

Vince lazily nuzzled her ear, pushing aside her long, dark hair to sink his teeth gently into the soft, pink lobe. "What's the matter, hon? I thought you were comfortable?"

She shot him her quick, charmingly crooked grin, and then leaned away, toward the front door. "I thought I heard someone at the door."

He pulled her back against his shoulder. "Probably just the new people in Seven bringing up the last of their things."

Halley suddenly shivered.

Vince held her tighter. "What's the matter, did someone 'walk over your grave?' "

She kissed his throat. "I guess so, darling. I'm really not cold; what with you and the fire, how could I be? Where do you suppose that saying came from, anyway?"

He ran the flat of his hand expertly down her back, and over her buttocks, engrossed in the sensual feeling of her firm flesh beneath the thin, jersey jumpsuit. "What? Where did what come from?"

"That old saying, 'Someone is walking over your grave,' when you have a sudden chill?"

Vince shook his head, and turned her so that she was lying on his left arm, face up. Slowly, he began to unzip the jumpsuit. "Don't know. Something about premonition, I guess. Or I would guess, if my mind wasn't elsewhere."

Looking into his narrow, intense face, olive-skinned and gray-eyed, Halley was totally aware of the moment, and her emotions.

Vince was all that she had ever hoped for in a husband, and now that she had him, all that she wanted—

well, maybe not quite all. There was one more thing, the thing they both wanted, and that was to have a child. A child would make it *absolutely* perfect. That was why she had quit her well-paying job, and was going to stay home—being a housewife, relaxing, and, she hoped, getting pregnant.

Halley's doctor had told her that there was nothing organically wrong with her, and there was no reason, that he could see, why she shouldn't be able to conceive. He hadn't examined Vince yet, and Halley wanted to wait awhile before broaching the subject to her husband. The doctor had suggested that the demands of her job, and the difficulties inherent in the situation of two busy, working people trying to adjust their schedules, and to find time to be alone, might be a factor in her failure to conceive. So from now on, a new regime. Vince's recent raise took the financial onus off of her quitting, and he had been delighted by the idea of having her free to keep house, and, as he said with a leer, "cater to his needs." He had added, "I intend to screw you at least once every morning and possibly twice every night."

She smiled now and pulled his head down to meet her lips. Well, he certainly showed every sign of trying to live up to that promise. The only problem they had now was that Vince, a computer expert by profession, was so good at his job that he was in much demand throughout the country for consultations and lectures. As a matter of fact, he was flying to Chicago in the morning, and would be gone for several days.

As Vince's gentle fingers stripped away her clothing, Halley smiled in the firelight. Her body was already awakened and avid for his touch, the warmth of his mouth, the caresses of his fingers, and the hard thrust of his body into hers. She felt very hopeful. Surely, soon, their lovemaking would bear fruit.

Passion fruit, she thought to herself, and smiled again, before giving herself up to pleasure.

* * *

The scent of oranges and musk deepened. The woman was beautiful, and ripe. It would return. But for now, the call was still coming from above.

In the half of his apartment that served as his studio, Steven Street sat in a straight chair, staring at a large, still-wet canvas on an easel. There was no light in the room, except for the moonlight, which fell full upon the canvas, illuminating it softly, and adding a touch of eeriness to the face of the brown-skinned woman cradling empty arms, as if she held an invisible child. The soft light added depth to the woman's eyes, a depth that Steven knew would disappear as soon as the lights were turned on.

He rubbed his empty, complaining belly, and vaguely thought of fixing something to eat. He had been so busy, so engrossed in his work, that he hadn't wanted to stop for such a trifling thing as hunger. He had felt convinced, really sure, during the painting, that this time it would be different. This time, he would come up with "the real thing."

The real thing, to Steven Street, meant something really good; something he would not be ashamed to say he had done; something he would not be ashamed to show. But it was always the same. During the planning, the sketching, the actual painting, he felt that he had it, that it was going to work; but each time the finished canvas was the same. Empty of any real feeling of passion. Bland. Pretty. Superficial.

He kicked out at the easel. It fell to the floor with a satisfying crash, and the canvas rolled awkwardly to the corner, where it lay propped up against the wall, face up, not damaged in the least.

Well, he could always give it to Mother. She loved *all* of his paintings and thought him an undiscovered genius. Steven knew the truth. If he didn't have his mother's money propping him up, he would have starved to death months ago.

He turned on the lights, and went into the other

half of the apartment that he used for living quarters. Modern, comfortable, furnished by his mother, it looked like any other bachelor apartment.

As he opened and heated a can of chili in the kitchen, Steven wondered why he didn't follow the example of many of his friends. He had an income; he didn't need to work. He could have traveled with the other young, beautiful people; followed the sun and the girls, from coast to coast. He could be out right now, having a ball, being with warm, laughing people, instead of ripping his guts out and spreading them on canvas, only to find that somehow, in the spreading, they had turned to strawberry ice cream. Why couldn't he say, "To hell with it," and forget this crap?

Angrily he dumped the chili into a Mexican bowl and sprinkled it with cheese. Taking a few soda crackers from an open box, he carried the food into the living room. Although he felt like hell, Steven knew that he wouldn't give it up. Tomorrow would find him in the studio again, excited over a new concept, a new work, hoping that this time, pray God, *this* time he would come up with something worthwhile.

He got up, went over to the television set, and flipped it on. Kojak's bald head and sensual sneer filled the screen. Now there was one bastard whose life style was something that a man could admire.

Steven settled down to watch the program, hoping that it would lull him into a relaxed and sleepy state. He hadn't been sleeping well lately, and tomorrow he wanted to be rested. He had an idea for a new subject that just *might* work.

It did not stay long at the door of Apartment 5. There were possibilities here, too, but the call was getting stronger, the pull more urgent. It moved on to the next level.

• • •

Isaaic Aschermann could not get to sleep. All afternoon, he had been subjected to the thump and clatter of the new tenants moving in. Although the Barkley was a sound, well-constructed, old building, moving was an inevitably noisy process, and moving men were seldom light on their feet.

He turned restlessly in his comfortable bed. Tonight, the gentle supportive mattress, the smoothly ironed sheets, seemed to offer no comfort. He felt uneasy, and tense.

Bright moonlight, slipping in through a crack in the heavy drapes, struck his face and eyes. He threw back the comforter, arose stiffly from the bed, and padded to the window. He liked complete darkness when he slept.

When he reached the window, however, he pushed the drapes aside and looked out. The moon was full, and hung just over the skyline, in line with his window. The rain-cleansed air permitted a glorious view. Like a huge silver gong, pitted by a smith's hammer, it hung there, before his eyes. Aschermann shivered slightly. He had always been aware of the power of the moon, particularly a full moon. He could remember how, as a child, he would sneak from his narrow, hard bed, and climb out onto the fire escape, to lie in the moonlight, and dream his boyish dreams. And later, on archaeological digs in other countries, the moon had seemed to have a special signficance in relation to the ruins of the ancient civilizations around him. The moon, rising full over a vine-strangled temple in the Yucatan jungle, is not a sight to be easily forgotten.

Ashcermann sighed as he felt the familiar pang. He still missed the classroom; the bookish smell of the halls of the university; the eager questions of the undergraduates; and, most of all, the excitement of the digs. It was nonsense to make a man retire at a predetermined age. In all fairness, he had to admit that his health now made it impossible for him to work in the field; but dammit, he could still teach! Or maybe, he could no longer do even that; maybe he only thought he could.

He wondered what he would be doing now, how things would have worked out, if Rebecca had not died in the ovens of Auschwitz. Beautiful Rebecca, with her white skin and dark, doe's eyes; lovely Rebecca, who had promised, at sixteen, to wait for him, forever if necessary. But he had promised it would only be until he was finished with his schooling and was able to take care of her; lost Rebecca, whose father had chosen to return to Germany in 1933.

By the time Isaaic was ready to send for her, it was too late. Her father had been arrested as an enemy of the Third Reich, and his family had been imprisoned. Much later, he learned that she had died at Auschwitz. It had been years before he had stopped dreaming of her.

God, but he was gloomy tonight!

Even the moon, in its luminous beauty, seemed wrong, distorted in some way. He blinked his eyes, but the illusion would not be dispersed. Regretfully, he drew the drapes. No doubt it was simply another sign of the debilitation of advancing age.

He sighed again, and returned to his bed. There were so many signs now. The stiff knees, the pains in the back, the growing lack of physical stamina and strength.

Snug again in his bed, Aschermann felt a sudden chill shiver his body, and, responding to a habit he had thought long forgotten, he quickly whispered a prayer to the memuneh, the angelic spirits that his grandmother had taught him to believe in as a child. Feeling oddly comforted, he slipped gently into sleep.

It felt something that might be called apprehension, and fear. It drew back quickly from the door of Apartment 6. There was no pleasure here. There might be something else. Something harmful. Quickly it passed up to the next flight of stairs, the last flight, to the door of Apartment 7.

Martin Gerard stood on the terrace of his new apartment, and looked down at the city spread out before him. The wind that blew against his face still bore the bite of winter, and the city lights, and the headlights of cars, sparkled in air cleared by the rain, which had stopped only minutes before.

New York was a busy, vital, no-nonsense city, business-oriented. That was why he had chosen it. He wanted a contrast; something different from the hothouse atmosphere of Rome, a city that would have no similarities to the place and time he wished to forget.

When he had asked for a transfer, they had offered him a choice—Los Angeles or New York. He had toyed with the idea of Los Angeles. He knew it was safer, cleaner, and more pleasant, but he also knew that the warm summer nights, the smell of orange blossoms, were too much like Italy and certain to trigger memories that they all wanted to forget. No, it was better here. Hopefully, he would be able to lose himself in the press of his business affairs. Nina loved the theater and the museums, and she was a big-city girl at heart anyway. There should be plenty to keep her occupied, and take her mind off the past. Maybe in time, she would even be able to forgive him.

He sighed, and turned, going back into the warmth of the living room.

Nina glanced up from the box of books she was unpacking. She managed to look neat, and well-groomed, even involved in the midst of hard work. She frowned at him slightly.

"Martin, have you seen the crate of china?"

He shook his head. "Nope, I'll look for it."

Melissa came in from the hallway carrying a small, paper box. Her cheeks were pink, and her soft blonde hair was charmingly disheveled. Martin's spirits lifted at the sight of her. At least Melissa seemed untouched by all that had happened. He thought, as he always did when he looked at her, what a beautiful child she was. He could see Nina, too, soften at the sight of her daughter.

She went to Melissa and smoothed her hair. "What have you been up to, snippet?"

Melissa looked at her reproachfully. "Mother! You know I hate it when you call me that!"

Martin laughed, walked over to where they stood, and put an arm around each of their shoulders.

"She's growing up, Nina. A young lady has to have a little dignity."

Nina shrugged. "Oh, pooh! It will be a long time before Melissa's too old to be my little girl." She smiled and kissed the girl on the forehead.

Melissa and her father exchanged understanding glances.

Nina saw the look pass between father and daughter, and ignored it. She knew that Martin sympathized with Melissa's impatience to grow up, and she also knew that they both thought she was a little foolish about trying to keep Melissa a child as long as possible. Well, it was a natural thing. Children grew up all too soon, anyway. They grew up and then they left you, and then you were alone.

She shooed Melissa off to her bedroom, telling her she could unpack the box, which contained all her private treasures, tomorrow. As Martin went into the dining room to search for the crate of china, Nina sank down into one of the gold chairs, and let herself relax for a moment.

She could feel the tenseness of her body, the edgy tightness of nerve, bone, and muscle. She even knew why she kept herself geared to this pitch, why she kept busy every moment that she could. It was very simple. When she was very busy she could not think of other things, and it was very, very important that she did not think of other things. Maybe some day, when many years had passed, she would be able to think about what had happened in Rome—think about it and examine it. But not now. Definitely not now. Now she was going to concentrate on forgetting. She was going to keep busy; she was going to enjoy herself in this new home, in this new city. She was going to take care of Melissa, and Martin.

She was going to make them into a happy, cohesive family unit again, as they had been before Rome, as they had been before *it* happened.

Nina shivered, and hugged herself. For a moment she could feel something, something dreadful, pushing at the edges of her mind. She clamped down her steel wall, the wall she envisioned to block out the thoughts she did not want to think, the memories that she did not want to face. She was becoming quite adept at blocking things out. In a moment the feeling went away, and she sighed with relief. Things were going to be all right. They were going to be all right!

There was a sound in the air, a soft sound, like sighing. This was the place. Here was the call. It had found them again. This time it would not lose them.

TWO

Halley McGuire awoke in the morning to a half empty bed. Still partially asleep, she turned and reached for Vince, but the other side of the big bed was cool and unoccupied.

Drowsily, she sat up and pushed her hair out of her eyes. There was a note pinned to Vince's pillow. The morning was dark, and she had to turn on the bedside lamp to read the bold handwriting.

Hon:

Didn't wake you because you were so sound asleep, and you looked so pretty, I didn't have the heart. I'll be home day after tomorrow, and we'll take up where we left off.

Love, Vince.

Still holding the note in her hand, she smiled and snuggled back under the covers. The air was chilly, and the warmth of the bed was seductively comfortable. Maybe she would go back to sleep, but with that thought she came completely awake and stretched luxuriously.

Now, what should she do with her day? In the past there had been no question; it was jump up, swallow some breakfast, take her turn in the shower, dress, a quick kiss from Vince, and off to work. For just a moment she felt a little panicky at the thought of all the unstructured time that lay ahead of her. Well, if things went as they were supposed to, and she got pregnant, that problem would be solved.

She slid out of the warm bed and pulled on her robe. On the way to the kitchen she turned up the thermostat. Spring was late arriving in New York this year.

Halley loved her kitchen. It was bright, cheerful, and, despite the fact that it was located in a New York apartment, looked very much like her mother's country kitchen back in Wisconsin. Halley was an excellent cook, and the walls were hung with every utensil that she needed to ply her culinary skill.

Pulling aside the bright curtains, Halley peered through the kitchen window at the day outside. It was gray and dismal: a terrible day for going out, but a great day for baking.

Suddenly she had the most marvelous idea. She would bake a lovely bundt cake and take it to the new people upstairs. They would probably go into shock, or think that she had come to rob them, but she was going to do it. She laughed at herself when she realized the feeling of daring that accompanied her plan. Well, here, in this city, it *was* daring.

The cake was absolutely beautiful. Halley, her hair combed back and tied with a blue ribbon that matched her blouse, hoped that she looked properly respectable and harmless.

Because of the cake, she took the elevator. Its plush interior seemed to watch her disapprovingly. She smiled at herself in the mirrored walls.

As she approached the door of Apartment 7, she felt a few misgivings, but she shrugged them off. It was a calculated risk. They might think she was crazy, but they might, just might, be friendly and pleased.

The cake was heavy, and demanded both hands, so she pushed the bell with her elbow. She could hear the sound of the chimes inside the apartment.

The door was opened by an attractive woman who

appeared to be in her mid-thirties. She had large, cool, gray eyes, and smartly cut, taffy-colored hair. She opened the door wide, not keeping it on the chain, which Halley found both startling and charming. The women looked at Halley curiously. "Yes?" she said. Her voice was high and clear.

Halley smiled and held the cake forward. "I'm Halley McGuire, from downstairs. I just wanted to welcome you to the Barkley Plaza."

For a long moment the woman looked at Halley, then turned her eyes to the cake. Suddenly Halley felt like an utter fool. This was one of those smart, sophisticated; woman—you could see it in her face and in her expensive clothes; this was not the kind of woman to whom you brought a homemade cake.

Then the woman smiled, and Halley's whole impression of her changed. The gray eyes warmed, and her rather thin lips widened in a shy smile.

"Do come in," she said. She reached out for the cake, taking it from Halley's hands. "It looks wonderful. Thank you so much. Melissa will be ecstatic; she adores chocolate."

The interior of the apartment was cluttered with boxes and packing crates, but Halley thought the furniture was marvelous. All of the pieces seemed to be antiques, and had been beautifully cared for.

"Please sit down." The woman motioned to a lovely pearl-gray love seat. "I'm Nina Girard." She placed the cake on a packing crate and sat down opposite Halley.

"This is so kind of you. I had forgotten that people did this kind of nice thing; or that they used to."

Halley smiled. She was going to like this woman.

"I was afraid you'd think I was crazy," she said. "I did it on impulse."

Nina leaned forward. "Well, I'm glad that you did. You and your cake have brightened my morning considerably. Now *I* have an idea. Why don't I get some coffee and we'll have a piece of your cake and get acquainted?"

Halley started to her feet. "Oh no, I didn't mean to interfere with your unpacking. I know what it's like to try to get settled in a new place."

Nina waved her back to her seat. "Nonsense! I need a break. All this," she gestured at the crates, "is certainly not going to run away, and I'd like you to meet my daughter, Melissa."

"Well, in that case, fine." Halley settled back happily. Nina's cheeks were flushed with a becoming, rosy glow, and she appeared to be genuinely pleased with Halley's company. You see, Halley told herself, there *are* friendly people in New York. As Nina left the room to get the coffee, Halley realized that she had been lonely for the companionship of a woman friend. There were some things that you could only discuss with another woman, because only another woman would understand.

Halley knew the other tenants of the building, at least casually, but she had nothing in common with any of them except for old Mr. Aschermann, with whom she liked to discuss archaeology and history; two subjects that were hobbies of hers. The two girls in Apartment 2 were about her own age, but even though she was tolerant of life styles different than her own, she had to admit that she felt uncomfortable around them. It wasn't as though they weren't interesting, and they were perfectly nice people; it was just that the way they acted toward one another made her acutely conscious of their relationship, and that put her off.

The Kauffmans were simply out of the question. Not because they were older—after all, Mr. Aschermann was older than all of them—but *he* was a caustic, rather cold man, whom Halley found rather frightening, and Gertrude, his wife, was a prim, withdrawn woman with no personality whatsoever. Helga, the daughter, seldom seen but often heard, was an object of pity and embarrassment. Altogether an unlovely family.

The Bartolos were a great couple—sunny-natured, warm people—but their interests and hers were miles apart; and Steve Street, the artist who lived in 5, was so involved in his own affairs that he had little time to spare for contact with other people. So it was nice that the Gerards had moved in. Maybe when Vince came home she would ask them over to dinner; that is, if the child wasn't a complete monster.

Nina came back into the room carrying a large, silver tray. On the tray were three thin, china plates bearing large pieces of the cake, two cups and saucers, a glass of milk, and a graceful silver coffee pot, sugar, and creamer. She set the loaded tray down upon the polished coffee table in front of the love seat. "There," she said crisply. She poured the coffee, then straightened. "Go ahead. I'll get Melissa."

Halley spooned half a teaspoon of sugar into the delicate cup, and wondered desultorily what the child was like. If she were noisy, it could be unpleasant for Mr. Aschermann, who lived directly downstairs.

The child who preceded Nina Gerard into the room was almost startlingly beautiful. Small and slender, she had luminous, milk-white skin, and huge pansy-purple-blue eyes. Her hair, lustrous and pale, shone like a nimbus around her delicately boned, high-cheeked face. She was dressed in a pale-green dress that stopped a few inches above her slender, well-formed knees. Halley felt almost stunned by her beauty. The girl looked unreal, like the personification of an illustrator's dream of the perfect child.

The girl smiled shyly at Halley, and moved toward her, at her mother's urging.

Holding her hands behind her back, she looked directly into Halley's eyes. Nina stood just behind her daughter, with her hands on the child's shoulders. "Melissa, this nice lady is Halley McGuire. She lives downstairs, in Apartment Four, and she just brought us this lovely cake."

Melissa put out a small but strong-looking hand, and Halley took it into her own. "I'm very glad to meet you, Mrs. McGuire," Melissa said.

Halley noted that the child's voice was lower than she would have expected. The purple-blue eyes looking into hers reflected a poise and sophistication unusual in so young a child.

"I'm glad to meet you, too, Melissa." Halley released the child's hand with a feeling of reluctance. What a perfect, lovely child! She would be absolutely ecstatic if her own child even approached the beauty of this girl.

"Your mother told me that you like chocolate," she said, hoping to get the child to be less formal.

"I love it!" Melissa's open smile was all that Halley could have hoped for. In an instant, it transformed the rather adult little princess into a gamine.

"How old are you, Melissa," she asked, as the child picked up her cake and settled herself gracefully in a huge velvet chair.

Melissa sank her fork into the cake, then looked up. "Ten," she said, lifting the fork smoothly toward her mouth. Halley watched as the girl ate. Her manners were as beautiful as the child herself. Her appetite was healthy; she finished both her cake and milk, but she did it in such a ladylike manner that she appeared to be barely picking at the food. Halley, whose own appetite was hearty, envied her this ability. I'll have to take notes, she thought to herself, smiling.

Melissa set her neatly cleaned plate and glass down upon the tray, and wiped her mouth daintily with her napkin. "I'm a Cancer, Mother's a Pisces, and Daddy's a Capricorn. What sign are you?"

The pansy eyes looked expectantly into Halley's eyes, and Halley, startled by the question, rummaged vainly in her mind for the answer.

"I'm afraid I'm not much into astrology," she said

apologetically. My birthday is November second. If that's any help."

Melissa nodded. "Then you're a Scorpio. That's a water sign." Her small face was serious, and Halley laughed somewhat uncomfortably.

"Is that bad or something, being a Scorpio?"

The pansy eyes were momentarily veiled by pale lashes. "Scorpio is a very interesting sign. Scorpio's are . . ." She hesitated, then said, "complicated."

Nina Girard smiled and reached over to hug the child's shoulders.

"I don't know where she learns all these things."

Melissa sat back in the large chair. She grinned, and again for the moment looked like an average ten year old. "Yes you do," she said. "You know you always say I'm an 'inveterate' bookworm." She hesitated only slightly over the pronunciation of the long adjective.

Both of the women laughed. Halley felt relaxed and at home, but she realized that she must leave and let the other woman get on with her unpacking.

Halley was just mentally framing her goodby, when Nina emitted a sharp exclamation and looked at her watch.

"Oh, my God! I'd forgotten that I have to go downtown to take care of some business. My appointment is for one o'clock, and it's after twelve."

Halley jumped to her feet. "I'm so sorry!"

Nina shook her head. "Not your fault; mine. I really don't want to go. Melissa, you'd better get ready."

"Mama, I don't feel so well."

Both women looked at the child who was leaning back in the large, blue chair. The blue fabric accented her luminous pallor, but now a rosy flush brushed her cheekbones and her eyes had a glazed look.

"Oh my," said Halley, "I hope it wasn't my cake."

Quickly Nina pressed experienced fingers against the girl's forehead. She shot a quick smile at Halley. "You can relax. It's not the cake. She seems to be running a fever." At that moment, Melissa sniffed.

"Probably a cold." Nina glanced at Halley and shrugged. "Wouldn't you know? I guess I'd better call and cancel my appointment."

Halley leaned forward. "No, don't! I'll stay with Melissa."

Nina hesitated. "I hate to impose, but this *is* important. Are you sure you won't mind?"

Halley grinned. "I'll love it. I miss my own younger brothers and sisters, and besides, I can use the practice. I'm trying to have a child of my own."

The small lines that had been forming around Nina's eyes and mouth suddenly smoothed out.

"All right. I won't be long. I really appreciate this."

Halley waved aside her thanks. "It's no bother. After all, what are neighbors for?"

"Well now," Halley said. "I think it might be a good idea for you to take an aspirin, and lie down for a while."

Melissa smiled wanly and nodded. "I guess so."

"Where's your room?"

Melissa got up and led the way to her room, which was at the end of a hallway. It was a pretty, bright room, even though it was filled with a clutter of unpacked cartons. The four-poster, canopied bed, painted white and gold, was the bed that Halley had dreamed about but never had as a child. There was a delicate matching dresser and two fragile night tables. When everything was in its place, it would be the perfect room for the perfect little girl. Halley couldn't help experiencing a touch of envy on behalf of herself as a child.

"It's a lovely room," she said, leading Melissa toward the bed.

Melissa glanced up at her. "Yes, it is nice," she said in a serious, adult way that amused Halley.

"Now, I don't think you'd better lie down in that pretty dress. Where's your robe?"

Melissa pointed toward the closet. The closet door

stood partly open. Inside, Halley found a multitude of pastel dresses, small patent leather shoes, boots, coats, caps—it was unbelievable, particularly when you considered that the child would soon outgrow the clothing and it would have to be replaced.

Melissa looked at her, a serious expression on her small face.

"I don't even wear them all," she said as if she knew what Halley was thinking. "But Momma keeps buying them. My robe's on a hook at the side."

Halley found the robe, a soft, lavender, brushed-nylon garment with a high bodice and a full skirt. Feeling the fabric, she could guess the approximate cost.

Melissa had pulled her dress over her head, and sat revealed in pale blue panties, fringed with what looked like imported lace. Her narrow, breastless body gleamed like fine satin.

Again, Halley was caught by the girl's beauty. If her looks did not change, someday Melissa would be one of the world's most beautiful women.

Melissa offered her slender arm, and Halley slipped the soft robe over it, around the narrow shoulders, and onto the other arm. Melissa started doing the buttons, as Haley removed her black, patent leather shoes and stockings.

Melissa leaned back against the pillows, and Halley pulled the beautiful crocheted coverlet over her legs.

"Now, I'll get you the aspirin—that is if you'll tell me where it is."

Melissa pointed to the bathroom door next to the closet, and Halley, after tucking the coverlet around the child's legs, went to find the aspirin.

The search took her a few minutes, as the medicines were in a box which was still packed. When she returned to the bedroom, she saw that Melissa was holding a small carton on her lap. The girl looked up and smiled.

"I didn't get out of bed," she said earnestly. "The

box was there, on the chair." She pointed to the chair next to the bed. Halley set the aspirin bottle on the night table. "Are those your special things?"

Melissa nodded. "My special things. I carried them all the way from Rome on my lap. When you ship things, sometimes they get broken."

"They certainly do," Halley agreed. "Now, I'll get you something to wash down the aspirin. Where's the kitchen?"

"On the other side of the living room," Melissa's face seemed more flushed. Halley put a hand to her forehead, but it seemed no hotter than before. "I'll be back in a minute."

Melissa smiled, and turned her attention to opening the carton.

When Halley returned with a glass of orange juice, Melissa had the carton open, and various objects spread around her on the bed.

Halley had to admit that she was curious. Just what things would such a pampered, privileged child consider special?

As Halley put the juice on the night stand, she looked at the articles on the bed. She couldn't help but smile. As might have been expected, the beautiful child loved beautiful things. A scarf, filmy as the rainbow, whose colors it echoed; a long, silver chain with a silver pendant; a tiny, jeweled box; a figurine, whose form Halley could not make out, as it was partly covered by the scarf; and a magnificently carved wooden chest, about eight inches long. These were museum pieces, collectors' items, not things for a child to play with!

Halley let out her breath in a long sigh. "Those are really very special things," she said wryly. "They're very lovely."

Melissa looked at her, smiling shyly. "They are, aren't they?" She rubbed her fingers over the polished surface of the small chest. "Would you like to know where I got them all?"

"I'd love to, but first, the aspirin."

Melissa opened her mouth obediently, and Halley placed the tablet on the child's tongue and handed her the juice. Melissa drank it down, then leaned back against the pillows.

"I got this scarf in Paris. It's a 'designer original.'" She spoke the last two words as if quoting. "Mother always lets me get something—a memento—from every place we go. Isn't it beautiful?" She waved it through the air. "It looks just like a piece of rainbow, doesn't it?"

Halley nodded. "I was thinking just that."

Melissa picked up the figurine. The small, perfectly proportioned figure was that of a woman with the head of a cat.

"Bast," said Halley.

Melissa nodded. "I got it when we went to Egypt." Then she picked up the silver pendant and swung it so that it caught the light. "This came from England." She stopped the pendant's movement. "See those?" she said and pointed to the two hybrid figures standing back to back, forming the pendant. "Those are griffins!"

Halley smiled. "They certainly are. My, you do know a lot for a young lady."

Melissa's sudden grin again made her look engagingly ordinary. "I do, don't I?" she said.

"And where did you get the lovely box?"

Melissa's small fingers delicately traced the design on the box.

"In Italy. It's my favorite treasure." She leaned forward conspiratorily. "Do you know why?"

"No," said Halley. "Tell me."

Melissa's voice was a whisper. "Because *he* gave it to me!"

Halley lowered her voice also. "Who is *he*?"

"Dion. He gave it to me, and told me that I should keep it close to me forever!" She said the last words triumphantly.

Halley tried to keep her expression serious. "Well, I must say that is very romantic. Is there anything in the box?"

Melissa nodded, turned the box around so that the front faced Halley, and lifted the lid.

Inside the box, on a bed of velvet, nestled a small, onyx carving. It was oval in shape, and the design was very convoluted and sinuous. At first glance, it was impossible to make out what the design represented.

Slowly Halley became aware of a soft, pleasant scent. She inhaled deeply. Why, it smelled like ripe oranges, ripe oranges, and incense; or a musky perfume!

Melissa was holding the box toward her, staring at her intently. For some reason she could not explain, Halley was aware that she was uncomfortable. It suddenly seemed unnaturally warm in the room, and the heavy perfume had become intensely cloying. Also, she was aware of the fact that she was reluctant to touch the carving, although why, she had no idea.

Finally, forcing herself, she reached forward and picked up the stone. It felt warm and vital in the palm of her hand, the pattern suddenly like a living thing. As she stared at the complicated design, suddenly the pattern became clear. The carving was a representation of two lovers, bodies intertwined in the most intimate of embraces. Hastily she put the stone back into its velvet nest. As she did so, her eyes met Melissa's. The child smiled sweetly. "Isn't it pretty?"

Halley swallowed. "Yes, lovely." She couldn't resist asking the question, "Do you know what the carvings mean?"

Melissa shook her head from side to side. "Oh, they aren't meant to be anything, I guess. Just a design." She carefully closed the box and slid down until her head rested upon the pillows. "I'm getting kind of sleepy. I guess I'll take a nap now."

Halley, her lips set firmly in an expression of disapproval, pulled the coverlet up around the girl's shoulders. Now what kind of an idiot would give an erotic carving to a small girl? Evidently Melissa didn't realize what the carving depicted, but surely her parents had seen the thing. She reached down to remove the box from the bed, but Melissa covered it with her hand. "No, I like to sleep with it next to me." Halley stood still for a moment as the girl's eyelids closed. Should she mention the box and its contents to Nina Girard? Well, it really wasn't any of her business. She yawned, realizing that she too felt very drowsy.

She left the bedroom, closing the door softly behind her, and yawned again. It was probably the heat in the apartment. Evidently, Nina Girard liked to keep the thermostat set high. It was much, much too hot.

Halley went to the kitchen and got herself a glass of water. She could still smell that scent. She drank the water thirstily, feeling odder by the minute. Not only was she drowsy, but she felt strange and sort of spacey, like she had been drinking or something. Maybe she was coming down with the flu; sometimes it hit her like this.

At that moment she heard the sound of a key in the front door, and Nina Girard came into the room, her cheeks pink from the outdoor cold.

Halley stifled another yawn and went to meet her. After reassuring Nina that taking care of Melissa had been no trouble, and promising that she and Vince would come to dinner one evening, Halley said goodbye. She wanted to get to her own apartment and lie down.

As the elevator moved slowly down to the fourth floor, Halley looked at herself in the mirrored walls, searching for pallor or other signs of illness. For an instant she experienced a feeling of vertigo as her image in the mirror seemed to swirl and move. She had a sudden glimpse of her face, vivid with color, her hair tousled; and for just a moment—a moment so brief she could not be certain it happened—she thought she saw another face as well, a male face, with great, dark, mocking eyes.

Halley shook her head, as if trying to shake out the disturbing image. The elevator doors opened, and she stumbled as she stepped over the sill. She really did feel awfully strange.

Inside her apartment, in her bedroom, she was too sleepy to draw down the spread; she simply dropped across the bed, and surrendered to the drowsy feeling that had been pressing in on her. Before she sank entirely into sleep, she noticed that the odd, orangy scent seemed to have followed her from the Girards' apartment.

THREE

The movement of the bed aroused Halley only partially, just enough to make her peripherally aware of the fact that someone was in the room with her, and was seated on the bed, beside her.

Still cradled in the warm comfort of the dream she had been experiencing, she was only slightly surprised that Vince was home. Briefly, as if just touching her awareness, came the thought that he must have finished with his business early. She murmured his name, or thought she did. She was so deliciously drowsy that she was not certain, and really didn't care.

In this pleasant state, she felt the touch of his hand as his fingers slid down her back. His touch was warm and gentle and felt good against her bare skin. He bent and kissed her ear, as his hand continued down her back and over her bottom. She was mildly surprised that his hand was unhindered by clothing, but the thought seemed too complicated to follow. She knew that she should wake up and greet him properly, but this thought too drifted away into the soft haze that surrounded her.

His hands were on her waist now, and he was turning her over. She let herself be moved, not opening her eyes, and lay passive as he leaned over and kissed her lips. She was subliminally aware that he was not wearing his usual shaving lotion, but something different, something warm and spicey. She accepted his kiss, which was long and passionate. His lips were warm, almost hot, and his tongue pressed between her lips and teeth with an insistent sensuality that aroused her body, while her mind remained drowzy and detached.

His lips moved down her throat and over her breasts. His tongue teased her nipples, then moved down her stòmach, abdomen, and into the secret place; until she moaned her desire that he enter her. She heard her own voice, strange and peculiarly unhuman sounding, as if she was listening from a far place. She felt him astride her, felt him enter her gently. He seemed to fill her as he never had before. She came to climax quickly, feeling the hot rush of fluid inside as he joined her. She relaxed back into the pillows, as his hands lingeringly left her body. In a moment, she knew, she would be back asleep. She hoped that Vince wouldn't mind. It had been lovely, being made love to like this. She felt passive and sublimely satisfied as she drifted back to sleep.

Steven Street put down his palette knife and stood back from the large canvas resting on the easel in front of him. It was growing dark, and the light was going, but it did not matter. It was finished.

He wiped his hands on the towel at his belt, not taking his eyes from the painting. He was tired, but for the first time in months he felt really alive.

Dammit! It was *good*! Different than anything he had ever done, but with a strength, a reality about it that none of his other work had ever touched; even though the subject carried more than a touch of the fantastic, and even though the idea for the painting had come to him out of nowhere.

He had been sitting there—lying almost—in the large chair with his feet up on the ottoman, feeling drained, angry, and hopeless, and he had dozed off; or at least he thought he had.

As he sprawled there, his mind empty of thought, a

scene had come into his mind. It was almost as if he was suddenly looking through a secret window into someone else's room, a bedroom. There on the bed was a beautiful woman, slender and dark-haired, lying on the blue coverlet of a king-sized bed. She was on her side, her hands tenderly curled in the sweet vulnerability of sleep. She looked very lovely curved against the blue of the spread, with her dark hair swirled around her head in a graceful fan.

Then, as he watched, she moaned and sat up. He could see her face, eyes wide and sleep-drugged, unseeing. Then she smiled—a strange Mona Lisalike curving of the lips—and began to remove her clothing slowly and sensously. He could feel himself growing aroused as she removed her blouse, disclosing round, ripe breasts, rosy nippled and perfect. Slowly, with deliberate, sensous movements, she slid out of her long pants and briefs. He could feel his heart pounding as the dark triangle of pubic hair and her slender, well-shaped legs were exposed. She flung the garments to the floor, near the bed; then lay back, arms outstretched, like a sacrifice. Her eyes were closed now, but her lips still bore the same anticipatory smile.

Then, he saw that she was not alone. There was someone else, a man, sitting on the edge of the bed. Surely he had not been there before. Steven blinked his eyes. For some reason, it was difficult to focus on this second figure. He had an impression of height, broad shoulders, dark skin, but no matter. What mattered was what he was doing to the girl. Desire coursed through Steven's body. My God, what he would give to be in that young man's place!

But then the artist took over. What a magnificent picture they made—the two beautiful bodies intertwined there on that blue bedspread—the bronze of his body, the pale ivory of hers, the placement of their limbs. Steven caugh a glimpse of the man's upright organ and felt a sense of wonder. My God, what an instrument!

He remembered leaping from his chair as he awoke to the sight of his own studio, awake, but still possessed by the vividness of the dream, as his own swelling member attested.

Feeling like a sleepwalker, he had grabbed his palette and paints and squeezed out the worms of vivid color, still seeing the girl's face as she had come to climax, still seeing the beautifully curved musculature of the male as he had mounted her. Hurridly he began to lay the paint upon the canvas. He must capture that tender violence and rapture.

And he had. Now, as he looked at the painting, Steven felt a sense of wonder. By God, it *was* good!

On a field of blue lay the woman, smiling mysteriously, eyes closed, body open to the male who was poised above her, just entering her body. Against the pale, clearly delineated body of the woman, the male body was darker, less clear, suggesting a mutability, an ambiguousness, that made the figure mysterious and slightly frightening, like a figure in a dream.

Steven saw that he had given the male figure horns, short stubs that glinted among the black curls above the beautiful, but not completely defined, face. He drew in his breath, realizing that he had painted an archetype—the dream prince, the demon lover who has inhabited the fantasies of women for thousands of years. If this painting conveyed to others what it conveyed to him, if others could see in it the power that he saw, well he just might make it as a painter after all.

My God, he had to get someone to look at it, someone who knew something, someone whose opinion he could trust. He picked up the phone and called the Winslow Gallery. When the secretary answered, he asked to talk to Wilma King.

* * *

Halley was cold, and suddenly very much awake. Confused for the moment by the disorientation of a quick awakening, she stared at the window, which was almost dark. Why, it must be late. Had she slept all afternoon?

Aware of the cold again, she looked down at her naked body curled on top of the bed. Then she remembered and smiled. Vince had come home early. She stretched mightily, thinking that at least he might have covered her, and wondered where he was; probably in the kitchen, getting something to eat. Sex always gave Vince an appetite.

Getting up from the bed, she padded to the thermostat and turned it up a few degrees, then went into the bathroom, where she washed away the signs of her recent seduction—for that's the way she felt.

Funny, wasn't it? After three years of marriage, to feel that her husband had seduced her. Still it was a nice feeling; romantic.

She looked at her face in the bathroom mirror—pink-cheeked and bright-eyed. She and Vince should have good-looking children; and maybe, if she were very lucky, at this very minute she might be harboring the genesis of their first child.

She stuck out her tongue at the expectant face looking back at her from the glass. "Romantic," she murmured happily.

Hair brushed and lips glossed, she pulled a warm caftan over her head and opened the bathroom door, calling out, "Vince . . ."

The words died on her lips. The rest of the apartment was dark; dark and cold. Feeling a peculiar panic, Halley flicked on the lights, calling Vince's name again and again as she went from room to room. The apartment was empty. There was no sign of Vince.

In the living room she dropped down onto the gold sofa and drew her legs up under her. Where could he have gone? She stared blankly at the front door, until, with a sudden cold awareness, she found that she was looking at the deadbolt, which was firmly drawn. If the door was still locked from the inside—as she always kept it when she was alone—how had Vince gotten in? *How had he gotten in*?

She sat there for a long moment, eyes still fixed on the door. Had she been dreaming? She shook her head and leaned forward, hiding behind the dark curtain of her hair. She remembered waking, or at least partially waking, and despite her drowsiness the experience had been very real.

Suddenly she pulled up her caftan and pressed her hand against the soft hair of her pubic mound. There had been semen. She had washed it away; or was that part of the dream too?

A wave of confusion swept over her. Since it was obvious that no one had entered the apartment, the only possible conclusion was that she had been dreaming. Gingerly she touched the experience in her mind. Her body felt *used.* She had lain down fully clothed! Oh, God, but she wished Vince was here!

Wilma King stood well back from the painting, the slender fingers of her left hand propping up her strong, stubborn chin, as her right hand cradled her left elbow. Steven Street stood beside her, nervous as a bridegroom, awaiting her opinion.

When the silence seemed to stretch interminably, Steven prompted her. "Well, Wilma? What do you think? Am I crazy, or is it really good?" He hoped that she would never know the effort it took for him to say those words so casually.

Wilma dropped her arms and turned to him with a hundred-watt smile that livened her rather plain face into near beauty.

"You're not crazy Steven. It *is* good! *Very* good!"

She moved closer to the canvas, then stepped away again, shaking her head. "I can't get over it. It's such a departure from your usual style and subject matter;

but I love it. It has power and a sort of gut-level appeal."

She turned to him. "Now, how soon can you have some more for me? I think it would be best to get together enough canvases for a showing before we try to sell them, don't you?"

Steven looked at her, dumfounded. More? Could he do more? The inspiration for this one had come out of nowhere—could he do it again? He began to sweat.

"Of course," he said, taking her arm. I'll do enough for a show, and then we'll spring me upon the public in a blaze of glory. I'll be a sensation!"

She laughed, and kissed his cheek. "You will, you know. I'll stake my professional reputation on it."

He smiled and kissed her back. He could tell that if he urged her she would stay, but he felt drained and exhausted, incapable of coping with any kind of a personal exchange at this time. He just wanted to be alone to think about what was happening. He just wanted to be alone so that he could figure out whether or not he would be able to paint like this again.

FOUR

In the bedroom of the first-floor apartment, Sal Bartolo yawned and knuckled the residue of sleep from his eyes. Turning toward his wife, he noted with pleasure that she was just as attractive in sleep as she was when awake. Her short, dark hair was touseled and sexy-looking, and her face was peaceful and rosy. The covers were pushed down on the outside of the bed, and one firm, plump shoulder was exposed.

Sal gazed at the shoulder with proprietary appreciation, and debated whether or not he should wake her for a quick one before breakfast. No matter what time of day or night, whether she was sleeping, ironing, doing dishes, or watching television, Ursula never seemed to mind being interrupted for sex. Sal always listened to the jokes—"My wife always has a headache. Do you know how to stop a girl from having sex? Marry her!"—with smiling complacency. Maybe that's how other women were, but not his Ursula.

Suddenly, he blinked uncomfortably, as the sight or Ursula's white shoulder triggered a throught—no, a fragment of a dream. Broken images of soft flesh and eager lips came for a moment to the forefront of his mind. Grimacing, he pushed them away. So he'd had a sexy dream. Lots of guys did. He gave a brief moment to the thought that he, Sal Bartolo, seldom had such dreams—probably because he didn't need to. So it was unusual, but so what? He didn't want to think about it. What he wanted to think about was Ursula and her soft shoulders and plump breasts and . . . smiling, he lifted the covers and slid over against the warm body of his wife. Ursula smiled and snuggled closer without even opening her eyes.

Tracy Cummings slid out of bed and slipped the flowing caftan over her body in what seemed to be one fluid movement. Barefoot, she padded through the living room into the kitchen, where she put the kettle on to boil, and rummaged in the refrigerator for the makings of breakfast.

The two girls had, early on, decided that each of them would do her own cooking—except for dinner, which they took turns preparing.

Usually, the two women awakened at approximately the same time, and breakfasted together; but this morning Tracy was just as glad that Elva was still asleep. She had experienced a very pleasant, very vivid dream last night, and as was often the case with her dreams, the mood and feeling stayed with her.

Tracy's dreams were invariably vivid; she usually remembered them, and they often seemed almost as real as her waking life. If the dream were pleasant, she basked in the remembered warmth of it the whole day; if unpleasant, the bad feeling stayed with her, just as much as it would have if the dream incident had been real.

This dream now . . . her hand stopped just short of putting a slice of whole grain bread into the toaster. This dream had been something else. She had been in a garden—a lush, opulent sort of old-fashioned garden, like you never saw anymore. Tracy stood frozen as her mind turned inward, following the chain of tantalizing bits and pieces that she could remember from the dream.

She had been lying on the grass near a marble fountain. There had been birds singing, and the air had smelled of flowers. A young man, skin smooth as satin and eyes like black velvet, had been making love to her there on the grass, and it had been wonderful; more wonderful than any lovemaking she had ever known.

She jumped as the whistle on the tea kettle noisily announced that the water was boiling. Quickly she removed the kettle from the burner and turned off the flame.

She found it difficult to concentrate on the ordinary mechanics of her morning procedure. She had to fight the desire to go back to bed, to think about the dream until she was caught up in it again.

She shook her head, feeling a little guilty. She had not even looked at a man since she met Elva. With Elva it seemed that she had found what she had always been searching for—a sharing, warm relationship. The sex part had seemed to come as a natural extension of the feeling that the two of them had for each other. It hadn't really seemed strange or unnatural, even when she had pondered it; as she had. Examining the relationship in the light of her early upbringing, it should have seemed abhorent. Intellectually she recognized this, but emotionally she did not feel this way. She had never had a satisfactory relationship with a man. Of course she was young, but most girls had been in love dozens of times by the time they were her age. And most of the girls she knew had not only been in love, but had been involved in several affairs of varying intensity. Tracy had kept wondering when it was going to happen to her. And then she met Elva. . . .

She made herself put the bread into the toaster and push down the timer.

"Morning, sunshine! What on earth are you doing up at the crack of dawn?"

Tracy jumped, hitting her hip bone on the knob of the silverware drawer. She turned to see Elva, sleep-touseled and long-legged in her black shorty nightgown, standing in the doorway. The blonde girl yawned and stretched like an awakening cat.

"Mmmm. I slept like the veritable dead last night. Fell asleep and didn't know a thing until I woke up."

She padded toward Tracy and put her sleep-warm arm over the other girl's shoulder. Tracy felt herself stiffen guiltily, and then, consciously, made herself relax. My God! She was acting as guilty as if she had really had an affair last night. This was ridiculous. She smiled and pulled up the shoulder strap of Elva's gown.

"Sit down, baby. A cup of coffee will fix you up."

Elva yawned again, and sat down. "It'd better. At these prices it had better be a goddammed miracle cure!"

She smiled, and combed her hair with her fingers. "Have you noticed how much better it tastes since it's worth its weight in gold?"

Tracy mixed two cups of instant and put one of them in front of Elva. "Hey, baby?"

Elva took a long swallow from the steaming cup. "Mmmm?"

"I'd like to have a meeting tonight. Are you going to be home at the usual time?"

Elva swallowed her coffee before answering. She tried to keep her voice noncommital. "Don't you think it's kind of short notice? I mean, Maryann's out of town, and Billy and George have theatre tickets tonight. Remember?"

Tracy's slim fingers fidgeted with the handle of her cup. "Yeah, I remember, but I thought we could ask someone else for a change. Maybe someone from the building."

She looked up, her words coming out in a rush. "I know it's the last minute, Elva, but I have this feeling . . . I think it's important! You know I wouldn't make it so rush-rush if I didn't think it were important." She looked apologetically at the other girl. "It's as if I can hear something out there, calling!"

Elva put down her cup and took Tracy's hand "I know, Tracy, I know. Well, we'll see what we can do."

Her sigh was covered by Tracy's words. "Thanks, Elva. I'm not working today, so I'll see who I can get, and I'll have everything ready. You won't have to do a thing."

Elva smiled and nodded, and Tracy didn't seem to notice that Elva's heart was not in it. Elva found the "meetings"—which was what Tracy called her séances—even more embarrassing than the sessions with the Ouija board, and she only participated because they meant so much to Tracy. She should have known last night that one would be coming up.

"Well, I just hope you can get someone to come," she said, feeling like the rankest hypocrite.

"Oh, I will!" Tracy smiled. "I have a feeling."

Elva sighed again and reached for a piece of Tracy's toast.

Isaaic Aschermann, attempting to adjust his eyes to the dim light, took a firm grip upon the warm hand offered him and allowed himself to be led into the room.

He could hear the low murmur of voices, and as his eyes finally adjusted, he saw the pretty little McGuire girl from 4, and the artist fellow from 3, talking on the sofa.

The room was illuminated by at least a dozen candles, which cast an interesting—if to his way of thinking, inadequate—light upon the glossy, black table that had been pulled into the center of the room. The scent of incense was strong in the air, and Isaaic resisted an impulse to sneeze. Tracy always insisted upon all the accouterments for her meetings, and he had to admit that she knew how to create an atmosphere.

He released her hand, and turned to pat her shoulder. "Thank you, my dear. I believe I can see my way now."

Tracy's full-throated laugh warmed the air near his left ear, as she planted a kiss on his cheek. "Oh, I'm on to you, Isaaic. It's just that you like to hold my hand."

Aschermann chuckled and gave the expected response. "Well, it's not often that a man of my age gets to hold the hand of a lovely young girl. It's one of the privileges of age."

Tracy laughed again, and Isaaic smiled wryly. How glibly the trite phrases tripped from his tongue. The privileges of age did not balance the indignities; but there was no use in telling young people this. It would only make them unhappy.

He genuinely liked Tracy and Elva, despite their unconventional life style. The years had taught him tolerance, if nothing else. He had experienced enough difficulty in living his own life. He certainly did not have the presumption to tell others how to live theirs.

He found a spot on the couch, next to the McGuire girl. Such a pretty girl; but she looked tired—or was it this dammed half-light?

She turned to him. "Hi, Mr. Aschermann! I didn't know you went in for the occult."

Isaaic smiled. "Isaaic, please. I feel old enough without the polite 'Misters' from all of you young people. Once in a while I come to one of Tracy's meetings. It sort of keeps my hand in. After all, I used to make my living studying dead cultures—it's not so different talking to dead people."

He felt a warm body push against his shoulder. Tracy had seated herself next to him on the arm of the couch. "Hey, come on Isaaic. That's not fair. You know it's more than that!"

Isaaic smiled at her, then turned to face Halley. "She's right. I'm being flippant."

Steven Street leaned around Halley. "How is it more than that? I've never sat in on one of these things, and I'd like to know what to expect." He laughed rather nervously.

Tracy looked at him seriously. "There are forces in the world, powerful forces for both good and evil. Some cultures have called them 'angels'; some 'demons.' Some of us believe that we can contact these forces; that we can draw upon their power and use it. That's what magic is all about. The American Indian believed it. The African knew it. Of course, sometimes you contact other, lesser forces, life forces of those who have gone over to the other side. These forces can answer questions, things like that. Sometimes, if you're a sensitive, you can feel them trying to get in touch with you, and that's what I've been feeling. That's why I'm having a meeting tonight. Understand?"

Street shook his head doubtfully. "I'm not sure. Are you saying that you can feel some sort of ghost or spirit calling you in some kind of way; and that we're all going to try to help you get in touch with it?"

Tracy lightly punched his arm. "That's about it. Just remember to keep an open mind, to concentrate on whatever I say, or whatever questions I ask. Okay?"

Street nodded and sat back. "Got it."

Elva came in from the kitchen carrying a tray with five glasses, each filled with a deep, amber liquid. She put the tray down upon the coffee table, then went to the stereo. In a few seconds a faint, eerie music insinuated itself into the background. Isaaic found himself convulsed by a shiver. Halley McGuire put her hand upon his arm. "Are you all right?"

"Fine," he said as he took the glass of wine that Elva was offering. The mead slid warmly down hi[illegible] throat and the moment was over; but for just a seco[illegible] he had experienced a cold feeling of revulsion [illegible] fear, as if an old enemy had walked into the room[illegible] was reminded of the way he had felt night befor[illegible] the night when the Gerards had moved in. In tr[illegible] explain the feeling to himself, the only words h[illegible] come up with were "psychic unease"—a feelin[illegible] was not well with his world.

Isaaic had always had an open mind i[illegible] psychic phenomena, and he followed with[illegible] latest articles published on the subject.

many of his friends active in the field, he possessed considerable psychic ability himself. Thinking of this, he admitted that he had been trying to stifle a sense of discomfort about tonight's meeting. Perhaps it was an old man's foolishness, but he had an uncomfortable feeling that tonight's session might prove disastrous in some way.

"All right. Everybody to the table, and join hands!"

Following Tracy's directive, he offered his arm to Halley McGuire, who graciously accepted. He escorted her to the table, then seated himself next to her. There was a fat, purple candle squatting in a silver dish in the center of the table. By its light, Halley's face looked white and drawn, but her hand in his was warm and firm.

Steven Street seated himself to Isaaic's right. His grip was strong, but his hand was as soft as a woman's. Isaaic had seen some of the man's work—all mournful eyes and soulful faces, in pastels. His work lacked passion and vigor. Next to Street was Tracy, who already had her eyes closed, preparing herself for trance. On Tracy's right was Elva, looking patient ...ored. Isaaic knew that she didn't care for any of ... she went along. A supportive person. That

... reassuringly at Halley and Street. The ...openly, but Street's upward move... entirely a gesture. His hand in ... Relax, my boy, relax, Isaaic

... I tell you it is all right ... over the table, and ... to flicker. "You ...ou may do so." ... and only the ... the room. Isaaic ... suddenly seemed ... was conscious of a feeling of pressure. The air felt heavy, as it sometimes did before a storm.

Through her fingers, he could feel Halley moving; then he felt the pressure of her grip increase. He looked at Tracy. Her slender body had stiffened, and he could see the points of her delicate breasts beneath the thin stuff of her sleeveless top. The sight evoked no feeling save asthetic appreciation. Alas, he thought. Another of the privileges of age.

Tracy's mouth opened and closed, as if she were trying to speak. When her voice came forth, it was very soft, a whisper. "I am open. I am the way. Speak through me. We gather to hear your words. I am the door, you are the key. Speak through me."

As she spoke the last words, her body began to twist and bend, her slender arms pulled between Elva, whose face showed an expression of alarm, and Steven Street, who looked appalled.

Isaaic felt his heart beat faster, and he was again assailed by the cold feeling that he was coming to think of as a premonition of doom.

"Don't let him—don't let him—you'll be sorry—you will—you will—don't let him in—get rid of it—get rid of it—it calls to him—she calls to him . . ."

The voice, high and clear, Isaaic recognized as that of Minka, Tracy's usual spirit contact—but the words were spoken so rapidly, were so run together, that he had difficulty in making sense of them. It was as if Minka was trying to get certain information out before someone or something stopped her; and Tracy's writhing body seemed to verify the fact that at least two beings, or forces, were struggling for possession of her vocal apparatus.

Tracy's lips lifted in a rictus as the words strained through her clenched teeth in Minka's high voice; "Nonononononononononononon . . ."

It was an eerie and unnerving sound, and both of Isaaic's hands felt as if they were being broken by the grips of Halley and Street. He knew how they felt—

the hair on the back of his own neck was rising, and the base of his spine felt cool. He could not take his eyes from Tracy's face. Her features seemed as fluid as water.

Then her jaw relaxed, her mouth fell open, and her face assumed a sensuous, somehow feline expression. Her lips opened loosely, then smiled.

"I am here. You have called, and I have come. You will serve me; I will serve you!"

The voice, deeper than Tracy's, masculine in sound, rolled sonorously out of Tracy's mouth. A sensual chuckle spilled from between her parted lips. "We will serve one another well!"

The words themselves were not threatening, but something in the tone caused a coldness to spread in Isaaic's bowels. This time Tracy had gone too far. They had called up something that was far better left alone—he was sure of it.

He closed his eyes for a moment, unable to focus his train of thought. The crash of the outer door, as it hit the wall, roused him to full, heart-pounding awareness. All of them except Tracy turned in astonishment. He knew that his own mouth must be agape even as the others were.

In the doorway stood the stocky, disheveled figure of Helga Kauffman. The moving candlelight reflected from her flat, unseeing eyes. She seemed totally unaware that there were others in the room.

For a long moment, they all seemed caught in stasis. No one dropped hands, and Tracy was still in trance.

As the girl began to slowly move, to walk toward the table, Isaaic felt a surge of revulsion. Her walk was a parody of a streetwalker's sexy, hip-swinging strut. Performed by Helga's gross body, the movements were obscene.

The girl stopped in the back of the room by the long pile of cushions that served as seating. Arms raised above her head, face to the group at the table, she began to move her pelvis in an awkward, forward-tilted grind; then quickly, with more fluidity than one would have thought she possessed, she reached down and pulled off her shapeless dress. She wore nothing beneath it, and the tallowlike folds at waist and belly were cruelly delineated by the light from the candle on the table by her side.

Again she began the lascivious pelvic grind, and her stubby hands began to fondle her own shapeless breasts. A low, crooning sound came from her as she stretched out her arms as if to a lover standing before her.

Isaaic blinked his eyes. It must be a trick of the light, he thought; but for a moment it looked as if something had grabbed her, pushing her backward with the force of an embrace. She fell back upon the pile of cushions, spreading her heavy thighs as if to receive. . . .

"No!" a voice cried out, and he felt his left hand released. Halley was staggering to her feet, her face a mask of shock and disgust.

Tracy cried out, as if in pain, and collapsed in her chair. Elva bent toward her and Street and Isaaic both got to their feet.

Isaaic's immediate concern was for Tracy. He knew that it was harmful to a medium to have the circle contact broken while still in trance; but before he could make a move to help, he heard the sound of running feet, and Mrs. Kauffman, closely followed by Dr. Kauffman, burst into the room.

FIVE

In the Kauffman apartment, Helga had been put to bed in her room. Ernest Kauffman had forced the girl to swallow two Librium, but the heavy, animalistic sobs had not stopped, they could be heard even in the living room as Kauffman attempted to read the evening paper, using the tabloid to block out his wife's accusing stare.

"You were supposed to be watching her!" The woman's voice was dull and accusatory. "I don't go out often—you know I don't go out often. Couldn't you just once . . ."

Kauffman, irritated and bored, laid the paper down in his lap. When he spoke his voice was cold. "There was nothing I could do, Gertrude," he said with condescending patience. "As I have already told you, the girl was in her room. The door was shut. She was watching television quite placidly. I was in the living room—just as I am now—attempting to read the paper—just as I am now. I had no reason to suspect any problem. Her door burst open and she came out, moving very quickly. She was past me and out the door before I was really aware of what was happening. I ran after her, but she was already in the apartment of the two *lesbos.* I hardly think that I am to blame. If you would let me put her in a home, as I have so often . . ."

Gertrude's hands shot up to her mouth, and a strangled sob issued from behind her fingers. "You don't care! You don't care about her! You never even call her by her name. She's not an animal; she's a human being!"

Kauffman nodded, his eyebrows slightly raised and his expression one of studied calm. "A flawed human being, Gertrude. A damaged human being. You saw what happened. You saw what she did in front of those people!"

Gertrude moaned into her hands, her body rocking back and forth. "What can we do? What can we do? I'm so ashamed. How can I face them again?"

Kauffman permitted himself a smile. Personally, he did not consider the girl's actions all that terrible. The other tenants knew that she was subnormal. Certainly they would talk about it, but only for a while. He was far more interested in the *reasons* for her behavior—this sudden action, this volition, was entirely unlike her. Tonight she had acted much as she had the other day in the living room, on the day that the Gerard family moved in—as if she saw something or someone invisible to the rest of them. He was interested in studying the phenomena further. Perhaps there was a paper in it—but at this moment he was using the incident against his wife. Gertrude, dear, dull, dry Gertrude, who was so ashamed of her sex; perhaps if she became embarrassed enough by the girl's behavior, she would consent to having her put into an institution. He hurried to impress his point while Gertrude was vulnerable.

"If she is going to do this kind of thing often, it will be difficult," he said almost kindly. "We will have to keep her door locked, keep a watch on her at all times."

Gertrude's hands dropped. Her face was stricken. "But you know how she hates being locked in. The noise . . ."

Kauffman nodded. "Yes, there is that to consider." When forced to stay behind locked doors Helga screamed hoarsely and incessantly, and pounded upon the walls. "But what alternative have we?" he added gently.

Gertrude again buried her face in her hands, and Kauffman retreated behind his paper, a faint smile on his face. He felt that he had breached the wall of his wife's determination. For the while, that would do. In the meantime, he would study the girl and make notes for an article. He began to hum under his breath.

Halley wasn't feeling at all well, and she gratefully accepted Isaaic Aschermann's offer to see her to her apartment.

As they stopped in front of her door, and she fumbled in her purse for the key, he peered into her face anxiously. "Is your husband home, child?"

She shook her head, angrily blinking back weak tears. Early in the afternoon, Vince had called, telling her that he would have to stay another day, and would not be home until tomorrow.

She didn't know why this news upset her so. He had been gone longer than this before, and she certainly had not gone to pieces then. What was the matter with her? For an instant her mind skimmed dangerously close to the incident of the day before—the dream, or whatever it was—but she resolutely turned her thoughts away. Somehow she found the incident extremely threatening, and she did not want to examine it too closely.

"He's on a business trip," she said to Mr. Aschermann. Where was that damn key?

Mr. Aschermann gently touched her arm. "I have an excellent idea. You don't appear to be ready for sleep yet, and neither am I. Why don't you join me in a cup of chocolate, and we can discuss this evening's rather bizarre episode? What do you say?"

Halley hesitated only a minute. She certainly did not want to be alone, and she knew that Mr. Aschermann was trying to be kind, to reassure her about the evening's events, which she had to admit had frightened her. "I'd love to," she said gratefully, dropping the just-found key back into her purse.

Halley had not been in Mr. Aschermann's apartment before, and she examined the contents of the living room with interest, while he prepared the chocolate in the kitchen.

The room was filled with mementos of his profession. The furniture was tasteful, but subdued, as if to show off the really important aspect of the room—the artifacts that lined the many shelves and claimed places of importance upon table tops.

On the coffee table squated an expertly crafted terra-cotta figure with a rounded, Buddhalike body, and a fat, baby face. The mouth of the figure was drawn down at the corners and the lips were open; but Halley could not tell if the face was meant to express anger or tears.

"Here we are." Mr. Aschermann came into the room, bearing a large silver tray upon which sat a slender silver pot, a pair of delicate china cups and saucers, and a plate of cookies.

He placed the tray upon the table next to the terracotta figure. "I see you're admiring my friend. The piece is Olmec, and shows the 'jaguar' mouth, a typical feature of Olmec art." His voice had drifted into a faintly pedagogic tone, and Halley for the first time realized that the old man must miss his work.

He poured her a cup of the rich, fragrant chocolate and handed it to her. "There. That will fix you right up. My old grandmother swore by this as a general soother and comforter."

Halley accepted the cup, grateful for his perception. She very definitely felt in need of soothing and comforting.

The chocolate was hot and not too sweet, and the warmth of it in her stomach did seem to make her feel a little better. She took a deep breath. Aschermann looked at her over his cup.

"This has been a very exciting evening," he said

wryly. "I have attended Tracy's little soirées before, but never with such interesting results. I imagine the effect was a little startling for your first experience."

Halley nodded ruefully. "Tracy came up this afternoon and asked me if I'd like to come. Vince had just called and said he wouldn't be home, so I thought, why not? Now I wish I'd said no." She shivered. "It was really weird—that strange voice coming out of Tracy—that really got to me, and then when the Kauffman girl came in and started . . . well, started all that, it was just too much!"

Aschermann shook his head. "Poor child. As far as I know she has never done anything like *this* before." His voice was thoughtful and his face pensive. "It was almost as if she were answering a call. Did you notice how she came running in—no hesitation—as if she knew where she were going? And her actions—she acted almost as if there were really someone there with her. Very strange."

Halley shivered again, and nodded. "I noticed. You don't suppose that *thing*, whatever it was that Tracy called up—you don't suppose that it was *really* there, do you?"

Aschermann shrugged. "In the many years that I spent in strange corners of the world, I saw many things happen that we, in our society, would call impossible. At the risk of frightening you, I have to admit that yes, I do believe that Tracy called up, or contacted, *something* tonight—call it a spirit, a force, whatever you will, but I believe that *something* other than the five of us was in that room, and I can't help but wonder if it wasn't that something that brought Helga downstairs to the girls' apartment."

"But the things she was *doing*!" Halley blushed. "I mean, well, they were sexual. Can a spirit be sexual?"

Aschermann smiled and put down his cup. "Have you never heard of incubi and succubi?"

Halley thought a moment before answering. "I think so. The incubus, anyway, but that's just a myth, isn't it? Doesn't it have something to do with nightmares?"

Aschermann's eyes sparkled. She could tell he was enjoying having a pupil to instruct. "Just so. The incubus is often pictured as a monster sitting on some poor maiden's chest, and there is a connection with the nightmare; but the basic identity of the incubus or succubus is that of a demon or spirit who takes on the form of a man or woman in order to have sexual congress with humans."

Halley made a moue of distaste. "And you think that this being or spirit that Tracy called up is one of those? An incubus?"

Aschermann shrugged and smiled ruefully. "I say that I believe it is possible. It would explain Helga Kauffman's behavior, and would not be out of character with the words that it spoke through Tracy's mouth."

"I will serve you, and you will serve me," Halley repeated thoughtfully. "Brrrrr." She rubbed her upper arms. "Well this has been very interesting, but I don't think it's cheered me up any. Maybe I'd better have another cup of comfort." She held out her cup, and Aschermann refilled it. As he set down the pot, he looked up at her.

"Now, Halley, you are a grown-up young woman. I thought I could be truthful with you. If I have frightened you, I am sorry. I sometimes forget that not everyone shares my boundless curiosity about the unusual. You should have told me to stop."

She could see that he was hurt, and hurried to reassure him. "Oh, no, Isaaic. It's been really fascinating. I was just sort of joking, you know. I mean, we're all fascinated by the unknown, even when it frightens us, or maybe because it does frighten us. I really wanted to know. I think it's easier to face things—whatever they are—if you know what you're facing." She smiled, and he returned her smile.

"Ah, that's better. Those are my sentiments exactly.

Of course, there are some of us who not only *want* to know, but find it absolutely necessary, that is why we become scientists of one kind or another, always seeking out answers to the strange questions."

Halley put down her cup. "Well, I think I'll be able to get to sleep now. Your grandmother was right about the chocolate."

Aschermann put down his cup and got up. "I'll see you downstairs. If you ever want to talk, or . . ." he seemed embarrassed, "if you should need my help, please call."

"Thanks," she said. He really was a nice old man, but why on earth should he think that she would need help?

She gratefully said good night to him at the door to her apartment. Once inside, she carefully pulled the heavy bolt, fastened the chain, and locked the dead-bolt lock. Usually this procedure filled her with a sense of comfort, a feeling that she was locking out the bad things of the world—leaving this, her place, cozy, warm and safe from danger; but tonight she had a cold shivery feeling that instead of locking the bad things out, she was locking something inside with her.

The living room was in order now, and Nina Gerard sat in the blue velvet chair with her feet upon the hassock, and looked around her.

The room looked lovely, and usually she took great pleasure and comfort from admiring the pleasant arrangement of her beautiful things; but tonight she felt a cold restlessness that canceled her usual good feeling.

Martin would be late—a business dinner—and Melissa was already in bed. Martin had wanted her to attend the dinner with him, but she had not yet found a local baby-sitter, and of course she could not leave Melissa alone.

She had also received an invitation to attend a séance, or some such thing, from one of the girls in the second-floor apartment. The girl, Tracy, she thought the name was, said she could bring Melissa down to rest in their bedroom, but Nina had politely refused. She had no desire to get involved with occult games. She certainly didn't need any reminders of what she thought to herself as "the trouble" in Italy.

Perhaps the Contessa's séance had had no bearing on the events that followed, but the series of happenings were irrevocably linked in Nina's mind.

For a moment she pictured the black-eyed, malicious face of the Contessa as it was on the day they had first met.

Nina blinked her eyes and pressed her palms to her temples. She must not think of the Contessa, or of anything connected with the time spent in that villa. She was getting one of her headaches again—she always did when she let those thoughts creep in.

Resolutely, she arose and started toward the bathroom. She would take a couple of aspirin and go to bed. She was overtired, she knew, from getting the new apartment into shape.

Passing Melissa's closed door, she was stopped by the sound of her daughter's voice raised in laughter; then a soft whispering, and the rustle of bedclothes. For just an instant, it sounded as if two voices were speaking, in low, secret tones. A cold hand seemed to touch Nina's vitals. Without further thought she grabbed the cold metal knob and opened the door.

Melissa looked up at her from the rumpled bed. The covers were pushed back, and Melissa's "treasures" were spread around her on the bed. The room seemed unnaturally warm after the coolness of the hallway, and the air smelled faintly of oranges. Nina made a gutteral sound in her throat—at the villa, in the hot Italian sun, the over-rich air had always seemed to smell of oranges.

Melissa's nightgown was rutched up above her hips, and her face was flushed.

Nina swallowed, and tried to keep her voice steady.

"What are you doing, Melissa? I thought you were asleep."

Melissa smiled, and put the trinket she was holding into the box by her side. "I just couldn't sleep, Mother. I just thought I would play with my things."

"Well put them away now. It's late!" Nina was amazed at her control.

She helped Melissa put the items back into the box, then pushed the box under the bed. She pulled down the child's nightgown, and smoothed over the covers. Melissa smiled at her sweetly.

As Nina turned out the light, preparatory to closing the door, Melissa called out, "I'm sorry that I bothered you, Mama. Good night!"

As Nina closed the door she felt her stomach contract as if she was going to retch. Was it happening again, or was it just her imagination? Was she making too much of a perfectly harmless incident? The heat, the smell, were they only in her imagination?

She hurried into the bathroom and shook three aspirins into her shaking hand. Then, for good measure, she shook out two Seconals. She had to sleep—had to quiet her mind. Everything was going to be all right—it simply had to be, because she knew that she could not handle it if it wasn't.

Steven Street paced the floor with almost feverish intensity, pausing now and then to stare at the painting propped against the easel. The light from a small table lamp illuminated the work, giving the painted figures a peculiar kind of life.

His mind was fired by the evening's experiences; he could not put the image of Helga Kauffman's gross form writhing on the cushions out of his mind. Despite the girl's lumpish exterior, there had been a compelling sensuality to her straining figure, white and grotesquely female against the brightly covered pillows. The way she had moved—as if there were someone, a lover, in her arms.

He stopped again and looked at the painting of the man and woman, studying the expression on the woman's face—she looked almost sleep-drugged—looking at the handsome, almost gloating face of the man. A feeling of excitement began to rise in him. He could do a whole series, a series based upon the concept of the demon lover, the succubus, in his various forms.

Almost without volition he began laying out his paints and equipment. He removed the finished painting from the easel, and replaced it with a prepared canvas. Boldly he began to sketch in the outlines of Helga Kauffman's massive body.

Elva dumped the ashes of the burned incense into the wastebasket. Her fair face was paler than usual, and her mouth was set. Tracy watched apprehensively from the corner of the couch, where she sat curled in upon herself like a lovely, brown cat.

"Tracy, this has gone too far. I mean, this time it was just too much! That awful girl! Christ, you should have seen the looks on our friends' faces!"

Tracy lowered her head. She was still shaken by the results of her séance. Of course, she never remembered what happened while she was in trance, but the shock of the broken circle, coupled with the sight of the nude Helga sprawled on the floor cushions, had left her weak and drained. In this condition, she had been open to the trauma and shock being experienced by the others.

She put the fingers of both hands over her eyes. "Hey, I'm frightened enough, Elva. You don't need to go on. I'm not going to do it again."

Elva walked over to kneel at the other girl's side. "Do you mean that, Trace?"

Tracy nodded. "That was the *end.* I don't know what I called up, or what I've gotten us into. I've got a little power, and I can communicate, but I know I'm not ready to handle whatever it was that we brought in here tonight. I just hope it's gone, and stays away!"

She shivered, and Elva put an arm around her shoulders. "Shhh, it's all right, baby. It's gone now. It won't come back."

"Sure." Tracy tried to smile. "Well, I think I'll go to bed. I feel sort of cold."

Elva watched as Tracy went into the bedroom. Well, thank God! At least some good had come out of tonight's embarrassing foolishness. No more "meetings." She smiled as she went about straightening up the room.

SIX

Halley closed the book lying on the table in front of her and pressed the palms of her hands to her eyes. After two hours of reading, she felt more confused than ever.

After her last conversation with Professor Aschermann, she had gone to the local library and, feeling somewhat sheepish, had looked through the card catalog under the word *incubi.*

To her surprise, she found several listings, all in books on demons, or witchcraft.

As she checked her books out, she had expected the librarian to look at her askance; but the librarian, showing no curiosity, had stamped the cards as if she checked out this kind of thing every day; and Halley, thinking about it, realized that she probably did.

Halley knew that there was a current resurgence of interest in the occult. You couldn't help reading about it in the daily papers, or seeing the television programs—it was just that she had never had any real interest in the subject.

She pushed the book away, and stood up, stretching. She felt a little hungry; but her stomach was still upset. For the last few mornings, she had felt nauseous upon arising. That, coupled with the fact that her period was late, was making her feel very apprehensive.

Apprehensive! She should be happy as a clam. This is what she had wanted—to have a baby. This was why she had quit her job—to have a baby, Vince's baby; and that was the problem.

She turned toward the window and looked out onto the street. The wind was blowing, and passersby were holding on to their hats and leaning into the wind.

It was ridiculous! It was completely mad! It was, because it had to be, perfect nonsense, but she could not put the incident of the dream—or whatever it was—out of her mind! It had been too real. She had never had a dream that real. And then that incident with Helga Kauffman during the séance . . .

She turned away from the window, and put the tea kettle over the burner of the stove, turning on the burner with one hand and reaching for the tea cannister with the other.

A tear slid out of the corner of her eye, and trailed wetly down her cheek. She should be happy, contented, anxious to find out if she were really pregnant; but here she was, putting off seeing her doctor, worrying whether or not her baby had been conceived by an incubus! Unbelievable!

And Vince; she hadn't even told him that she thought she was pregnant. The thought of Vince caused another tear to follow the first. It was over two weeks now since he had returned from his trip. She had been so anxious for his return; wanting the comfort of him; wanting his arms around her—and then he had arrived.

She had been busy all that afternoon fixing a special dinner—all the things that Vince liked, a good wine, his favorite dessert.

She had bathed and scented herself carefully, put her makeup on with special attention, and worn the slinky-soft blue jersey robe that he liked so well.

When she heard his key in the lock, she rushed to throw open the bolt, and was in his arms almost before he entered the room. He dropped his suitcase and kissed her hungrily; then held her at arms length. "Well, now *this* is worth coming home to."

He sniffed. "What's that wonderful smell?"

She laughed—oh it was so good to have him home—and squeezed his arm. "That's dinner, my love. All your favorites; but you're supposed to smell *me* first!"

"You don't have to ask me twice," he said, burying his face in her neck and hair. "Mmmmmm. Fabulous! Better than dinner, anytime."

His lips trailed up her throat and chin and found her mouth, as his hands moved from her back, around her waist, and then up to her breasts. Still holding her in this fashion, he began to walk her gently backward, toward the bedroom. She pulled away momentarily, to whisper "The dinner . . ." but her words were stilled by his lips, and she happily and willingly let herself be moved backward until the backs of her knees struck the edge of the bed.

He released her just long enough to slip the robe from her shoulders and arms, and to quickly strip off his own clothing; and then they were together, body against body—the lovely, sensuous feel of warm flesh against flesh—and she sighed, so happy now. She was where she belonged.

It was marvelous for the first few minutes, and then she found herself, despite the enjoyment she had always taken in Vince's lovemaking, thinking of that other afternoon, and that other lover—the dream lover—and wishing that Vince would do to her what the other had done, in the way that the other had done it.

Horrified, she tried to immerse herself in the current act, in the feeling of her husband's hands, in his lips, in his strength as he penetrated her; but the tiny seed planted by the thought would not be displaced. When Vince finally slid from her with a contented sigh, she was left with a nagging sense of dissatisfaction. Sex with Vince had not been completely right for her since.

• • •

The sound of furiously boiling water drew Halley's attention to the kettle on the stove. The water had almost all boiled away. She turned off the burner, and stood staring at the stove for a moment; then walked over to the telephone hanging against the wall.

The telephone on the other end rang four times, and she was about to hang up, when Professor Aschermann's voice said "Hello" in her ear.

With a great feeling of relief, she said, "Hi. This is Halley."

Aschermann's voice sounded friendly and somehow comforting. "Why, hello there. How are you, my dear?"

Halley suppressed a sigh. "I know I'm supposed to say 'fine' but truthfully, not so hot. Are you busy? Would you mind if I come up for a few minutes?"

Aschermann chuckled. "No, I'm not busy; and I would be delighted to have you come up for as long as you like. Shall I put on the chocolate?"

"Please."

"Then I'll see you in a few minutes."

Isaaic was smiling as he put down the telephone. It was true that he would enjoy seeing Halley. He liked the girl. She was warm and outgoing—a caring person.

He went into his kitchen and got the milk out of the refrigerator and the chocolate from the cupboard. There was something troubling Halley, he could tell; something more than the understandable fear or apprehension caused by witnessing the peculiar behavior of the Kauffman girl at the séance. He thought to himself that he would not be surprised if it had something to do with the strange force, or tension, that he was becoming increasingly aware of—a presence that seemed to fill the whole building. He could feel it in the hallways and the lobby, and even in the basement laundry room. If he had been pressed to put it into words, he could have said only that there was something in the building that had not been there before.

Something strange. Something alien. Something that prickled the hair on the back of his neck and caused him to have disturbing dreams at night—dreams that he could not remember upon arising, but that left him with a feeling of lassitude when he awoke.

His doorbell rang while the chocolate was heating, and he opened the door and let Halley in. She looked charming, in denim pants and a simple, blue shirt, open at the throat; but he noted that her face was pale, and her eyes too bright. He took her hand.

"Come in, come in. The chocolate is on, and it's nice and warm in the living room." He added this last because her hand in his was icy cold.

She followed him through the entry way in to the living room, and curled up on the sofa in front of the coffee table.

Aschermann left the room and returned with the chocolate, some apples, and half of a Gouda cheese, all of which he put down in front of Halley.

"There, lunch. I'll bet you haven't had any yet."

Halley smiled and shook her head. "No, I haven't. Thanks." She cut a wedge of the cheese and began to nibble at it. He could see that she wanted to talk, but was reluctant to start.

"You know," he said, "I feel that there is something going on in the building, something very odd."

Halley raised her eyebrows in a quizzical expression. "Mr. Bartolo is cheating on his wife?"

Isaaic's full laugh boomed through the room. "Now, that would be shocking, wouldn't it! Such marital devotion I have seldom seen. Such felicity! Such mutual happiness!"

Halley shrugged, her expression slightly petulant. "Maybe it's just mutual blindness. I don't think they really see anything except each other."

Isaaic looked at her questioningly. "But the world has always claimed that love is blind. Why be surprised? And why be displeased?"

Halley looked flustered. "I'm not displeased. Whatever gave you that idea?"

Isaaic smiled. "Becuase of the expression on your pretty face, my dear. You looked quite cross when you spoke of the Bartolos' felicity."

Halley's eyes opened wide. "I did? Well, I suppose maybe I did at that. I mean, I was feeling cranky about it for some reason. I can't imagine why."

Isaaic handed her a cup of chocolate. "Can't you, my dear?"

She lowered her eyes as she sipped at the chocolate. "Well, maybe I can, at that."

Isaaic chuckled. "I thought so. How's the chocolate?"

Halley raised her cup as if in a toast. "Excellent, as always." She put the cup and saucer down on the table.

"You know, after we talked last, I went to the library and got a book on demonology, and one on witchcraft, and read the chapters on incubi and succubi."

Isaaic nodded approvingly. "And did you find what you were looking for?

She shook her head. "Not really. After reading all that stuff, I'm more confused than ever. In both books, the writers quote about a dozen sources, and most of the sources seem to contradict each other."

"Yes, there was a period when theologians argued about the nature of sexual demons much as they did about the number of angels who could gather on the head of a pin. But didn't you get anything out of the books?"

Halley picked up her chocolate, and took a mouthful; holding it for a moment to savor the flavor, then swallowed and felt the warm sweetness trickle down her throat.

"Well, the only thing that seemed really definite was pretty much what you told me that night; that there are sexual demons, or spirits, or elementals, that take on a human form in order to have sex with human beings, and that they most often, but not always, come at night—that much they all seem to agree on. After that it seemed to be each man for himself."

Isaaic raised his eyebrows, and nodded. "Yes, there are many stories. Perhaps I can help you find your way through the maze. I have a small book written by one of my graduate students, Patrick Ernst, titled *The Night Visitor*. Patrick has sorted through the stories, and has come to some conclusions of his own, with which I happen to agree. I think it will help you to make sense out of the mishmash of material on the subject."

Isaaic got up from the sofa and went to one of the ceiling-high bookcases that lined the walls. He returned with a slim volume bound in red, and handed it to Halley.

"Now, there is one thing you might remember. Demons, including incubi and succubi—and there is some question as to whether they are actually demons in the usual sense of the word—predate Christianity by many, many years. The earliest sources say that they were angels who fell because of lust for women. Incidentally, the word 'demon' originally meant only 'replete with wisdom.' If a demon were good, he was called an *eudemon*; if evil, *cacodemon*."

He smiled. "So you see, in a way they were not so very different than human beings, being both good and bad. Also, in early stories, they were usually depicted as very pleasing to the eye, and were often said to be devoted lovers."

Halley leaned forward. "But what about the other stories, the ones that say that they are devils, and that they are ugly, and look like animals, and that having sex with them is unpleasant?"

Isaaic returned to his seat, and poured himself a second cup of chocolate. "I believe you will find most of them attributed to supposed witches persecuted during the Christian 'witch trials,' or to Christian theologians. The Christian religion is, shall we say, particularly intolerant of so-called sins of the flesh. At any rate, you will find all that mentioned in the book, and put better than I can say it.

"Another cup of chocolate?"

Halley, smiling, held her cup forward.

On the floor below, Steven Street stood, dead-tired but happy, looking at the paintings that lined the walls of his studio. In fifteen days, he had completed twelve paintings. All together, in one room like this, they constituted an assault upon the senses, an assault that was gut-level in its impact, for all of the canvases preached the same message—sensuality and sex in their purest forms.

Looking at the glowing bodies, the wanton legs, and smooth breasts, Steven felt his own sex swell and push against the confines of his jeans. He immediately thought of Wilma King. He had to know if the paintings were as good as he thought they were, and if Wilma thought she could get him a spot in the next gallery show.

As he dialed her number, the pressure at his crotch grew until it was well nigh unbearable, and he had to rearrange himself to attain a degree of comfort. As the telephone rang, he found himself muttering, "Answer. *Answer!*"

At the sound of Wilma's voice, he felt a great surge of relief. He hadn't realized just how much he needed to make contact with another human being, after spending two weeks closed up in his studio. For a moment, while the telephone was ringing, he had had the frightening feeling that if she did not answer, it would mean that he did not really exist.

"Wilma," he said, "it's Steven. I've done it. I have a dozen paintings, and as far as I can tell, they're all as good as the first one."

Wilma's delighted response was all that he had

hoped for. As soon as she had stopped talking, he spoke hurriedly.

"Can you come over? Right now? I've got to see if you think they're as good as I do; and besides I'd—well, I'd like to see you."

"Fine," she said. "A half hour."

It seemed like the longest half hour of his life.

When Wilma finally knocked at his door, he had a bottle of wine chilling in an ice bucket, and he had showered and put on clean clothes.

As she came into the room, he resisted the urge to immediately push her onto the couch and make love to her. Instead, he let her look at the paintings—anxious and curious to see if they affected her as much as they did him.

"My God!" she breathed. "They're fantastic. They're so . . . so erotic! My God, Steven, these will knock their eyes out. They . . ."

Suddenly, she seemed to become aware of him standing close to her; and as she glanced down, she could not fail to see his condition. Her expression softened, and she turned into his arms. Her words were stopped by the pressure of his lips; she offered no complaint as his hands probed down the band of her skirt, and stroked the smooth skin of her upper buttocks.

The button on her skirt popped, and Steven pulled down the zipper. She helped him push the garment to the floor, and unbuttoned her blouse herself, so that he would not tear it in his impatience.

Afterward, as they lay exhausted upon the couch, she whispered in his ear. "The gallery is having a show for a few artists next week. With these, I'm sure I can get you a spot. Oh, Steven! You'll be famous!"

He liked hearing the words, but in his own mind, he already knew he was a success. The paintings were *good,* and that was what mattered.

Feeling himself again engorging, he trailed his fingers across her slightly rounded belly, and down to the light fuzz of pubic hair.

"Oh, Steven!" she said, and moved against him. He could feel the answering heat rising in her body.

As Nina Girard squeezed the bath sponge and let the perfumed water trickle down between her small but well-formed breasts, her thoughts were on the evening ahead. This would be their first night out alone, for her and Martin, since they had moved into the new apartment.

Martin had obtained tickets for a new musical that they both wanted to see, and they were going out to dinner before the show. She still felt hesitant about leaving Melissa with a sitter; but Martin had called a reliable agency, and there was really no way Nina could refuse. Martin already thought that she was pathologically protective of Melissa; and if she made another excuse, he might find out just how shaky her emotional state really was. Things were still strained between her and Martin, although both of them did their best to pretend that their relationship was as it had always been.

She stirred restlessly in the water. She knew that Martin felt that Melissa had not really been hurt by what had happened in Italy—that she had not suffered any trauma—and Nina had to admit that the child seemed normal enough. She was just as happy, bright, and inquisitive as she had always been; but what was going on underneath? Children were so expert at hiding things from adults. . . .

There had been an incident in Nina's own childhood—an old friend of her father's, a handsome, robust man, had, when her parents were not around, tried to touch her in places that she knew very well were not to be touched, and had taken her up upon his lap, where a strange, hard protuberance had made her feel afraid and guilty, as she became conscious of it growing beneath her childish buttocks.

Although the man made her very uncomfortable, Nina remembered that she had never once considered telling her parents. She had worked it out alone, as best she could, avoiding the man when he came to the house, and being very careful never to be left alone with him, if she could not avoid him. Eventually her family had moved away, and the man no longer came to call.

Nina pulled the stopper in the tub, and rose to her feet, water sliding down over her narrow hips and slender legs. Wrapping herself in a huge, fluffy, white towel, she stepped out onto the bath rug.

As she turned, she saw her reflection in the floor-length mirror: a slender, graceful woman in a towel sarong, with a smaller towel wrapped turbanlike around her head.

Slowly, she unfastened the towel swathing her body, and let it fall to the foor. Critically, she looked at herself. Her body was still firm, still youthful, still desirable.

She thought back to the last time she and Martin had made love. It had been several weeks—her doing or his? She really didn't know. Did she still want him that way? Sexually? She wasn't sure. She only knew that there was a terrible tension in her, that her nerves felt like taut silver wires, and that a constant pressure existed at her temples.

She picked up the towel, and rubbed her skin briskly. Why was she feeling this way? What was wrong with her? Her family was together, they had this beautiful new apartment; and she knew, despite what had happened, that her husband still loved her. So why this feeling of pressure, this feeling that she was under a constant siege, that she was fighting some kind of battle of which she was unaware, upon a battleground that she did not recognize?

She shivered, despite the heat of the bathroom heater. As she reached for her robe, she could not keep her thoughts from turning to the thing she brooded about most. What about the sounds and voices which she heard, or thought she heard, in Melissa's room?

Several times within the past two weeks she had again heard what she was certain was the sound of another voice—not Melissa's—in the child's room; but each time when she had opened the door, there was no one there but Melissa herself, looking flushed and secretive, sitting among those treasures of hers in a room that felt unnaturally hot and smelled of ripe oranges.

Each time, Nina had wanted to scream, to shake Melissa, to make her daughter tell her . . . tell her what? That she, Nina, was going crazy? That guilt and fear were making her lose her mind? Because she did feel guilty. If she had taken better *care* of Melissa, if she had watched over her more closely, perhaps it would never have happened.

Nina gave an involuntary groan as the vise of pain gripped her forehead, and made her close her eyes. What had she been thinking of? It didn't matter. Nothing mattered now except the pain in her head.

Quickly, she turned to the medicine cabinet, and reached for the bottle of headache tablets. She washed two down with water, then stumbled to her bed. She *had* to be all right for tonight, or Martin would think she was making excuses again. As she stretched out upon her back, she tried to remember what she had been thinking about before the headache came, but she could not.

SEVEN

Of Adam's first wife, Lilith, it is told
(The witch he loved before the gift of Eve)
That, 'ere the snake's, her sweet tongue could deceive,
And her enchanted hair was the first gold.
—D.G. Rossetti, English poet (1828–1882)

Halley read the words aloud, and smiled. She found the poem very beautiful; more like a passage from a fairytale than a record of demonology.

She lifted the book higher on her raised knees, settled deeper into the cushions of the couch, and read on.

Since sex has always been of outstanding concern to the human race, it should not be found surprising that a great interest has always been shown in incubi and succubi, the demons who assume human form in order to have sexual intercourse with human beings.

According to some sources, an incubus is an angel who fell because of lust for women. In France, he is called *follet*; in Germany, *alp*; in Spain, *duende*; and in Italy, *folletto*. He is, essentially, a spirit, or demon, who seeks sexual intercourse with women. The corresponding demon who seeks out men is called the succubus.

* * *

Fascinated, Halley pushed the hair back from her eyes, unaware of how late the hour was growing.

Most authorities seem to agree that the sexual demons can assume either the male or female shape; sometimes appearing to a man in the form of a woman (succubus) taking his sperm, then, in the form of a man (incubus) ejaculating this sperm into a woman.

In the past, many theories have been put forth as to how a spirit can become a body. The most generally accepted seems to be that the demons collect human seman emitted in nocturnal emissions or during masturbation, and use it to create bodies for themselves.

No matter how the spirit creates a corporeal form, the idea that demons and humans can have relations even has the authority of the Bible behind it. Genesis VI 4: "The sons of God came into the daughters of men, and they bore children to them."

There are many legends of offspring being born of such unions: Merlin, the magician; Robert, the father of William the Conqueror; Luther; Romulus and Remus; the whole race of the Huns; and the inhabitants of the island of Cyprus, to name a few.

As you can see from the above list, such offspring were neither necessarily evil, or ill-formed; but on the contrary were possessed of extraordinary abilities and powers; causing one to wonder even more about the nature of their demon fathers.

Many legends have described the incubus/succubus as being very beautiful in appearance; sometimes assuming the shape of a loved or desired partner. These same tales say that once a human has been intimate with an incubus or succubus, he or she will never again be satisfied with a human partner.

On the other hand, descriptions of demon lovers given during the Christian witch trials almost always describe the incubus as 'black,' 'ugly,' and 'cold,' and describe the demon's sex organs as 'cold,' 'hard,' and 'painful.'

To this, I can only say that it would be well to bear in mind the fact that these stories were elicited under torture; were greatly influenced by the Christian faith and philosophy; and were usually recorded by churchmen, who had, shall we say, a vested interest in making such liaisons unpopular.

The earlier tales seem to show the incubus and succubus as attractive, alluring creatures—somewhere between demons and men. Even Sinistrari, the seventeenth-century theologian and expert of the day, had a theory that they were not demons at all, but rural spirits and sylvan dieties; beings of a different and lower nature, motivated solely by lust and lasciviousness, and not by the desire to degrade man; a motive attributed to these spirits by other churchmen . . ."

"Hey! Unfasten the chain!"

Halley dropped the book and jumped to her feet. The front door was partway open, and Vince's voice was issuing through the crack, as the door strained against the chain of the bolt.

Halley, flustered, and caught offguard, stuffed the book under the sofa cushions and smoothed back her hair. Quickly, she ran to the door, and unfastened the chain.

Vince came into the room, bringing with him an aura of cold air. She kissed his cool cheek, which was reddened by the wind, and helped him off with his coat.

"It's still cold out there," he said, rubbing his cold

nose against her warm neck. "I think spring has forgotten us this year."

She held him close, trying to bring all her attention to bear upon him; trying to forget for a moment about the material she had been reading.

He held her away from him, and looked at her. "Hey, you're not dressed!"

Halley's hand flew to her mouth. "Omigod! I forgot!"

He looked at her for a moment, his expression slightly puzzled. "Hey, that isn't like you, Halley. You never forget a date to go out to a show; particularly when I've promised to take you to dinner afterward."

Halley forced herself to smile. Oh God! It *wasn't* like her to forget something like this—not like her at all. She was going to have to get her act together. "It'll only take me fifteen minutes," she said brightly. "Just long enough for you to shave and shower."

"Hah!" Vince snorted as he headed for the bedroom, removing his tie as he went. "If you can do it in fifteen minutes, I'll even order champagne for dinner!"

Fifteen minutes later, Halley looked at her reflection approvingly, and then turned to look at Vince, who had just finished putting on his jacket.

"We both look beautiful," she said decisively.

He grinned. "Yeah, I know. I just hope that the audience is sophisticated enough to appreciate us."

Halley made a face at him. "Even if they aren't, don't you want to look beautiful for me?"

He leaned over and kissed her on the nose. "I thought you told me that I always look good to you. At least that's what you said last night."

Halley playfully pushed him away, and reached for her shawl. "Well, you know how it is. A woman will say anything in the heat of passion."

He gave her a mock leer. "Yeah!"

As Halley smiled back at him, she thought about last night. It had been better for her—almost the way it was before—and, obviously, it had been good for Vince. A little more time, that was all it would take—a little more time, and things would be the same; except for one thing. She still hadn't told Vince that she was pregnant, even though now she was certain of the fact. Her doctor had verified it yesterday.

She shivered slightly as she thought of the material she had just read.

"Hey, come on. You were the one who was originally hot to trot to this event, or have you forgotten that too?"

Halley gave a guilty start, then turned her most dazzling smile on her husband, as she took his arm.

The evening was an unqualified success. The show was entertaining, the dinner excellent, and, true to his promise, Vince had ordered champagne, a full bottle, with the meal. By the time their cab let them off in front of the Barkley, Halley was feeling that all was right with the world, and that her worries had been nothing but neurotic maunderings. She clung happily to Vince's hand as they entered the lobby, and walked toward the elevator.

Just as the elevator door opened, Steven Street and an attractive woman came through the outside door. "Hey!" Street waved his hand. "Hold it up!"

As the couple came toward them, Halley noticed that they seemed to be feeling every bit as good as she and Vince. When the elevator doors opened, they all piled inside with a certain amount of good-natured jostling.

Vince, his arms around Halley's shoulders, smiled at Street. "Well, you seem to have been celebrating."

Street nodded with the careful seriousness of the intoxicated. "Darn right! Something to celebrate too." He looked down at the woman by his side. "Hey, Wilma, shall I tell them?"

She shrugged. "Why not? But first maybe you should introduce us."

By the time Steve made the necessary introductions,

the elevator came to a halt at Vince and Halley's floor. Street reached out and held the door so the elevator would not move.

"I've finally got something really worth showing!" he said. "Got some paintings that will knock them on their asses. Wilma, here, is getting me into a show. It's really going to be something!"

Vince nodded, still smiling. "Fan-tas-tic! We're very happy for you. We'll come to the show, won't we Halley?"

Street waved his free hand, and Wilma laughingly supported him as he momentarily lost his balance. "Why wait for the show? Come on up to my place. We'll all have a drink to celebrate, and I'll let you be the first ones in the Barkley to see the work of the new Steven Street."

Halley looked inquiringly at Vince, and he shrugged good-naturedly. "Why not? It's not every day that we get to attend a private showing. We'll take a peek, and have one for the road. The night is still young."

Steven let the elevator door close and pushed the button for the fifth floor. Laughing, they all trooped out when the door opened, and after only a few minutes of difficulty, Steven managed to unlock his door and let them into his apartment.

Halley was feeling happier and more relaxed than she had felt in weeks. She enjoyed this kind of spontaneous, unplanned event, and thought it was a perfect ending to a lovely evening.

Inside the apartment, Steven turned on only the large lamp near the sofa, leaving the rest of the room in semi-darkness. He busied himself opening the liquor cabinet, and asking what everyone wanted to drink. When they all had a filled glass in their hands, he raised his own glass in a toast.

"Here's to success!"

They all echoed his words. Halley took a swallow of her drink as the others did likewise.

Street pointed to the couch and the squat, comfortable chair across from it. "Come on, sit down. Make yourselves comfortable."

Halley set her glass down on the coffee table. "No!" she said. "The pictures first! It's not fair to keep us in suspense."

Wilma laughed, and touched Steven's arm. "Come on, Steven, you know you're dying to show off."

Street grinned. "You're right. I can't stand the suspense, either. All right. Here goes. Prepare to be astonished!"

With a dramatic flourish, he walked over to the wall, and touched the light switch. The room was immediately illuminated, and they all blinked their eyes at the sudden glare.

As Halley's eyes adjusted, she could see the pictures—bright masses of color, against the pale, cream walls. The room was silent as they all moved to study the paintings.

Halley looked at the one just across from her; a large canvas with a multi-colored background. Her eyes focused on the figure in the painting. For a frightening moment she was back in Tracy's and Elva's apartment, staring in horror at the nude form of Helga Kauffman; for it was Helga—no matter that she wore a slightly different face—that sprawled in naked abandon across the bright pillows.

Yet, the picture was not gross—the longer Halley stared at it, the more this impressed her. The flesh tones of Helga's heavy limbs were Rubenesque, bathed in a lambent light that seemed to come from within the flesh. The overall effect was one of great sensuality.

She turned from the painting to look at Steven. "It's fantastic!" she said. "I've never seen anything quite like it!"

Steven's eyes were glowing. "Thank you," he said. "I think they're good, and Wilma thinks they're good but . . ." He shrugged.

Halley nodded. "I know what you mean. "It's nice to know that outsiders, the public, think they're good too. There's a special kind of satisfaction in that."

"Vince?" She turned away from Steven and Wilma to where Vince was standing in front of a long, blue-backgrounded canvas. His stance seemed peculiar—rigid and strained. She could not properly see his face.

"Vince, what do you think of them? Aren't they marvelous?"

Vince turned his face toward her, and she almost gasped with shock. His features were set and his eyes were cold. It was the face of a stranger. She quickly glanced at Steven and Wilma to see if they noticed her husband's strange demeanor. By the expressions on their faces, they too seemed to see something odd in his behavior.

"What do I think of the paintings?" His words were strangely clipped and measured. "I'll show you what I think of your paintings. . . ."

As Vince spoke these last words, he advanced upon Street and swung his fist toward the other man's jaw.

Both Halley and Wilma gasped at the solid *thwack* of bone against bone, and Wilma moved toward Street as he staggered backward and fell heavily against the wall.

The two women stared aghast at Vince, she stood facing them like an enemy.

Street groaned, and his head sagged. Halley, feeling stunned and frightened, felt also a rising anger and embarrassment.

"Vince! What in the name of heaven are you . . . ?"

"What did you expect me to do?" he almost hissed the words. "How did you expect me to behave when I see my wife," he repeated the words, "my wife! Like that!"

He spat the last word, and Halley, wondering if he was going mad, turned her eyes in the direction of his angry gesture. The painting behind him? It had something to do with that?

Slowly, she turned and walked past Vince, to stand in front of the canvas.

Looking at it, her insides seemed to shrivel, and her bowels felt weak. For a moment she thought she would fall; but she could not take her eyes from the scene depicted there on the canvas in front of her; for she saw herself as she had never seen herself before—sprawled limbs pale against the blue coverlet that she knew so well; her face, to her, almost unrecognizable in an ecstacy of abandonment; and above her the darker figure, forcefully masculine, poised to . . .

She reached for the wall, and leaned her head against the cool plaster, as the memory of her dream came back to her—that strange afternoon. She knew with a horrible certainty that defied reason that this painting depicted the occurrence of that afternoon, and yet how? How could Steven Street have painted that scene?

The room was silent behind her. Slowly she turned and faced her husband's anger and Steven's and Wilma's confusion.

"You bitch!" Vince's voice was raw with anger and pain. "So this is how you spend the time while I'm away!"

"No, Vince! No!" But even as she spoke the words, she knew how unconvincing they sounded in the face of the bald, concrete fact of the painting.

For a long moment the two of them stood frozen, facing one another like combatants; and then Vince, with a muttered oath, spun around and left the apartment, slamming the door behind him.

Halley looked at Steven and Wilma with stricken eyes. "I'm sorry," she said. "I'll . . ." But not really knowing what she would or could do to untangle this painful situation, she only shook her head and blindly followed Vince out of the room.

Steven, still sitting on the floor, rubbed his jaw gingerly. "What in the name of hell?"

Wilma shook her head. It was the picture; something about that picture.

She helped Steven to his feet, and they both walked over to view the canvas more closely.

Steven shook his head, and then groaned. "That sonofabitch! I think he cracked my jaw!" He looked at the painting and touched his jaw again. "Now what in the holy hell could he have seen in that canvas to set him off like that?"

Wilma, looking at the central figure, shrugged and smiled wryly. "Maybe it's because the woman in the painting is his wife." she said.

EIGHT

The pen, with which he had been taking notes, dropped from Ernest Kauffman's fingers, and the hand holding his notebook hung lax by his side.

The notebook was three-quarters filled now, and in Kauffman's bold, clear hand, detailed the day-to-day behavior of his daughter, Helga, as she struggled through the stages of the strange fixation that possessed her.

There had been no more difficulty with Gertrude, since his veiled threat to lock the girl in her room; in fact, Gertrude seemed finally to have accepted the inevitable, and had been going out now and then, indulging in small pleasures such as going to shows or visiting friends, pleasures that she had not allowed herself before.

Kauffman had been careful to keep a close watch on the girl during these times when Gertrude was absent; and there had been no more incidents like the unfortunate affair in the *lesbos* apartment.

Not that Helga's behavior had changed—far from it—she was behaving in a more deviant fashion than ever; each day seemed to draw her into greater excesses of sexual behavior, which Kauffman recorded religiously.

At times, in his coldly logical way, he questioned his increasing involvement and growing lack of detachment in the case; but after examining his motives, he felt assured that he would be foolish to miss this opportunity to study at first hand the phenomenon of hysterical sexual behavior. One of the things that intrigued him was that Helga's symtoms were so similar to the behavior exhibited by the nuns of Loudun, in the seventeenth century.

Now, as he stood half-crouched before his daughter's open bedroom door, his mind was engrossed not with the article, or his notes, but with the girl, Helga, herself. He had been watching now for perhaps half an hour, and the progression of events had him in an almost hypnotic state.

Never in all of his sexual life—before or after marriage—had Kauffman done, or seen done, the things this girl was doing, or that seemingly were being done to her, before his eyes. And the eerie, the uncomfortably strange thing was that if he did not believe the evidence of his own eyes, he would have sworn that she was doing these things with someone else. The way she held her arms, as if a solid body rested between them; the way her breasts flattened, as if someone was pressing against them; the way her legs spread, pushing upward her spread sex—he could almost see the male organ driving into that rough nest. And the odor . . . the odor of sex was in the room. He could smell it from where he stood.

Now, she turned on the bed—grunting, an eager, animal sound—until her buttocks faced him, as she rose on her knees and elbows, spreading her legs wide.

Kauffman drew in his breath as he watched what happened next; the cheeks of her buttocks parted, as if invisible fingers were separating the flesh and pushing the cheeks upward. He could almost see the entering organ pushing and spreading the inner lips, and the sounds—the wet, smacking sounds of flesh against moist flesh; the girl's groaning sounds of pleasure.

The notebook dropped from Kauffman's hand, to lie unnoticed beside the pen. He was unaware of the sweat that beaded his brow, and of his increased heartbeat and respiration. He felt dizzy and disoriented; but he could not take his eyes from the scene being enacted in front of him.

There was one strangled cry from the girl, and then the sounds stopped. For a moment she stayed in the same position; then she flopped over on her back, her face and body wet with perspiration. She lay sprawled, panting happily, her face still bearing a smile of enjoyment.

Still Kauffman watched. She lay quiet now, lower legs dangling off of the edge of her narrow bed, thighs spread; and then she lifted herself upon her elbows, raised her head, and looked directly at him.

A galvanizing shock coursed through Kauffman's body, as his eyes met hers. Her eyes were green and glass-clear, and knowing—so very knowing. He felt as if she were seeing into all of the dark corners of his soul, seeking out his hidden passions, looking for—

They were not Helga's eyes! Helga's eyes were a muddy brown. *This girl was not Helga!* It was clear to him now; why had he not seen it before? This girl's hair was blonde and thick, and her body was solid but well-formed. Her breasts were large and white, with round, pink aureoles, and although her hips were generous, her waist was narrow and compact. She was the perfect example of womanhood, and she was looking at him with desire in her eyes.

He felt himself engorging—felt his whole body expanding—she smiled at him invitingly, licking her pink lips with a moist, pointed tongue.

One of her hands began fondling her breast, while the other slid down to disappear between her legs.

Kauffman suddenly became aware of the sound of his own blood pounding in his ears. As she pulled her hand out from its damp crevice and beckoned toward him, he could see the moist sheen of her fingers in the light.

Slowly, heavily, he walked toward her, until he stood over her body, as she lay back upon the bed.

His eyes greedily examined the expanse of pink flesh, as he inhaled the intoxicating odor of her sex, and then he could bear no more.

With an explosive grunt, he yanked open his trousers and shorts and let them fall to the floor, as his painfully tumescent organ sprang free and erect.

As he fell upon her open body, he felt a sense of power he had never known. Her sex seemed to seek out and engulf him, and as he plunged in mindless, overwhelming lust—a surrender he had always desired, but never before dared—he was hardly aware of the terrible blow that ended his life even as his body was still moving.

Gertrude Kauffman got off of the bus with a spring in her step. It had been a lovely afternoon; one of the most pleasant she had spent in a very long time. She and an old school friend, Edna, had eaten lunch at Schrafts and then gone to a matinée. She couldn't even remember the last time she had done something like this—taken off a whole afternoon just to enjoy herself. She hadn't thought of Ernest or Helga, not even once, in the whole afternoon; and even though now she felt the first pricklings of guilt, she wasn't sorry. It had been just lovely.

Perhaps Ernest was right, after all. Perhaps she devoted too much of her time and herself to the care of Helga. Perhaps she should finally admit to herself that this was it! That this was what Helga was, and would be forever more—a not-quite-finished human being!

It was difficult to face, yes; but she was not as stupid as Ernest seemed to think; she very well realized the futility of the hope that she had been nourishing at her breast for years—the hope that by some miracle, some divine intervention, Helga would change, become normal. Still, it had been almost impossible for Gertrude to give up this hope.

Now she had begun to think that giving up the

struggle, facing reality—as Ernest would put it—might have its rewards. Times like this afternoon, quiet enjoyments, friends, the taking up again of her own life, which she had, in a sense, been holding in abeyance while she waited for the miracle—perhaps it might be worth it after all!

As she passed a shop window, she caught sight of her figure in the plate glass, and straightened her shoulders. Such a mouse! Such a nonentity, that woman there in the reflection, in her practical coat and unflattering hat; a woman who walked with an apologetic stoop, as if afraid to be noticed.

The cold ache of depression replaced the warm glow she had been feeling. How had this come about? How had the cheerful, rather pretty girl she had once been, a girl who had had expectations of life, how had she come to be this characterless, dowdy, little woman in the window? And Ernest, how had the intelligent, serious young psychology student she had met and fallen in love with turned into the rigid, unfeeling man she now lived with?

He had been so handsome then; a young exchange student from Germany, with a strong accent, and searching, penetrating eyes that seemed to see into her soul. He *was* serious, yes, and practical; but she had been certain that the seriousness covered a sensitive soul, and practicality, to a nice, middle-class girl of solid German background, was surely a desirable characteristic.

She approached the Barkley, and mounted the steps.

Just when had she realized that the seriousness covered only rigidity, and that the practicality had turned to hardness? She only knew that it had been a long, long time ago.

She opened the door, and entered the foyer.

Well, perhaps now it was time for *her* to be a bit hard, a bit practical. Perhaps it was now time for her to think of herself, of the rest of her life. She would start by letting Ernest watch the girl more often, while she, Gertrude, enjoyed more time to herself. That last talk, the one after Helga had . . . well, it had made her think. Yes, made her really think!

The elevator arrived and the doors opened. She hesitated before she stepped into the carpeted interior. For one quick, flashing moment she wished that she did not have to go back; that she might walk away and leave them, leave them both! But the thought passed quickly, and she stepped between the waiting doors.

On her own floor, she took out her keys, and let herself into the apartment.

Ernest was not in the living room, and the place seemed unusually silent, until she walked across the room, and headed down the hallway toward Helga's room.

In the middle of the hallway, she paused, shoulders and body settling unconsciously into the familiar pattern of resignation.

From behind Helga's closed doors, she could hear sounds that could only mean that the girl was abusing herself again. Mingled feelings of pity and disgust turned Gertrude's expression sour. Should she go in and stop the girl, or ignore it? Ernest said that Helga must express her sexuality, but it was disgusting all the same.

As she vacillated, Gertrude heard the other sounds, the harsh, unmistakably male gruntings of a man in rut.

She could feel the heat stain her face and neck, while wild thoughts crossed and re-crossed her mind. Someone had gotten into the apartment, and was attacking her daughter! Where was Ernest? Had he gone out and left Helga alone? He had promised to look after her! He had *promised*! What should she do? What *could* she do?

Helga's voice rose over the sound of the man's animal grunting, in a cry, that to Gertrude's ears, was a cry of pain.

Wildly she looked around for a weapon to defend her child, and her eyes fell upon the heavy bronze statue of Rodin's Thinker, which occupied its usual position in a niche in the hall wall.

Grasping the figure firmly by the head, feeling somewhat reassured by the hefty weight of it in her hand, she approached Helga's door upon trembling legs.

As she paused, with her hand upon the door knob, she thought that she would fall. Her heart plunged against her ribs like a captured animal, and she felt dizzy and faint.

Then, Helga cried out again, and Gertrude turned the knob, and threw open the bedroom door.

The sight that met her eyes could not be believed. For what seemed an interminable time, she could only gape in frozen silence as she gazed upon the tableau on the bed.

Helga, nude and sweating, hair a wild tangle, limbs flailing, was writhing and thrusting her body feverishly against that of the man lying prone upon her; and she was smiling—smiling in idiot, foolish, lascivious delight at what the man was doing to her!

And on top of her, hairy buttocks bared and pumping, trousers awkwardly around his ankles, uttering ugly, animal sounds of both appetite and satisfaction was Ernest Kauffman! Gertrude's husband! Helga's father!

As Gertrude stood there, frozen with shock, eyes bulging, mouth open, breath failing; as she felt her mind being destroyed by each pumping thrust, by each thump of flesh against flesh; as her reason, refusing to face what her eyes told her she was seeing, slid and slipped away, the pair on the bed were totally oblivious of her presence.

Slowly, almost gently, she felt her right hand—the one holding the statue—rising.

Standing erect now, she walked forward almost gracefully, until she was directly behind and to the right of the sweating, humping male figure.

When she was in just the right spot, when the angle was perfect, she brought the statue down upon his head with terrible force.

Her expression did not change, as his skull crushed, and his blood spurted over the bed and walls, and over her own neat blouse and skirt. With eyes that did not blink, she watched her hand as it brought the heavy statue down again, and again, and again. She had a faint, vacant smile upon her face.

NINE

Halley awoke slowly and unwillingly. She finally opened her eyes to a glare of sunlight, and to the whirring click of her clock radio—a sound which seemed unnaturally loud to her over-sensitive ears and painful head.

The clock said 2:00 P.M., and it took Halley a moment to adjust to the fact that she had slept through most of the day.

She looked down at herself with shock and surprise—she was still wearing her evening clothes. Then the events of the night before returned with painful clarity, and she groaned.

After leaving Steven Street's apartment, she had paced the floor, waiting for Vince to come home; and when he still had not returned by four o'clock, she had finally thrown herself across their bed, and cried herself into a restless, dream-filled sleep.

Cautiously she put her feet to the floor and stood upright. Every step she took was like a blow to her painful head. She made it to the dresser, peered at her image in the wide mirror, and did not like what she saw.

She tried to pull a brush through her hair, but finding that even her hair hurt, gave it up, and settled for wiping away her smeared eye makeup and lipstick. Then, able to wait no longer, she opened the bedroom door, hoping to find Vince asleep on the couch in the living room. The room was as empty and neat as it had been the night before.

Her insides felt cold and shriveled. Where was Vince? Where had he stayed last night? What was happening to them? Why couldn't he have talked to her? Why couldn't he have let her explain? But how was she to do that? Her shoulders slumped. How could she explain what she did not understand herself.

Slowly, she walked into the bathroom, and got a tissue. She could understand that the picture had been a shock to him—God knows it had been a shock to her—but she found it hard to forgive his lack of trust. Together they could have worked it out, found the answer.

She blew her nose, and threw the tissue into the waste basket. The answer had to lie in Steven Street's apartment; in Steven Street, himself. He had painted the picture, and she would have to learn how, and why.

Not bothering to change her clothes, Halley went out into the hall, locking the apartment door behind her. She waited several minutes for the elevator, but it seemed to be stuck on the third floor; so she opted for the stairwell, and lifting her long skirt, climbed up to Steven's floor.

She knocked loudly on his door, and was finally admitted by a subdued Wilma King.

"I've got to talk to Steven," Halley said firmly. Wilma nodded, and moved aside to let her go into the living room.

Steven was half lying on the couch. His jaw was now black and blue, and looked swollen.

"Oh, my God!" Halley looked at him helplessly. "I'm so sorry. I don't know what got into Vince; he's usually not like that."

Wilma smiled wryly. "I don't suppose he ordinarily sees many pictures of his wife in the arms of another man!"

Halley closed her eyes for a moment, and tried to

make herself speak intelligently. "Yes, that's the first thing; Steven, why did you paint that picture? Where did you get the idea for it?"

Both women looked at Steven expectantly, and he lowered his eyes, seemingly reluctant to meet their gaze.

"Come on, Steven. She has a right to know. Besides, I'm curious too." Wilma moved to his side, and sat down beside him. "I get the impression that you didn't even realize that the woman in the painting was Halley?"

Steven nodded, and slowly raised his eyes. "That's right. I didn't. I still don't see that the girl in that painting looks that much like Halley!" He said the words defensively.

Wilma shook her head, a look of exasperation upon her face. "Steven, you've got to be blind, or you're lying in your teeth! That girl is the spitting image of Halley. Both Halley and Vince can see it; why can't you?"

"How did you come to paint it?" Halley asked stubbornly. "After all this, I think you owe me that much, Steven."

Steven sighed. "This is going to sound corny, but that painting came to me in sort of a dream; like an inspiration."

Wilma looked at him doubtfully. "Oh, come on now, Steven."

He looked up quickly, and winced at the motion. "Honestly! I'm telling you the truth. I was sitting there in the big chair. It was late, and I was disgusted with the way my work was going. And then I fell asleep, or half asleep. I seemed to see this scene in my mind—just as if I were watching a film or something. There was this young woman on a blue coverlet, lying there nude, and then I saw a male figure, not clearly, but I could see that he was there. When I woke up, or whatever, I thought of what a great painting it would make. I painted all night, and that," he gestured, "is the result." He shook his head. "I've never really seen that much of Halley and Vince, and I swear to God that it never dawned on me that the girl was Halley."

His face turned red above the swollen jaw. "I mean, I've never seen her . . . you know, that way. I've only seen her with her hair tied back and in casual, sporty clothes. Oh, hell! You know what I mean!"

Halley nodded, and caught her lower lip between her teeth. "I believe you, Steven. For reasons of my own—which I don't feel like talking about right now—I believe you."

For a long moment they all remained motionless, staring at one another, at a loss for further words to explain the strange happenings of the evening before.

Then, Wilma rose to her feet. "Halley, do something for me, will you? Look at the other paintings, and see if you recognize any of the subjects."

Halley shrugged. "Sure, but I already know one; the portrait of Helga, there on the pillows." She pointed.

Wilma looked at Steven questioningly.

Steven raised one hand, as if to stave off further comment. "Yes, it's Helga. I did that one deliberately, but I changed her face so that she would not be recognizable. That night at Elva's and Tracy's, well, I could see what a great composition it would make, but I didn't want to upset the girl's parents, so I changed her appearance in the painting."

He looked at Halley. "You probably only recognize her because you were there that night, and remember the incident."

Halley smiled tiredly at Wilma. "He's right. I don't think that anyone who wasn't there that night would know it was Helga."

They moved on to the next painting, a wide canvas depicting two female figures; one pale and luminescent, one golden and tawny. They lay face to face, but apart, on what appeared to be a red velvet bedspread. The two girls were reaching toward one another, an expression of yearning on both of their faces; but between the figures, overlapping the pale figure, and embracing the tawny figure, was the faint body of a man, a very beautiful, but masculine man; and it was difficult to tell whether the darker female figure was embracing him, or reaching through him, to the other girl. The painting was both disturbing and arresting, and as Halley could immediately tell, the female figures were excellent likenesses of Tracy and Elva.

Halley looked at Steven with a question in her eyes. "It's the girls!" she said. "It's Tracy and Elva!"

Steven frowned and shook his head. "No! You're wrong! It's just because one is fair and the other dark."

He peered closely at the painting, and shook his head confidently. "Look at it again. It doesn't look like them at all."

Wilma looked at Halley, and Halley nodded. "It's them, all right. A photograph couldn't look any more like them."

Steven, flustered now, moved them on to the next painting, a dark canvas upon which a pale, glowing child shimmered like a ghost figure, an innocent, fair-haired child, with guileless, blue eyes and perfect features. The child, like the figures in the other paintings, was nude, and she was playing at some innocent game—spread about her were boxes and trinkets that Halley immediately recognized—and around the childish figure, appearing to surround her, to hold her, to touch her, was another figure that almost, but not quite, faded into the darker background; a male figure whose smiling face was not that of a father or brother, but more that of a lover; and as Halley looked at the figure of the child, so innocently involved in her play, she noticed the girl's smile, the way the child's figure leaned back, against and into the male figure, unaware, or not caring that one of the man's hands was slipping over one white thigh, and that the other was almost invisibly touching the breastless torso.

Halley shivered violently. The painting disturbed her more than she could say. "It's Melissa," she whispered. "Melissa Girard."

"Who's Melissa Girard," asked Wilma.

"She lives upstairs, in the top apartment. She's only a child." Halley said the last four words in a voice that exposed her feelings of shock and outrage. Both women turned toward Steven, who was now sweating.

He backed away from them, something like panic in his eyes. "My God! What do you think I am? I don't even know the kid. I haven't met any of the Girard family. How could I . . . ?" He paused, his face a mask of conflicting emotions.

"Exactly," said Wilma quietly. "How could you have painted her, and how could you have painted these others? It seems like they are all here, all of the tenants of the building. All of them in these paintings!"

Steven looked wildly around the room. "It can't be! It just can't be! Some of them I've never even met!"

Halley, moving past the other paintings, stopped in front of the last. Her voice, when she spoke, was emotionless, as if too much feeling had shorted out her emotions. "Even you're here, Steven. This last one is of you!"

Steven's eyes widened, and his voice was hoarse. "That's impossible. I might not know some of the other tenants, but I sure as hell know myself!"

He strode to her side, and looked across her shoulder at the picture in front of her.

The figure of a man stood spread-legged in front of an easel. Upon the easel was a painting of a beautiful, long-haired woman with a bold face. The male figure was holding the sides of the inner painting with his hands, and the woman in the painting was reaching toward him, seemingly coming out of the painting, reaching forward, ready to touch. . . .

"That's not me! It's not anybody I know. I didn't even use a model." Steven was shaking his head wildly from side to side. "How can you say that's me!"

Wilma gently took his arm and led him to the couch. "It's all right, Steven. Just take it easy. We'll figure this out."

He pulled his arm away from her, and frowned. "What is there to figure out? None of those people in the paintings are who she says they are. She's doing this for some reason of her own!"

Halley pressed her hands to her mouth. She felt as if her head and her heart both hurt, and she felt dulled by her own confusion.

Wilma slowly pushed Steven back against the cushions of the couch, and shook her head. "No, Steven. We're going to have to face it. That man in the painting is you, and I'm certain that Halley isn't lying about the others. There is something going on here, something very strange, and I think that we had better get to the bottom of it!"

Isaaic Aschermann turned the corner and saw the police cars and the ambulance in front of the Barkley. He felt the heaviness of premonition in his chest. He knew with a terrible certainty that the tension he had felt building in the apartment house the past few weeks, had broken. Who had broken it, and how, he did not know; but his gut told him that the ambulance was not there for a stranger, a visitor to the Barkley; it was there for one of them, one of the tenants.

As he hurried toward the building, his mind turned over the names and faces. Dear God, please let it not be young Halley, for whom he had developed a paternal affection, or her husband, or . . . dear God! Who was it, and what had happened?

By the time he reached the front of the building, he was panting, and his heart was racing at a frightening speed. Carefully he took three deep breaths, stopping, as he felt a heavy hand touch his arm.

"Would you please move along, sir? We have an emergency here."

Isaaic looked up to see a tall, ruddy-faced young man in a police uniform looking down at him, not unkindly.

"I live here, officer," he said. "I am just getting home. What has happened?"

The young policeman's face showed sympathy. "I'm not allowed to discuss it, sir. If you will just wait a few minutes the lobby will be clear, and you can return to your apartment."

Isaaic leaned weakly against the fender of a car parked by the curb. In a moment, the lobby doors swung open, and two young men in white came out, carrying a litter upon which lay a completly covered form.

Isaaic drew in a deep breath. The face was covered. That meant whoever it was, was dead. He noticed that the figure was large, too large to be any of the women.

The brisk young men in white closed the door of the ambulance, and the vehicle roared away. The policemen got into their cars, and the small crowd of spectators began to disburse.

Still Isaaic stood, unmoving. Much as he longed for the comfort of his apartment, he hesitated to enter those doors which had just emitted the finality of death.

Finally, slowly, he mounted the steps. Inside, in the lobby, he found the Bartolos. Sal was vacuuming the floor, and Ursula was comforting a potted palm, which evidently had gotten jostled during police processes. Both of their faces, which usually wore smiles, were pale and set. Ursula's eyes looked as if she might cry, given the slightest provocation.

They both turned as Isaaic came into the lobby.

"Who was it?" he asked simply.

Sal's usual hearty rumble was subdued as he answered. "Dr. Kauffman."

"Well, then." Isaaic sighed. "How did it happen?"

Sal lowered his eyes, and Ursula shook her head. The

tears, which had been waiting in the shine of her eyes, welled up and spilled over. "I'll finish up out here later, Sal."

Her look beseeched Isaaic's understanding, as she almost ran into her apartment.

"It's been pretty hard on Ursula," Sal said slowly, and then the words came more quickly, as if he wanted to get them out, be done with them. "You see, she saw it all—I mean she saw Kauffman, after his wife . . ." He swallowed. "She got this call from the Kauffman's apartment. It was Mrs. Kauffman, very calm, just like she was calling about something wrong with the plumbing. She calls, and asks Ursula if Ursula would come up and clean up a 'mess' in her apartment. That's what she called it, a mess!

"Now I'm the super, right? And Ursula and I both help the tenants in any way we can, but messes in their apartments are usually their own business. But you know Ursula, she can't say no to anyone. She thought it was kind of strange, but she went on up to the Kauffman apartment, to see what Mrs. Kauffman was talking about, and Mrs. Kauffman met her at the door, just as calm as you please—Ursula says—with her face and clothes all splattered with blood! Right then, Ursula says she got a very funny feeling, but Mrs. Kauffman just led her into the girl's, Helga's, bedroom . . ." Sal took a great, shuddering breath, and swallowed.

"Well, there he was, Kauffman, with his head bashed in, and his blood and brains all . . ."

Isaaic raised his hand, palm forward, and turned his head away. "Enough. Enough!" he said softly.

Sal lowered his head and his face turned a dark, beet red. "Well, like I said, there he was, and on the floor beside him was a statue with blood all over it. Well, Ursula right away called the police, but the whole thing has had a real bad effect on her!"

Isaaic put his hand on the larger man's shoulder. "I'm sure it did. It was a terrible thing to see. It was a terrible thing to have happen. Did they, did the police, know why?"

Sal flushed again, the color rising up from his throat and staining his cheeks. He shrugged, seemingly at a loss for words.

Isaaic squeezed the man's shoulder affectionately. "Well, you go in to her, Sal, and take care of her. This can all wait," he gestured at the lobby, "I'm sure."

Sal bit his lower lip. "They got footprints all over the lobby. There's never been anything like this happen at the Barkley since we've been here!" These last words burst out of him, propelled by pain.

"It will be all right, Sal. These things happen. Bad things happen, things that we cannot prevent, and that we are not responsible for."

"We've always kept a respectable place," Sal whispered, as he turned and followed his wife into their apartment.

As the elevator moved upward, Isaaic mulled over what Sal had told him, and most of all, what he had *not* told him.

Isaaic had long ago admitted to himself that he was, by nature, a curious man. Perhaps that was one of the reasons he had gone into the field of archaeology—a field where the main interest is the uncovering of secrets—but it was more than curiosity that fueled his need to know the circumstances surrounding the death of Ernest Kauffman, for he felt, with a cold certainty, that Kauffman's death was in some way connected with what Isaaic had come to refer to as "the presence" that invaded the apartment house.

It seemed evident to Isaaic that Ursula Bartolo had seen something other than just the dead body of Ernest Kauffman. Her husband's blushing evasiveness made that clear, but she would never talk of it, as she would not speak of anything that might tarnish the name of the Barkley Plaza. The death of a man could not be hidden, but the situation surrounding that death could be covered over; appearances could be changed. The puzzle gnawed at him as he entered his apartment.

He was conscious of a feeling of great depression and unease. He wondered if any of the other tenants were aware of the tragedy, and thought first of all of Halley. Perhaps he should call her, just to see how she was.

The telephone in the McGuire apartment rang several times before anyone answered. Isaaic was grateful that it was Halley who answered; he didn't really know the husband well, and would not have known quite what to say, if Vince had answered.

Halley's voice sounded faint and strained. "Hello?"

"Halley, it's me, Isaaic. I just thought I'd call and see how you are."

Her soft chuckle sounded forced and mirthless. "You really are psychic, aren't you? Now don't tell me you *sensed* something was wrong with me."

He shrugged, although she could not see the gesture. "A good Jewish father always knows when something is wrong with one of his children. So what's the problem?"

She sighed heavily. "It's a long story, Doc. A real two-pot-of-chocolate tale. Can I come on up?"

"Of course. I'll get out the things."

"I'll be right up."

Isaaic hung up the phone. He felt gratified. Already her voice sounded better.

Halley arrived at his door looking like a poor cousin to her usual self. She was wearing a faded caftan, and her hair was uncombed. Her face was pale, and her eyes red, as if she had been crying; however she managed a smile for Isaaic as he let her in.

Her story was indeed a long and a strange one; beginning with the afternoon she had acted as babysitter for Melissa, the afternoon of the dream depicted so eerily in the painting by Steven Street, and ending with her fears about the paternity of her unborn child.

Despite the bizarre quality of her tale, Isaaic found no difficulty in believing any of it.

When she was finished, he told her, as simply as he could, of Kauffman's death; thinking that it would be better coming from him than from the evening news or the morning paper. Her face whitened as she listened.

"It's all tied together somehow, isn't it?" she said softly.

He nodded. "I believe so; and I also believe that it will go on; that other things will happen, if we don't do something to stop it. We must find out what, or who, is responsible. I think it is time that the tenants of the Barkley Plaza get together and hold a meeting. A meeting at which we all must be very honest; where we all must tell of any strange or unusual things which have happened to us within the past few weeks!"

Halley looked at him over her cup, her eyes wide and dark.

"You're right," she said.

TEN

It was a subdued group that met Isaaic's eyes when he entered the Bartolos' comfortably funrished apartment on Monday evening.

Tracy and Elva sat hand-in-hand on the small love seat. Tracy's usually smiling face was serious, and Elva, looking pale and tense, nervously chain-smoked with her free hand.

Halley and Vince McGuire were sitting on opposite ends of the long sofa, and Isaaic took the seat between them. As he looked at Halley, he could feel the tension that emanated from the two young people.

He looked across the room, to where Nina Girard and Melissa were seated on straight-backed dining room chairs. Nina seemed harassed, and her fine-featured face was drawn; but Melissa looked perfectly at home and at ease, her slender legs dangling from the chair seat, not quite reaching the floor.

To Isaaic's right, Steven Street lay back in a large recliner, while Wilma King sat near him on a matching hassock. Steven seemed drained and lethargic, but Wilma's feelings were not apparent.

Isaaic sighed, suddenly aware of the absence of the Kauffmans. He could see again in his mind's eye the headlines of the morning paper: PSYCHIATRIST'S WIFE SLAYS MATE IN PRESENCE OF DAUGHTER! The article that followed was mildly lurid; but he was convinced that it would have been much more so, except for the intervention of Ursula Bartolo.

He turned and smiled at Ursula, but she would not meet his eyes, and, after giving him a grudging smile quickly lowered her head.

It seemed to Isaaic that all of the tenants were reluctant to meet the eyes of their neighbors. Gone was the friendly, open camaraderie that had existed before. Now, everyone seemed to have secrets.

Sal Bartolo, looking anxious and nervous, got up from his chair near the door and faced the group.

"Well," he said hesitantly. "I guess you all know why we're here."

Elva snuffed out her cigarette with a quick thrust, and tossed back her long, silver hair. "No. I can't say that we do, Sal. Just why are we here?"

Tracy shot Elva an inscrutable glance from beneath the dark fringe of her eyelashes, and Sal, flushing and startled, stammered out, "Uh . . . well . . ." before running out of words completely. He shot a pleading glance around the room, but Isaaic was the only one who would meet his eyes directly.

Isaaic sighed deeply, and stood up. It appeared that it was going to be up to him to bring the problem out into the open, where they all could face it.

"Dear friends and neighbors," he said, smiling and gesturing to include them all, "this will be much easier, and we will get much more done, if we do not play games with one another."

Sal, a grateful expression upon his open features, sat back down, and Isaaic realized the floor was now completely his.

"Now, is there anyone here who does not know of the unfortunate death of Ernest Kauffman?"

No one raised a hand, or made a sound.

"Is there anyone present who does not find that death unexpected and shocking?"

Again no hand was raised, and no one looked directly at him.

"One more question. Is there anyone in this room who has *not* had an unusual or strange experience—

something out of the ordinary—happen to him or her, within the past few weeks?"

Sal and Ursula Bartolo looked at one another nervously, and there was some shuffling of feet and clearing of throats.

Suddenly, Nina Girard moved forward in her chair, and, focusing on a spot somewhere over Isaaic's shoulder, said, "What are you getting at, Mr. Aschermann? What are you trying to prove here?" Her voice was high, and full of tension.

Isaaic shrugged and smiled. "*I* am not trying to prove anything, Mrs. Girard; but as one of you, one of the tenants of this building, I cannot help but be aware, and concerned, that something very peculiar has been happening on these premises. I, myself, have experienced certain odd feelings, and I happen to know that others"—he carefully avoided looking at Halley, or Steven Street—"have also had things happen to them that seem to defy the usual laws by which the world runs.

"What I am trying to do, is to get you, each and every one of you, to compare notes, to tell us here, in open session, anything you might know, anything, strange you might have experienced recently, so that we may find out just what this thing is that seems to be stalking us!"

Nina Girard laughed harshly, and all eyes turned to her. "This thing that is stalking us? Isn't that more than a little melodramatic, Mr. Aschermann? Just what do you think is going on? Do you think that the Barkley is harboring some kind of madman?"

Isaaic, determined to be patient, shook his head. "No, Mrs. Girard, not a madman; at least not in the usually accepted meaning of the word. I suppose you might say that right now, I am simply trying to get you to admit that *something* is wrong! If you will admit that, then we can get down to the business of trying to find out what it is."

Halley cleared her throat. "He's right, you know.

Don't fight him. Do as he asks." She looked around at the others. "I'll even go first."

Halley spoke softly but clearly. She told of her feeling of strangeness on the afternoon when she had stayed with Melissa; she even told about the dream experience, leaving out the sexual part, making it seem that the experience had consisted only of the presence of someone, or something, in her locked room. She also told them of the picture that Steven Street had painted, looking at him apologetically as she did so.

When she was finished, Steven took the floor. "What she said about the picture, is true," he said firmly; and then went on with his own story, which he told simply and concisely.

When Steven concluded his contribution and sat down, Isaaic was pleased to see Vince reach for Halley's hand, and move next to her on the couch.

Into the silence following Steven Street's statement, Isaaic interjected his own remarks and conjectures, starting with his feelings of depression, and his belief that a "presence" had come into the building, on the night of the Girard's arrival.

Isaaic's last word was barely spoken, when Steven Street broke in. "You know, I did my first painting on that same night! The night that the Girards moved in!"

Halley looked up, her eyes bright with awareness, and Isaaic knew that she, too, had made some connection. He felt excitement rise in him. He felt that they were making an important discovery.

The room immediately came alive with the buzz of voices, through which Nina Girard's tense soprano cut sharply. "Well, if you are implying that someone in my family has, or had, anything to do with all this nonsense, you're crazier than Mrs. Kauffman. Come on, Melissa!"

Pulling the child by the hand, Nina left the room. The remaining tenants stared thoughtfully after her.

"Methinks the lady doth protest too much!" murmured Wilma King.

"Shhh, now! Hush! We must do this in an orderly fashion." Isaaic unconsciously used his lecturing tone, and the group quickly quieted.

"Now, I think we are getting someplace. Let's start with Apartment One. Mr. and Mrs. Bartolo, did either of you have an unusual or strange experience on the night that the Girards moved in?"

Ursula instantly shook her head, but Sal puzzled over the question for a moment. Finally, "Well, not really an experience, I guess, but I did have some funny dreams that night!" He blushed. "I mean, I don't even usually remember my dreams, but they were really real, and they . . . well, they kind of bothered me, a little . . . if you know what I mean."

"Thank you, Sal. Now, second floor. Tracy and Elva, how about you?"

Elva shook her head. "Nothing!" she said firmly.

Tracy looked at her in surprise. "What do you mean, nothing, girl? You know that was the night that someone tried to take the control away from Minka."

She turned toward Isaaic. "When I asked who it was, it said, 'I am Legion!' We were working the Ouija board," she explained to the rest of the group. "It was real scary." This last, defiantly, she said to Elva.

"Yes. Thank you, Tracy. And Number Three, the Kauffmans. We'll never know for sure, but I can't help but wonder if that wasn't the first night that Helga Kauffman first exhibited her strange sexual behavior!

"Then, Four. Steven, you've already stated that you did your first new painting that night, and Halley and I have already told you of our experiences. That leaves only the Girards, and it seems that Mrs. Girard does not care to talk about it. Does anyone know where Mr. Girard is?"

Halley nodded and spoke up. "Away on a business trip. Maybe I can . . . well, maybe I can talk to her.

She's really a very nice person. It's just that she's upset and . . ."

"Yeah. A little too upset, if you ask me," Steven Street grumbled. "What's she hiding, anyway?"

Issaic, seeing the suspicion beginning to gather, raised his arms. "No! No! Now, we must not rush into accusations. We must go about this logically. We are not witch-hunting here!"

Elva snubbed out another cigarette, and laughed mockingly. "Aren't we? You've told us the same as that, you know. You've implied that there is some kind of evil *presence*; witch, demon, or whatever, in our building. Why not come right out and say it? Tell us what you're thinking, Isaaic."

Isaaic took a deep breath. "All right," he said, "I shall. I only hesitate because of the fact that most of you will find what I am going to say unacceptable, if not unbelievable. What I think, ladies and gentlemen, is that the Barkley Plaza is, and has been, for the past month, host to an incubus!"

A very pregnant silence greeted Isaaic's last word. Sal Bartolo, his forehead wrinkled in concentration, looked at Isaaic in confusion. "Incubus, Dr. Aschermann? What's an incubus?"

Isaaic clasped his hands behind his back in a gesture that any of his ex-students could have readily identified. "An incubus, Sal, is a sexual demon. A creature who takes on human form in order to have sexual union with mortal men and women."

Sal shot an embarrassed glance at Ursula, and his face reddened. "Oh," he said apologetically. Then, "I still don't understand!"

Elva Miller lit still another cigarette, and broke the match into the ashtray. "Why do you say, incubus, Isaaic? Why not succubus? If I didn't know you better, I'd accuse you of being a male supremist!" Although she spoke lightly no one laughed.

"I am trying to make it as simple as possible, Elva," said Isaaic reprovingly. "This is not, I assure you, a laughing matter. Think about what happened to the Kauffmans, and then consider the possibility that their recent tragedy may not be the last to occur in the Barkley, if we do nothing!"

Steven Street got to his feet, and walked over to stand by Isaaic. "I, for one, don't know an incubus from an outubus, but I do know that something pretty peculiar is going on in this building, something outside of my experience, and I sure as hell want to find out what it is. As I told you a few minutes ago, I'm involved. I don't want to be, but I am! If any of you doubt what Mr. Aschermann has been saying, well, you can drop by my apartment after this meeting and I'll show you a few pictures which may change your mind!"

Halley tentatively raised her hand. "Isaaic, when we were talking about incubi and succubi, I thought you seemed to believe that they were not demons, per se." She looked around at the others. "Dr. Aschermann and I have talked about this before."

She looked back at Isaaic. "I mean, I got the impression from your conversation, and from that book you lent me, that such creatures weren't necessarily evil, and that they did not necessarily want to do humans harm—so, how does that equate with all this?"

Isaaic nodded. "A fair question. The only answer I have to that is that someone doesn't have to *intend* to do you harm to hurt you. My own feeling is that a creature such as an incubus would be completely amoral, entirely careless of the effect of its actions upon the people with whom it comes in contact. But to us, however, the creatures' intentions are academic. What matters is the result of the contact, and I'm afraid that for some of us, the result has been tragic!"

Halley waved her hand. "I think that we should ask Isaaic to take charge of this . . . well . . . this investigation."

"I agree!" said Steven Street.

"And I think that if there is anybody here who

hasn't spoken up, anyone who has had an experience, but is afraid to talk about it in front of the rest of us, they should go to Isaaic in private, and tell him their story. It seems to me that we need all the information we can get; and we all know that Isaaic can be trusted to protect a confidence. What do you say? Isaaic's the only one of us who has had any experience with such things."

"Except for my roommate, who probably called up the dammed thing!" Elva's voice was cutting. Tracy pulled her hand away from the other girl's hand, and gave her a hurt look.

"If I did, it wasn't knowingly! I think Halley and Dr. Aschermann are right. I think we should all admit that we've felt something is wrong; that we've all had strange experiences; and that we don't know what to do about it. I've been having dreams too. Dreams that bother me, and I want them to stop."

Elva gave Tracy a curious look. "Do you really?"

Tracy looked away from the other girl. "Yes, really. I want to feel in control of my own life again. I think we should ask Dr. Aschermann to take charge. Let's vote on it!"

Isaaic raised both of his hands, palms forward. "First, how many of you agree that there *is* something to investigate?"

All present, save for Elva, raised their hands.

"And how many of you want me to take charge of an investigation to find out what it is?"

This time all hands were raised. Tracy smiled at Elva, and patted her shoulder.

Standing in front of these people, his friends and neighbors, Isaaic sighed, knowing that the real trouble, for him, might be just beginning.

Before pressing the button for the elevator, Vince pulled Halley close, and kissed her on the forehead. "I'm sorry, honey! I know that words aren't nearly enough, but at least it's a start. It's just that when I saw that picture . . . well, it made me a little crazy! I'll make it up to you. I promise!"

Halley clung to him with tears in her eyes. "Oh, Vince. The way you looked at me! I can't tell you how . . ."

"Hush, baby." He smoothed her hair back from her face. "It's going to be all right. I can see now, after listening to Aschermann, that it has something to do with Street, and not you at all."

Halley looked up into his eyes with a sinking feeling. He didn't understand any of it! "But . . ." she said.

He stilled her lips with his finger. "Never mind now. It's all going to be fine."

But Halley, knowing things that her husband did not, was far from being reassured.

As they reached their apartment, Halley could hear the phone ringing insistently on the other side of the door.

As he opened the door, Vince smiled at Halley. "Whoever it is, get rid of them. We have a lot of making up to do."

Halley returned his smile reflexively. She was very relieved to have Vince reacting normally again, but her mind was filled with other things. Quickly, she picked up the phone, anxious to still it's ringing.

"Halley?" It was Nina Girard's voice, sounding thin and taut as strung wire. "Are you busy? Can I talk to you for a few minutes?" And, as Halley hesitated, "I simply *have* to talk to someone, and you're the only one I really know!"

"I'll be right up." Halley hung up the phone, and turned to face a puzzled Vince.

"Hey, babe, what do you mean you'll be right up? Who was that, anyway?"

Halley moved close to him, and put her arms around his waist. "It was Nina Girard. She needs me to stay with Melissa for a few minutes. It's really an emergency, and I'm the only one she knows well enough to call on."

Halley was amazed at the ease with which the half lie tripped from her tongue. "I'll only be about a half hour or so, and in the meantime, you can take a hot bath, and be all relaxed for when I come back." She moved against him suggestively, and felt him respond.

"All right. But make it fast. I have a lot of apologizing to do, and it may take some time." He pulled her close, then released her. "So go do your errand of mercy. Just remember that you have a husband waiting for you, who needs a little mercy too."

When Nina opened her apartment door, Halley's first thought was, My God! She looks terrible!

Nina's usually perfectly groomed hair was disheveled and stringy, and her face was an unhealthy white, devoid of makeup.

"Nina, what is it?"

Nina almost pulled her into the room. "Oh, Halley! Oh, God! I'm so glad you came. I think I'm going crazy! I really do. I guess I need someone to tell me I'm not, or at least that's what I hope you will tell me; but after I've talked to you, maybe you won't. I mean, maybe *you'll* think I'm crazy too."

"Shhh, now." Halley found herself making soothing noises, instinctively trying to calm the overwrought woman. "You're not going crazy. You've just got something bothering you that needs to be talked out. We'll have some tea—where do you keep it?—and you'll tell me all about it, and we'll work it out."

As Nina distractedly led Halley to the tea cannister in the kitchen, Halley surrepticiously watched her. Nina really looked as if she had reached the end of her rope, physically and mentally, and Halley wondered if she was up to handling the situation. But it was too late now to back away.

When they were both seated in the living room with ceramic mugs of hot, honeyed tea, Halley leaned forward and touched the older woman's hand.

At the touch, Nina winced, and then began to talk, as if the words, bottled up inside her for so long, were coming out under great, internal pressure.

"I just couldn't tell Dr. Aschermann, not in front of everyone. In fact, I haven't been able to tell anyone, not even Martin. But I can't go on this way! I simply can't!"

Her words faded into great, wracking sobs, and Halley, empathetically feeling Nina's pain, felt like crying also. "It's all right. It's all right," she murmured. "Let it out. You have to let it out."

Nina pulled a tissue out of the pocket of her robe, and wiped her eyes and nose. "It's Melissa, or maybe I should say, not Melissa, herself, but . . ." She leaned forward. "I hear noises in her room. The sound of voices. Laughing. Two voices, Melissa's and . . . and a man's."

She looked pleadingly into Halley's eyes, as if begging her to believe, and Halley, finding her story no stranger than her own recent experiences, did.

"Yes, Nina. And when you go into the room?"

Nina's shoulders sagged. "There's no one there but Melissa. Just Melissa, looking secret and excited, with all of those, those . . ."

She threw the wadded tissue to the floor. "Those damned trinkets of hers spread around her on the bed, and that box, she always has that box open on her lap." She paused, a strange expression crossing her face, as if she was trying to remember something that eluded her.

"And the room is hot," said Halley softly, "and smells of oranges."

Nina glanced up quickly, fear in her eyes. "How could you know?"

"Because I saw and felt it too, that afternoon when you had me sit with Melissa."

Nina lay back against the cushions. "Thank God! Then it's not all my imagination! Every time I go into her room—after I've heard the other voice—the room is hot as a greenhouse, even though the thermostat is set on seventy, and I almost gag on the smell." Her nostrils flared. "That smell reminds me of something, Halley, but I can't remember what." She put her fingers to her temples and closed her eyes. "There is so much that I can't seem to remember lately."

"Nina, how long has this been going on?"

Nina took a swallow of the hot tea, and her voice grew stronger. "Since we moved in here." There was something evasive in her tone, that caught Halley's attention.

"Did it ever happen before that? Before you moved in here?"

Nina hesitated, then shook her head. "Not exactly."

Halley persisted. "What do you mean, not exactly?"

"Well, before we came back to the States, we were in Italy. Just outside Rome."

Halley, sensing that there was something important that Nina was not telling me, kept on. "Nina, I can see that you're reluctant to talk about this, but I think you should. I think you *need* to. Did something unusual happen to you, or to Melissa, in Italy?"

Again Nina hesitated before answering, and a puzzled, frightened expression animated her features for a moment, and then all expression vanished. With relaxed features and blank eyes, Nina said flatly. "In Italy, my husband was unfaithful to me."

Halley felt both chilled and confused. Nina's words seemed out of context. Halley was sure that it had been a difficult admission for Nina to make, but what did it have to do with Melissa, and the strange voice in her room?

Hesitantly, made to feel a little frightened by the flat look in Nina's eyes, Halley said, "Did Melissa have any trouble in Italy? Did anything happen to Melissa?"

Nina drew back as if struck, and for a moment her eyes came alive. "Yesssssss!" the word was drawn out of her, as if painfully.

Halley felt her breath catch in her throat. She wanted nothing so much as to get up and run back to her own apartment, but her curiosity, and compassion for Nina, would not let her stop. "What happened? Nina, you must tell me. What happened in Italy?"

Nina, leaning back against the cushions, drew further back still, as if someone, or something was physically exerting pressure upon her. She opened her mouth, and Halley could see her tongue moving, but no sounds came from her throat. She shook her head wildly. "Can't!" finally exploded out of her with gutteral resonance, and then her body slumped forward, as if the pressure against it had been released.

"My God!" Halley said. "Nina, are you all right?"

Nina nodded weakly, and began to cry silently.

Halley moved closer to the other woman, and put her arm around Nina's thin shoulders. "Nina, something is very wrong here."

Nina raised her head slightly. "I know!"

"Does this always happen when you try to talk about it?" Halley asked the question tentatively, wondering if the query wound bring on another paroxysm, but Nina only shook her head. "I don't know. I never tried before."

She fought to bring her voice under control. "The strange thing is, I don't even know what it was I tried to tell you. I . . . I've never told Martin, or Melissa, but I don't really remember many of the things that happened while we were in Italy. I remember some things; but there are large blank spots. Sometimes Martin or Melissa will mention something that happened to us all, and I have to pretend that I remember. It's terrifying!"

Halley sighed. "Wow. Sort of a selective amnesia."

Nina nodded. "Apparently."

"But you know that *something* happened in Italy; something beside the fact that your husband was unfaithful to you?"

Nina flushed. "Yes. I know it, and I know that I

must not let it happen again; that I must protect my family against . . ." She gestured helplessly. "You see? I can't even keep the subject in focus. It's maddening! The most awful feeling, like having an itch in a place that you can't scratch."

Halley laughed, but the laughter was sympathetic. "Do you think that this thing, whatever it was, that happened, has something to do with what's going on now—the voice in Melissa's room, the heat, the smell?"

Her "yes" was only a faint whisper.

Halley took a deep breath. "Now, Nina, I want you to listen to me. I think you need help, professional help."

Nina smiled sadly. "So, you do think I'm crazy."

"No, wait until I'm finished. Not that kind of help, exactly. I think that whatever happened to you in Italy was so traumatic that you've blocked it out." As she said this, she had a vision of Nina's body being pressed back against the cushions of the couch by an apparent outside force. She shook the image away.

"I've also got a feeling that it has a lot to do with what is going on in this building right now!"

Nina's expression changed, and Halley touched her arm. "I don't mean that it's your fault in any way, yours or anyone in your family—but I do think there's a connection!

"Now, I would like your permission to tell Dr. Aschermann what you've told me, and to ask him for his help. He knows a lot of people at the university, and I'll bet he can find someone to help you. What do you say?"

Nina turned her head aside. "I don't know. I'm afraid!"

Halley took the older woman's hand in hers. "Don't be afraid. Whatever you find out can't be any worse than what you're going through right now, can it? You've admitted that you're on the verge of cracking up. Let me talk to Dr. Aschermann!"

Slowly, Nina nodded. "All right. I've got to do something! I *can't* go on like this any longer!"

Halley gave Nina's hand a squeeze. "Good! I'll talk to Dr. Aschermann right now, and I'll call you later tonight."

ELEVEN

Dr. Sidney Allbright was a slender, gentle-looking young man with sympathetic eyes and a warm smile. He looked far too young, in Nina's opinion, to have a Ph.D. in Psychology; but Dr. Aschermann had assured her that Allbright was one of the best in the business, and a specialist in the use of hypnosis as a psychiatric tool.

She looked across the desk at him now, and his level gaze and kind expression alleviated the nervousness she had been carrying with her all the way to this meeting in his office at the university.

"So you think hypnosis is the answer?" she asked.

He raised a quizzical eyebrow. "I would say, rather, that it is a tool, to help us get at the answer. Right now, your conscious mind will not recall the details of your stay in Italy. Under hypnosis, I will send you back to the time you spent there; have you relive your experiences, talk of them."

She smiled slightly. "I feel like one of the three faces of Eve."

He nodded. "In a way, you are. We all have many faces, and often we don't show them all to all people."

She smiled again, but her hands began to twist nervously in her lap. "Will it hurt?" she asked, only half jokingly.

He laughed. "It shouldn't, at least not in the physical sense. If there is psychic unease, I can make you forget that."

"Psychic unease," she repeated. "I certainly have plenty of that right now, and I certainly would like to get rid of it. Well, when do we start?"

"How about right now? If you'll just lie down on the lounge, here, and make yourself comfortable . . ."

Nina moved over to the velours-covered lounge, and lay back against the pillowed end. It was surprisingly comfortable. She folded her hands across her stomach, and waited for Dr. Allbright's further instructions, watching him as he closed the blinds and dimmed the table lamp. As the light in the room grew dimmer, her tension mounted. Out of the corner of her eye, she could see Dr. Allbright seating himself beside her, near the desk. He moved his hand, and a soft tick-tock sound began to fill the room with regularity.

"Just listen to the metronome, Mrs. Girard. Listen to the sound—it sounds just like a clock, doesn't it?—just like time slipping away. It's a peaceful sound. As you listen to it, your body will begin to relax. You will feel very peaceful, very heavy and warm."

His voice was firm, yet soft; soothing, Nina decided. The tick-tock of the metronome sounded just like the the grandfather's clock that had stood on the landing of her parents' home.

"Your body is growing very heavy now, very relaxed. Your eyelids are growing heavy. Your eyes are closing."

Nina took a deep, easy breath. She felt wonderful—relaxed and unafraid. She felt herself drifting into sleep, as if she were easing gently down a long, slow slide.

"Now you are asleep, but you will still hear my voice. You will do what I tell you to do. Do you hear me, Mrs. Girard?"

"Yes, I hear you."

"Listen to the clock, Mrs. Girard. It is sending you backward into time. It is July of last year, Mrs. Girard. You and your family are just arriving in Italy. Are you there, Mrs. Girard? Can you see it?"

"Yes, I can see it."

"Tell me what you see and feel."

Some portion of Nina's mind registered the click and whir of a tape recorder starting up, as she began to talk.

Nina's feelings about Rome—in fact, about Italy in general—were ambivalent. True, there was great beauty here—everywhere the ruins, touchstones of the past, stood in damaged but seemingly eternal loveliness—but she could not get rid of the feeling that everything was too lush, too warm, too physical, here.

Martin laughingly told her that it was her New England upbringing, that her cool, ordered, Puritan spirit was outraged by this Latin opulence; and perhaps he was right. He also said that she would get over it, and there, perhaps, he was wrong.

It was not that she was not enjoying herself. She was thrilled by the chance to see the places she had read of in her youth and young womanhood; but she felt a holding back, a reserve, which was in no way shared by her husband and daughter.

It seemed to Nina that Martin and Melissa had, immediately upon their arrival, gone native. Martin already spoke a little Italian, and Melissa, bright sprite that she was, seemed to absorb the language like a sponge. They fit right in with these colorful, laughing people, and left Nina feeling a bit like a schoolmarmish outsider, sitting primly to one side, while the others enjoyed themselves.

Despite this original reluctance to yield herself up to the beauties of Italy, Nina's first impression of the small villa, which Martin had engaged for them outside Rome, was very favorable.

They arrived at the villa in late afternoon, and the sunlight—heavy and golden as some exotic liquid—seemed sprinkled upon the plantings of the lush garden, and lay pooled upon the terrazo patio.

In the center of the patio stood a white, marble

fountain. In the center of the fountain, a small marble boy squatted, holding a stone pitcher from which water burbled and fell away to the fountain bed below.

The villa itself was a two-storied, pink stucco concoction with rococo ornamentation, like swirls of decorative icing, around the windows and doors. It was lovely in a rather awful fashion.

Martin squeezed her shoulders. "It's our pink palazzo, darling. Isn't it great?"

She smiled, and covered his hands with hers. "Marvelous! It's just what an Italian villa should look like."

Melissa had already run ahead of them, through the garden and to the fountain. She leaned over and scooped up handfuls of the clear water, flinging it to the sky with delighted laughter. The drops shone like prisms in the clear, warm air; Nina didn't think she could ever remember being so happy. It would be lovely here, away from the city, which frightened her with its exuberance and strangeness. Here it would be peaceful and quiet. She could work on her needlepoint, tutor Melissa, maybe paint a little. Martin would go into the city to work, then come home at night, just as he always had. On weekends they would take trips to visit points of interest.

She squeezed his hand again. "I'm glad we came here, darling. I really am."

He pulled her close and kissed her neck back of her left ear. "I'm glad too, sweetheart."

They stood there for a long time, watching Melissa as she darted along the garden paths like some mad butterfly, laughing in excitement.

The villa was completely furnished—there was even a live-in maid—and moving in entailed only unpacking their clothing and personal belongings.

Despite the ornate, gilded furniture, despite the gold-framed mirrors and marble cupids, the interior had a certain insouciance that caught Nina's fancy. Melissa, of course, adored the place on sight, and even

Martin, usually somewhat oblivious to his surroundings, confessed that he found it "charming."

The first two weeks went by quickly, slipping away in a series of hot, peaceful days, and warm, perfumed nights.

Martin's new job was going well. The family soon settled into an easy routine, and except for one thing, life was almost idyllic.

This one thing was a problem that had been with Nina and Martin since their marriage—not a large problem really, but a circumstance that made their marriage less than perfect; and here, in Italy, it seemed to be intensified.

The problem, or the difficulty, lay in the fact that Martin wished that Nina would show more passion and abandon in their lovemaking. He never said so in so many words, but Nina could sense his unspoken disappointment. He had tried to encourage her; tried—she had to admit, subtly—to get her to "loosen" up, to let go, but the more she was conscious of this gentle pressure, the more self-conscious she became.

It was not that she did not feel passion, for she did. She loved her husband very much, and enjoyed having him fondle and make love to her. It was just that, for some reason, she could not let go. She could not forget herself—Nina Girard, Lady—even in bed.

Someone had once told her that every man wanted his woman to be three things: a cook in the kitchen; a lady in the parlor; and a whore in bed—and that a woman should never confuse the roles. Well, she was certainly a lady in the parlor, and even a cook in the kitchen—it was the third category that she had trouble with.

As soon as they were settled in, she began tutoring Melissa. At first she held the lessons in the small arbor that sat at the end of the garden; but she soon found that the location was not conducive to work of any sort. The breeze gently ruffling the leaves of the grapevine that covered the small building, the rich scent of the flowers, the sound of the fountain's musical rainfall—they were all well suited to engendering daydreams, but not at all to serious study. So Melissa's classes were conducted indoors, in the music room, where the view of the garden was not quite so distracting.

It was during one of their study sessions that Marie, the plump, apple-cheeked maid, came into the room to announce the presence of a guest. Her round face made serious by the importance of their caller, she formally announced: "The Contessa de Fiore," and presented Nina with a heavily embossed calling card.

Nina had not the slightest idea who the woman was, but one could hardly ignore such an impressive caller.

Matching Marie's formal manner, Nina nodded. "Show her in."

She looked at Melissa, and they both broke into giggles.

"It's just like a movie, Mama," Melissa whispered.

The door opened again, and a tall, angular woman, with pale, striking features swept into the room, bringing with her a cloud of heavy, musk-based perfume that made Nina want to cough.

The Contessa was of indeterminate age—whatever damage time had done was efficiently covered by the cosmetician's art—and her deep red hair was piled in an intricate, swirling mass atop her head. Her expression was somewhat cold, but her black eyes glowed intensely with life.

She swooped toward Nina in a sort of darting rush that was somewhat disconcerting, and held out a long-fingered, much be-ringed hand. Nina was not quite certain whether she was expected to shake the offered appendage, or kiss it. She settled for touching it with her own fingertips, and murmuring that it was a pleasure to make the Contessa's acquaintance.

The Contessa smiled, another disconcerting effect,

as the smile did not reach the dark, searching eyes. In a low, heavily accented voice, she said, "Mrs. Girard. So very glad to finally meet you—you and your so lovely little girl. Of course, having met your handsome husband when he rented my villa, I knew that his family would be equally attractive." She looked at Melissa searchingly, then turned those strange eyes to Nina. "Your child, if I may say so, is *unusually* lovely. You are to be congratulated."

Her dark, intense gaze brooked no disagreement, so Nina contented herself with smiling politely; however in her opinion true, natural beauty was a random gift from the gods, and since one did nothing to deserve it, it did not require a compliment. In addition, all of Melissa's young life she had been exposed to this sort of comment—well meant, but apt to cause an overdose of vanity, particularly in a young child. Nina did not want her daughter to grow up to be one of those young women who relied solely upon their personal beauty to obtain tribute from the world.

Nina was puzzled by her own inability to speak up to the Contessa, and yet she hated to admit that the woman intimidated her.

The Contessa swooped toward Melissa, and Nina was glad to see that the child held her ground, and offered her hand politely.

Then the woman turned back toward Nina. "Perhaps I should say who I am. I live in the large palazzo on the hilltop behind you. I am, what you call, your landlord, no?"

She favored them with another mirthless smile, and Nina found herself nodding dutifully. "Oh yes, of course."

The Contessa then swept around the room, as Nina and Melissa exchanged glances, trying not to smile. "Are you happy here? Is it to your satisfaction?"

"Oh yes, we love it. We all love it. It's so restful."

The woman nodded. "Ah, yes. A lovely spot. I particularly fancy the garden. Have you found someone to tend it for you yet?"

Nina felt startled. She hadn't really given a thought to the care of the garden—they had been there such a short time. Now she realized that they would have to have someone. The grounds were far too large for her to maintain herself, and Martin was home so little . . . "Well, no," she admitted. "Not yet, at any rate."

"I shall send someone." The words were a statement of fact, not a question. "The son of one of my staff. An excellent boy. He will work cheaply."

"Why . . . thank you." Nina wondered if Martin would approve, but there didn't seem to be any way to gracefully refuse the woman's offer. "Would you care for some tea, a cold drink?"

The Contessa shook her head. "Not today, thank you. I am on my way to Rome. I only wanted to greet you, and to ask you to come to my home for dinner on Friday. We will be holding a little séance after dinner. It might amuse you."

Nina found herself stammering. "Why, I think . . . that is I'm not certain we're free. I'll have to check with my husband."

The Contessa nodded. "I am sure he will want to accept. I will see you then." She turned to Melissa, and patted her hair. "You must come too. On one night of the week, you can be a grownup also, no?"

She looked at Nina with this last, and Nina found herself nodding, although she was definately opposed to the presence of children at adult gatherings.

"*Ciao!*" said the Contessa. "Till Friday, then."

"Till Friday," said Nina grudgingly, angry over the fact that the Contessa had bullied her—she could think of no other suitable word—in coming to a party that she did not really want to attend; and also into agreeing to allow Melissa to attend an adult gathering of complete strangers. Why had she been so spineless?

And then she caught Melissa's eye, and they broke

into mutual, sympathetic laughter, and she thought that she had never felt so close to her daughter.

Nina looked up at the facade of the Contessa's villa. Although it was constructed of what seemed to be the same pink stucco as their own, smaller, structure, there was no comparison as to grandness or elegance.

A white, gravel walk approached the building and divided to form an elegant, circular walkway in front of a pillared porch. In the center of the walkway was a formal garden, ordered and trimmed; but privately Nina preferred their own garden's reckless abundance.

A liveried butler admitted them through the wide, double doors, and they entered a vast, marble-floored entrance hall over which hung an enormous gilded chandelier. Heavy, thronelike chairs with velvet seats and backs rested against the walls, and gleaming marble statues graced the many pedestals placed in nooks and beside entryways.

To their right, a wide, marble staircase with a gilded bannister rose in a ponderous curve, to unseen heights.

Martin leaned over and whispered into Nina's ear. "I can't decide whether I'm on a movie set or at the museum."

Nina smiled, and took a firmer grip on Melissa's hand. The place was making her uneasy, and she didn't know why. It was plainly ridiculous, of course; they were barely into the building.

The butler showed them into a large, richly furnished room, already occupied by a great number of people. The sound of so many voices raised in animated conversation formed a cacophony that Nina found unnerving, but Martin and Melissa plunged into the group as they would into a friendly sea, pulling Nina behind them, until they were surrounded by the faces of strangers.

Nina admitted to herself that she was probably being imaginative, but she thought that she had never before seen so many out-of-the-ordinary countenances. The Contessa's friends all seemed to be of the type characterized by the word "eccentric." The general style of dress was what might have been referred to as flamboyant and exotic; and the general age, as the age of the Contessa herself, indeterminate—although it was quite clear that Melissa was the only child present.

Again, Nina felt a stab of resentment for being manuevered into bringing her daughter; she thought both the company and the hour unsuitable, but even Martin had sided with the Contessa. When he had heard that the Contessa had issued Melissa a special invitation, he had good-naturedly agreed with the child's pleas to attend.

Nina could see the Contessa on the other side of the room. She was sitting on a gilded, high-backed chair, upon a slight dais—for all the world like a member of royalty, holding court. Nina felt a bit embarrassed when she remembered that the Contessa was, indeed, royalty of a sort, but this, she thought, was carrying pomp a bit too far.

Martin was headed in the Contessa's direction, although it was rather slow-going in the crowded room. Despite the guests' animated interest in their conversations, Nina could see the side-long looks their passage occasioned. She found these glances oddly unnerving.

Then, they were through the crush, and into the relatively uncrowded space surrounding the Contessa and her court.

The Contessa looked down upon them, and gestured regally. For a brief moment, Nina humorously wondered if she was expected to curtsy. Martin held out his hand, and the Contessa took it, and shook it briskly. "Ah, Mr. Girard, and his so-charming family. I am so happy that you could come. Now, first, you must have some refreshments."

She clapped her hands, and a cadaverous waiter in

a resplendent, red velvet suit of livery, appeared at Nina's side, proffering a silver tray upon which rested several crystal glasses containing a pale golden liquid.

Gratefully, Nina took a glass. Her throat was tense and dry. Martin also took a glass, and as the waiter turned away with the tray, the Contessa motioned him back. "One for our small friend, also. It won't hurt her," this to Nina. "It is only a little light wine."

Nina, beginning to shake her head, was stopped by Martin's hand on her arm. "We'll let her have just one. After all, it's a special occasion."

Nina, again resentful—she was *definitely* against children being allowed to drink *any* intoxicating beverage—found herself unable to face the attention that public disagreement would bring. Melissa was given one of the glasses of wine.

The Contessa smiled at the child, obviously so delighted with her grown-up glass of wine, and motioned to her. "Come, little love. Sit here by me."

The woman moved to one side of the large chair, leaving a small space on the other. Melissa, without even looking at her mother, hopped up on the dais, and squeezed into the chair next to the Contessa.

Nina, fighting the urge to pull Melissa down from the seat, buried her face in her glass, and took several large swallows of the cool wine. Why was she feeling this way? The Contessa was simply a vain, overbearing woman, who enjoyed playing at royalty. Where was the harm?

Nina had several—she didn't really know how many—glasses of the mild-tasting wine, and from then on the evening became a sort of pleasant blur—faces melting into faces; conversations which she could not understand; a meal too rich, and accompanied by too much wine; a dinner partner, male, who kept touching her knees under the table; a dinner partner, female, who kept up an incomprehensible monologue.

She looked hopefully down the huge table to Martin, who was sitting about half-way down the opposite side, but he seemed deep in conversation with a horse-faced blonde in sequins. Melissa had been seated to the right of the Contessa, and Nina was somewhat annoyed to see that they seemed quite chatty.

After the meal—which seemed interminable—came the promised séance, which was held in the cavernous library.

Nina found the séance upsetting. She was not one of the ten guests who participated—holding hands around a polished table—but it disturbed her to see that Martin and Melissa were right there in the thick of things.

She put her hand to her head. She had drunk too much wine, and her temples throbbed unmercifully. She paid little attention to the activities at the table. It was too dim to see properly, as the only light came from a row of candles on a low console nearby. The participants all seemed to have their eyes closed, and they looked unpleasantly like corpses; particularly the fat, pasty, little woman, whom the Contessa had introduced as the medium.

Nina did not pay much attention to the rappings and table-thumpings, but she did take some notice when the medium turned stiff as a board, and began to talk in a hollow, deep voice. She was feeling too woozy to really pay attention, until she heard Melissa's voice cry out—a sharp, high cry—which brought Nina immediately to her feet.

The figures at the table were frozen into a tableau that seemed to waver with the fluctuating candle light. The sitters still had their eyes closed, and the medium was still rigid in her chair; but Melissa was on her feet, her mouth open, and her eyes wide. The expression on her face . . . what was it? Fear? Joy?

There was one thing Nina did know. Her child had cried out. She felt hands touching her; holding her; trying to stop her; but she broke away and ran, stumbling, to the table, to Melissa, and pulled the child's hands free of the sitters on either side of her.

Melissa blinked once, then looked up at her, as if there was nothing in the world wrong. "What's the matter, Mommy?" she said in her clear voice. And then Martin was beside them, and the Contessa was assuring her that it was not unusual for a spirit to possess one of the participants at a séance, and that no harm had come to Melissa. The rest of the guests were now shaking their heads, waving their arms, and speaking volubly in Italian.

The drive home was not altogether pleasant. Martin had his mouth set in the grim line that meant that he was annoyed, and Melissa was pouting at being dragged away from the séance, which she had thought was "fun."

Nina felt near to tears, and grossly misunderstood. She had reacted in what she considered a perfectly natural way, to what had seemed to be a threat to her daughter. Now, Martin and Melissa were acting as if she had done something gauche. She privately vowed that she would accept no more of the Contessa's invitations.

Later, thinking back on that night, Nina realized that it was just after the Contessa's party that things began to go wrong. Perhaps that wasn't quite the word for what happened; perhaps it would be more exact to say that things changed, slowly, and to Nina, insidiously.

The first incident, was the advent of the young gardener. The day after the Contessa's party, he appeared at the door of the Girard's villa. Martin had already left for the city, and Melissa was at the piano in the music room, carefully practicing Ravel's *Pavane pour une Infante Defunte*. The lovely, haunting melody had put Nina into a pensive mood; she had decided to go out into the garden, while the flowers were still fresh with the night's dew.

As she opened the door, she cried out, and her hand

flew to her mouth. A young man was standing on the doorstep, hand raised, as if halted in the act of knocking.

"I'm sorry," said Nina. "You startled me."

The young man smiled. "I am sorry too, signora. I would not purposely have startled you for the world." He answered in perfect, if heavily accented, English.

Nina knew she was staring; but could not seem to stop. The boy's beauty was like a blow: soft, black curls framed a face that was saved from prettiness by high, slanting cheekbones, and a strong jaw. His eyes were very large, very dark, and fringed by heavy, black lashes. Beneath a slightly curving, arrogant nose, his full lips were both sensuous and firm. The brown skin of his throat looked as smooth as velvet, and the muscles of his shoulders and arms, exposed by the sleeveless jersey he wore, were beautifully made.

Nina, who had never done such a thing in her life, found her eyes drawn to the point where his muscular legs joined, in the tight trousers. The considerable bulge there made her face grow hot. She turned away, so that he would not see her consternation, and walked a few steps back, into the house.

As if this was a signal for him to follow, the boy came after her into the room. As he came toward her, his rather sly smile told her that her discomfiture had not gone unnoticed. Well, she would have to put him in his place right now.

"What was it you wanted?" she asked coldly.

He smiled again, and took another step toward her. "Why, I am Dion, signora. The Contessa sent me. I have come to look after your garden."

He said these last words with the same intonation that he might have given the words, "I have come to be your lover." Nina felt her expression tighten. "Oh, yes," she said. "You will start today?" My God! What inane questions she was asking.

"Yes, signora, I will work until noon."

At that moment, the sound of the piano ceased, and

in its place Nina heard the sound of Melissa's running feet coming toward them. There was a strange, timeless moment, as Nina and the boy stared at one another, gazes locked, and then Melissa burst into the entry way.

"Mother, I'm finished. It's been a whole hour. I'm going over to Annette's. Her daddy got her a pony!"

Nina registered the words, and found them logical and sensible. Annette's parents owned the nearest villa, the equivalent of two blocks away, and the two girls often played together.

"All right," she answered automatically. "Be home by lunch time."

"Okay." Melissa flung a bright, curious glance at Dion, and skipped past him, out the door.

The young man's eyes flicked toward the child, then returned to lock again with Nina's eyes.

"Is your husband home?" he asked softly, not taking his eyes from hers.

Nina felt herself thrown off balance by the question, and began to stammer, "Ah, I . . . no, he's not home. Why do you ask?"

He shrugged, a gesture that carried so much more meaning than an English or an American shrug.

"I wanted to talk to him." Again, the laughter behind the words, as if they shared a common secret, as if he knew her thoughts. She flushed.

Again his eyes engaged hers, and for a moment she felt dizzy and disoriented. She closed her eyes, and heard the sound of the door closing. When she opened her eyes the boy was gone. She could see him through the window, walking toward the garden, with his tool box over his arm.

TWELVE

"How are you coming with Mrs. Girard? Are you getting to the heart of the matter?"

Sidney smiled. "Well, not quite the heart of the matter, as you put it, Isaaic. There seems to be a great deal of buried material, and all of it fascinating. The moment that woman's feet touched Italian soil, something seems to have started. I say 'something' because I don't know what to call it. She has given her permission for you to audit the tapes we've already done, and for you to be present at our next session. I tell you, it's one of the most interesting cases I've ever handled."

Isaaic nodded thoughtfully. "How many sessions do you think will be necessary before you locate the primary incident?"

Sidney moved around behind his desk. "I don't know. I'm having her go through it all, starting with her arrival in Rome. I think it's all important, and I don't want to push for the source of her problem, without getting the preliminary material. First of all, she would probably fight it—after all, she's got the incident, or whatever it is, pretty well hidden—and, then, it might be too much of a shock. I'd rather have her ease into it, so to speak. Don't forget, she's reliving this right along with the telling."

Isaaic gestured abruptly. "Yes, I know, but I have this feeling that time is running out. I can feel the pressure rising again among my friends in the building—it's almost a tangible thing—and after what happened to the Kauffmans, well, I'm afraid!"

Sidney leaned back in his chair, and smiled at his old friend. "Oh, come now, Isaaic, you, afraid? I've seen you face impossible situations, and remain unruffled. What's so special about this?"

Isaaic looked at him reproachfully. "I thought I explained the situation thoroughly, Sidney. Weren't you listening? If this force, this thing, is focused on the Girard family, or a particular member of the family, if this person is its connection, so to speak, and if we can discover who this person is, and break the connection, then perhaps it will leave, go back to wherever it came from—and only God knows where that is."

Sidney looked at his friend skeptically. "You know that I think your theory is fascinating, Isaaic, and I'll admit that you make an excellent case for the presence of a supranormal being, an incubus, if you will, being responsible for the phenomena that you have witnessed; but I believe that I could make just as good a case for mass hysteria, initiated by someone in the building and communicated to the other tenants. It certainly is not without precedent, you know. And just because Nina Girard is the one on the psychologist's couch does not necessarily mean that she is the one who initiated the delusion; it only means that she is highly strung and more open to the psychic pressures that have been engendered."

"I too, have thought of that, my boy. I am not quite senile yet, you know. But if you had been living in that building, as I have, I think you would agree with me that these phenomena are caused by an outside force. Also, over the many years of my career, I have learned to trust my feelings, my intuitions; and my intuitions, and my instincts tell me that there is a palpable entity in the Barkley that was not there before, and that it is causing harm and hurt to a number of people. You are welcome to your opinions. Keep them—as if I could stop you; but work with me as if you believe my hypothesis, and we will eventually find out which of our theories is the correct one. Eh?"

Sidney shook his head in admiration. "You're still a terror, Isaaic. I pity all those poor students that you bullied over the years."

Isaaic hid his smile behind a bogus cough, and both men leaned back, as Sidney clicked on the tape recorder, and Nina Girard's voice filled the room.

Nina was worried about Melissa's apparent fondness for Dion, the young gardener. Three times a week he came: Monday, Wednesday, and Friday, working from 8:00 A.M. until noon. The entire time he was on the premises, Melissa was at his side, talking, laughing, digging in the moist earth. Nina watched them from the window, seeing the two heads—one so fair, one so dark—bent together over the vivid flowers of the garden.

Admittedly, it made a lovely picture; yet every time Nina looked at them, she experienced a feeling of deep forboding that would not be reasoned away.

Trying to be fair, she asked herself just what it was that she was afraid of. Seduction? Surely a young man as handsome as Dion would have no trouble finding suitable female companionship nearer his own age. And although Melissa was a beautiful child, she was just that, only a child. Nina tried to assure herself that it was simply a case of a young man being kind to a friendly child; but the hollow feeling in the pit of her stomach, whenever she saw them together, did not seem to hear the words.

She attempted to change Melissa's study hours so that she would be otherwise occupied when Dion was working; but in this she was foiled by her own sense of fairness, which she had always employed when dealing with her daughter. When Melissa balked at changing her hours, when she logically pointed out that her studies were up to date, and suffered no ill effects from being conducted in the afternoons, instead of the mornings; when she wanted to know why her mother wished to change an already established regime, Nina had no answer for her, and did not feel right about utilizing the "because I say so" technique favored by less reasonable prents.

So, she did nothing to discourage the friendship between the two. She said nothing of her feelings to Melissa or to Martin; she simply watched. She watched very closely.

Then, another invitation from the Contessa came, hand delivered by Dion, when he came to work. Nina opened the crested envelope with distaste, already determined to plead illness, if necessary, to avoid another of the Contessa's functions.

The embossed card inside announced that "Mr. Martin Girard and family are invited to a masked ball on the night of June 21. Time, 8:00 P.M." Her heart sank. Martin seemed to like the Contessa—or at least to find her amusing. When Nina complained of her constant visits and invitations, he shrugged off her comments with the statement that "the old girl means well, and besides, there's not much else to do around here."

So each time they were invited to one of the Contessa's parties, they went. And each time Nina found the gathering either upsetting, or boring, or both; and each time she vowed that she would not attend again; and each time she found herself unable to avoid going. Angrily, she threw the latest invitation down on the entry-hall table. Martin was one of those people who enjoyed costume parties, while Nina always found them embarrassing. He was certain to want to go, and since the invitation was addressed "and family," the Contessa probably expected them to bring Melissa.

Resentment made its way up through Nina's usually calm exterior, and briefly she considered the possibility of destroying the invitation, of not mentioning it.

But of course someone, probably the Contessa, would mention it to Martin, and he would wonder why they hadn't received a royal summons—for that was the way Nina now thought of the Contessa's invitations.

Well, for the moment at least, to hell with it! She was going to take some aspirin, and lie down. For some reason, with the advent of warmer weather, she had been feeling unwell. Since her health was generally good, she found it particularly annoying. She had periods of deep lassitude, followed by headaches of blinding intensity. The only help seemed to come from lying down, in a darkened room. She went into the kitchen, to tell Marie to keep an eye on Melissa, then went upstairs to her room, where, with all the shades drawn, she sank into a restless and unsatisfying sleep.

On the day of the Contessa's masked ball, the sun rose in a cloudless sky, and gave a foretaste of what the Italian summer would feel like. Despite the lack of clouds, the air was humid, and Nina felt out of sorts and angry about having to attend the ball. Martin and Melissa were both looking forward to it so, she gave up her plan to play sick and had been working, ungraciously with Maria, to make them all ancient Roman costumes.

The costumes were finished now, and Nina hated hers. She thought it made her look like a sacrificial virgin. Martin's togalike outfit was just as bad. Only Melissa looked well in her short, one-shouldered tunic, with the crown of flowers in her hair, and strings of flowers around her neck.

Now, as she looked out of the window, Nina idly wondered what the occasion was. As far as she knew, June 21 was no special holiday; so why a masked ball?

When she had asked Martin, he had chucked her under the chin indulgently and, she thought, condescendingly. "My little Puritan," he said. "Does there have to be a reason for everything? Can't the Contessa be giving a masked ball simply because she is wild about masked balls?"

Outside of the window, Dion came into view, carrying a shovel. Nina drew away, to the side of the window, so he should not see her watching him. Still, she knew that he was aware of her scrutiny. Often, when she was watching, he would turn and gaze at the window, almost as if posing for her benefit. At these times she would turn away in embarrassment at the obvious sexuality of his poses. She felt angry with him; affronted by him, but since he did nothing overt, she could not fight back; could not chastise or dismiss him.

By the time Martin arrived home from the city, her head was beginning to ache; but she didn't dare tell him because he was sure to say she was faking it to get out of attending the ball.

Melissa was hopping around like a ping-pong ball, too excited to even eat the light supper that Nina had asked Maria to prepare because dinner at the party, she knew, would be late.

So, with considerable effort, Nina put a smile on her face, and the sacrificial virgin costume on her body, and tried not to dampen the spirits of her husband and daughter.

As they came up the drive, it became clear that tonight's gathering was going to be considerably larger than the Contessa's usual group. The circular drive was lined with cars, and light and sound were spilling out of the windows on all floors.

Melissa began bouncing up and down in her seat. "Oh, look, Mommy! Look!"

Nina's eyes followed the direction in which her daughter's finger was pointing and saw a bright, red, bull's head leaning out of the window.

"Oh, doesn't it look like fun?"

"Yes, darling. It certainly does." Nina sighed inwardly.

The entry way, the stairs and landings, and all of the rooms they passed seemed to be full of revelers; but the huge, main ballroom, with its vast expanse of carved ceiling, and mirrored walls, was jammed with dancers; cavorting, swirling figures that might have issued from a mad dream, or a fevered imagination. Satyrs danced with dominos; kings with wood nymphs; animals—in all shapes and sizes—with glittering creatures from the future. It was all quite dizzying, and the music, amplified so that it could be heard over the rolling susurus of conversation, blasted out a current disco number that made Nina's ears ache.

She looked down at Melissa, and saw that the child was wide-eyed with wonder and delight. She yanked at the skirt of her mother's costume. "It's just like *Alice in Wonderland*," she shouted. "Gee, Mommy . . . it's great!"

Nina smiled weakly, and looked up at Martin. He was smiling, and tapping his foot in time to the music. He turned toward her. "Come on, honey; let's dance."

He took her arm, but she moved back from him slightly. "What about Melissa? We can't just leave her here in this crush! We never should have let her come. This is no place for a child!"

The smile left his face, and for a moment he looked angry, but when he spoke, his voice was calm. "All right. This time I agree, this isn't the place for a kid; but we're here, for God's sake, and so is Melissa, and we might as well enjoy ourselves—or have you forgotten how?"

Nina flinched from the words as she would have from a blow. Again she was being put on the defensive. She felt tears come to her eyes, and a sharp retort to her tongue; but the moment was broken by the appearance of a small figure, not much taller than Melissa, in a Harlequin suit and black half-mask. "The Contessa asked me to tell you that since there are so many people, you might wish Melissa to go with me and the other, younger people, to a less crowded room."

The voice of this small person was piping and clear, yet disturbingly unchildlike. Nina stood looking down at him—she assumed it was a boy—startled and bemused. So there were other children here.

"We will take good care of her, signora. We have fruit, punch and cakes; and there will be games . . ."

The dark eyes looking up into hers were malicious and bright as the eyes of some small, night creature; but the facial expression was pleasant, and the voice polite. "I am called Mino." He bowed slightly from the waist; and Nina again was struck by his unchildlike poise.

At that moment she looked up, and saw the Contessa—she knew it was the Contessa by the red hair, and by the fact that she removed the mask that went with her very unusual costume—waving at her, and nodding, as if to say that what the child said came from her and with her approval.

"Great!" Martin put his arm around Nina's shoulder. "Now we can have our dance."

He propelled Nina out onto the floor as she looked back over her shoulder toward Melissa and Mino. Melissa had taken the boy's hand happily, and they were already nearly to the main door of the ballroom. Then Nina and Martin were swallowed up by the moving sea of humanity that jiggled and jounced to the deafening music that washed over them. As she began, automatically, to respond to the music, the lights dimmed, and then great splashes of color dazzled her eyes and confused her senses. Martin laughed. "Strobe lights."

She tried to cling to his arm, but he moved away from her, moving, as did the other dancers, in a semi-isolated ritual. As a wave of blue light bathed his face, she could see that he was smiling. In this press and crush of humanity, amidst this noise and movement, she could not remember ever having felt so alone.

As the evening wore on, it seemed to Nina that she had been dancing forever. The lights, the press of bodies, the grotesque bodies themselves—inhuman and other-worldly, animal-headed and fancifully masked—made the whole experience unreal and dreamlike.

Periodically, Martin would steer her to the refreshment table, where they ate and drank from the vast array of food and drink laid out for the guests.

At one point, Nina lost sight of Martin completely, cut off from him by a huge, jewel-plummaged bird, with a long, sharp beak, and wicked, black eyes. The creature—for she could not seem to think of it as a person in costume—circled around her, preening and bending its head in a curiously birdlike gesture. By the time she drew free of the thing, Martin was nowhere in sight, lost among the milling dancers. She stood, alone and lost, looking for some way to get free of the crowd.

At that moment, someone touched her arm, and she turned to face a striking figure, attired in a short toga, which displayed columnar brown male legs, and smooth, muscular shoulders. The man had thick, curling black hair that clung in tendrils to his neck, which glistened with a thin film of sweat. His hair was bound by a circlet of grape leaves, and his well-formed brown arms were adorned with carved bracelets of what seemed to be solid gold.

Dizzy and a bit frightened, Nina looked into the man's eyes. They were all she could see of the face, which was otherwise covered by a full mask, such as those worn by ancient Greek actors.

The carved, almost leering smile on the mask did not put her at ease, but the dark eyes that looked out at her held an expression that was at once tender, and insistent.

Before she could protest, the man had swept her

into his arms, and was moving with her, closely, in time to the music.

Shockingly, she became aware of his body against hers, the press of his maleness through the thin fabric of his costume, the warmth of his breath—which bore the odor of spices—against her cheek. His right hand pressed firmly against her back, forcing her breasts into contact with his chest.

She could feel a smothering panic rising in her, and desperately she turned her head, searching for Martin. As she did so, the young man's strong arms pressed her closer, and he began to draw her away, out of the crowd, toward an open doorway. Although she struggled against him, she was powerless to stop their inexorable progress toward that suddenly threatening door.

Then, seemingly out of nowhere, the Contessa appeared by their side. The Contessa's costume, that of a queen of some sort—Nina could not think what kind of queen would wear such a costume—was an ornate affair in purple and gold, with a high, flaring collar that served as a background for the face and head. A strange, towering crownlike arrangement, very fine and delicate, of golden wires, wavered over her head, giving an other-worldly look to the gold half-mask with upward-sweeping points.

Nina had not thought that she would ever welcome the sight of the Contessa, but at this moment she was extremely grateful for her presence.

"Contessa . . ." she said in as loud a voice as she could manage. "Please . . ."

The Contessa, instead of halting the young man as Nina had expected, only smiled, and followed along beside them as they moved, still, toward the door.

Then, with a light touch, she tapped the young man on the shoulder with her golden fan. "Now, Dion," she said chidingly. "You must not be so rough with Signora Girard. She . . ."

"Dion!" Nina pulled back, panic lending her

strength. This young man was Dion? The gardener? She glared at the Contessa in fear and confusion. "Make him let me go!" she shouted, but her words seemed lost in a crescendo of sound from the band. Why were they urging her toward that open doorway? Why didn't the Contessa see that she wanted to be rid of this boy? This man . . .

With the strength born of fear, Nina pushed at Dion's shoulders with her hands. At that moment, a drunken dancer, lurching sideways, fell against the young man, and Nina was able to break away.

Without a backward glance, driven by a fear she had no name for, she pushed through the dancers and made her way to the edge of the floor. Only then did she look back. She could see neither Dion or the Contessa among the mass of moving bodies.

Turning, she hurried toward the main door of the ballroom. What was Dion doing at the ball? Did the Contessa invite her servants to her parties? She felt terribly angry.

Suddenly, her mind turned to Melissa. Since she had finally gotten off that infernal dance floor, she could check on her daughter without Martin knowing or thinking she was being over-protective again.

Her heart still pounding, and her mind in confusion from her recent encounter, Nina almost ran through the maze of mirrored halls, opening doors as she came to them. Many of the rooms were occupied, some in ways so intimate that Nina was embarrassed and shocked. What if Melissa and the other children were to witness something like this?

Several times, Nina was certain that she heard the sound of children's voices. As she opened the door to one large, empty room, she saw a door on the opposite side of the room just closing, and caught a brief burst of childish laughter. But when she reached the door, which led into another empty room, she could find no one.

Tired now, and growing increasingly depressed,

Nina wandered back to the ballroom. Just inside the main door, she saw Martin, coming toward her. A vast relief filled her at the sight of his familiar and loved face.

"Oh, darling. I'm so glad to see you. I've been . . ."

He pulled her close, and gave her a squeeze. "Hey, where've you been? I've been looking everywhere for you. It's getting late, and I think it's time that we got Melissa home. Don't you?"

Nina choked off the words she had been about to speak. Telling him about what had happened would serve no purpose, save to dampen his own pleasure in the party, and, she knew, to annoy him—because what, after all, did she really have to tell? That a man in a bird suit had frightened her; that another man had held her too close, and that the Contessa hadn't stopped him; that she had been afraid; and that she couldn't find her daughter? Tired as she was, she knew it would sound like utter, hysterical, "woman-type" nonsense.

"Yes, dear," she said. "We had better pay our respects to the Contessa."

"Oh, I already have. I happened to see her, and knowing how hard it is to find anyone in this crowd, I told her then. Here's Melissa now."

Nina turned, and saw Melissa, walking sedately with the small Harlequin, coming toward them. It's all so very ordinary, she thought. Here we all are, perfectly unharmed, ready to leave the party. So why do I feel so strange? Why?

She looked searchingly at her husband and daughter, knowing that even if they knew the answer, she could not ask the question.

"Well, what do you think?" Sidney turned off the tape recorder, and sat down in his chair. "Do you think it could be the father, Mr. Girard?"

Isaaic pursed his lips. "We still don't have enough information to draw a conclusion. At this point, I would be more likely to think it is the child, Melissa. After all, the reason that Nina is here is because she hears a voice in the child's room. A male voice. And then, there's the heat, and the scent of oranges. Also, her mother is not the only one to have perceived the heat and the scent; another of our tenants had a similar experience while watching the child, and afterward, when she went to her own apartment . . . well, that is in confidence, but it does seem to me that the child could be the 'carrier,' so to speak."

"But we have to know more!"

"Yes, we must go on. We are still only scratching the surface. I think you should ask her to come again tomorrow."

Both men leaned back in their chairs and studied the tape recorder thoughtfully.

THIRTEEN

The weather kept growing hotter, and by mid-afternoon, the only bearable place in the house was the music room, where a large, six-bladed fan turned in slow circles just below the ceiling.

With the increasing hot weather, Nina found herself more and more often feeling unwell. She went to see a doctor in Rome, but he could find no physical cause for her headaches, for the lassitude, or lapses of memory, which preceded and succeeded them.

In the evenings, Martin, after making the drive from Rome in the heat, tended to be cranky and involved with the details of business. Only Melissa seemed oblivious of the heat and humidity. She kept up her usual schedule, energetic and good-natured as ever.

Despite her lack of energy, Nina still kept watch from the window when Dion was working in the garden. She knew that he was aware of her scrutiny, and she could sense that this amused him; but she could not seem to stop.

Then, on a Friday, just before the Saturday when they were expecting dinner guests, Maria, the maid, had to leave to attend a funeral in Palermo. There was nothing to do but to call the Contessa—much as Nina hated being indebted to her—and ask if she knew of someone to replace the girl. The Contessa, as always, had someone available—Lily, Dion's sister.

The Contessa told Nina not to worry, that the girl

would be there first thing next morning, and Nina thanked her with as much grace as she could muster.

On Saturday morning the temperature seemed to be down a bit, and Nina felt well for the first time in days.

At eight o'clock, Lily arrived, and Nina and Melissa both looked at her with a good deal of curiosity. Not surprisingly, she was every bit as beautiful a girl as her brother was a man—in fact, the resemblance was uncanny. If it were not for the long hair that hung nearly to the girl's waist, and the swell of her not inconsiderable bosom above the low-cut white blouse, they might have been identical twins.

Nina explained to the girl what she wished done, and Lily accepted her directions with a demure manner and respectful attitude—which was certainly a change from the attitude of her brother.

By the time the dinner guests arrived, the house was spotless, and an excellent dinner was ready to be served.

It was a small party, just a few people from Martin's office. The evening went smoothly, facilitated by Lily's excellent service.

Nina noticed that the men in the group, including Martin, eyed Lily appreciatively, but this was only natural; it would have been unusual if they had not taken notice of a girl as lovely as she.

It did seem to Nina that Martin looked at the girl a bit more than was necessary, and although she was not a jealous woman by nature, she was practical. There was no sense in putting temptation in a man's way. Privately, she vowed that as soon as Maria returned, Lily would go . . .

But Maria did not return. It seemed that she would have to remain in Palermo to attend to the household of her newly widowed brother; so there was nothing to do but ask Lily to remain.

"Did she tell you, the Contessa, that I can only work during the time that Dion does *not* work?" Lily asked, looking at Nina through her incredibly thick lashes.

"No," said Nina, feeling more than a little put out. "She said nothing about that!"

Lily lowered her head. "Well, you see, it is our grandmother. She is very old, and very unwell. We are all she has, and one of us must stay with her at all times, as she cannot care for herself. You understand?"

"Yes," said Nina grudgingly. It was clear that this was a duty that the young people must perform, so it seemed that she must adjust to their schedule or look for someone else to take their jobs. If she did this, the Contessa would be upset, and Martin would be upset because the Contessa was upset. Besides, it would mean breaking in someone new—it was just plain too much trouble. "All right," Nina said. "That will be fine, I guess. I've been used to having someone in the house to help full-time, but I suppose we can adjust."

And so it was left like that, and at first it seemed that it would, indeed, work out; but then the situation slowly began to change. Not with Dion—he still came regularly, and performed his duties efficiently enough—but with Lily.

Day by day her performance seemed to deteriorate, her work becoming sloppy, her manner sullen, and she never seemed to be around when Nina wanted her.

It finally became too much, and Nina told Martin that she was going to have to fire the girl.

She had expected some resistance—after all, the Contessa had suggested the girl—but she was surprised at the strength of Martin's attempt to defend Lily. "I'll talk to her," he said finally. "Don't worry about it. I'm sure she'll shape up."

Nina remained silent, although it was an effort. Hurt by his apparent interest in, and defense of, the girl, she simply withdrew, and let him take care of it.

She had to admit that whatever he said to Lily worked—the girl's usual standard of performance soon returned—but she still was unhappy about her husband's interest which so far, she had to admit, seemed harmless enough.

As the summer days wore on, the weather remained muggy and uncomfortable, but they were now beginning to adapt to it. Nina still had her headaches and periods of forgetfulness, but she was adapting to these too, and the chore of visiting a foreign doctor seemed more formidable than the headaches themselves. The only thing that *really* bothered her now was the puzzle of young Dion.

Although he never did anything, never said anything that she could legitimately take offense to, she could feel him there, at the edge of her mind, an insistent presence that pushed intimately against her psyche, with his sly smiles and sloe eyes. She wished that he would go, and then, in the next instant, feared his departure. The only way she could cope with the mixed feelings engendered by this apparent paradox, was to put the situation, and Dion, out of her mind as much as possible.

And then, on a Saturday morning about three weeks after the arrival of Lily, Nina awoke to a morning that was cool and fragrant, holding no promise of the heat to come. She bounced out of bed feeling rejuvenated and energetic for the first time in weeks.

The change in weather seemed to have affected everyone. Lily arrived early and prepared a large, heavy breakfast, which the whole family enjoyed.

After finishing her second cup of coffee, Nina smiled at her husband and daughter. "You know, I feel so good today; let's do something special!"

Melissa bounced up and down in her chair. "I *am* doing something special today, Mother. Teressa has invited me to her house to play this morning. She's the one with the doll collection. You know!"

Nina nodded. Yes, she knew. Teressa Cardoni was a child celebrity in the village because of her doll collection, and it was considered an honor and a privilege to be invited to visit and play with the beautiful dolls.

"Fantastic!" she said to Melissa. "You've made the big time. Well, Martin, what about you?"

He looked at her, his expression and the shrug of his shoulders expressing chagrin. "Sorry, honey. I have to finish these specs before Monday, and it's going to be a two-day job. I really wish I could. This is the first decent weather we've had in weeks."

Nina accepted his statement with a nod and a sigh. "Well then, I guess I'll just have to go into the city and do the shopping that I've been putting off ever since the weather turned so hot. There are at least a dozen things we need that I've been unable to get in the village. If I'm ever going to get them, it might as well be now. At least I'll have a nice drive."

Martin got up, moved to her side, and patted her shoulder. "That's my brave girl!"

The pleasant weather held for most of the morning, but by noon, the familiar, muggy heat began creeping back, and by the time Nina was on the road, headed for home, the air was exceptionally hot and humid.

The sky had turned overcast, and seemed to be lowering, like a vast, gray ceiling. The feeling of pressure added to the illusion, making Nina imagine that she and her small car might at a moment be flattened, like a bug, upon the roadway.

By the time she reached the small rise, overlooking their villa, the sky had turned a nasty yellow, and was issuing ominous rumblings that reverberated threateningly across the seemingly deserted landscape. Nina had not seen another car for what seemed like miles, and there was not a soul in sight, as she sped down the slope, hoping to reach the villa before the rain began to fall. She experienced the eerie feeling that at this moment she was the only person left in the world, and that she must quickly reach home, and her loved ones, before this feeling became fact.

The first raindrops, fat and warmly heavy, struck her cheeks and shoulders as she got out of the car. Quickly, she grabbed as many parcels as she could carry, then ran up the stairs and into the house.

Feeling somewhat exhilarated—there was something exciting in this pressure before the storm—she dropped the bundles on the dining room table, and pushed open the kitchen door, looking for Lily, so that the girl could bring in the rest.

The kitchen was clean and empty, strangely illuminated by the heavy yellow light coming in through the kitchen window.

Nina let the kitchen door swing shut, noticing that the house was almost completely silent—a strange, secret silence that seemed to Nina unusual. Where was Martin? Where was Melissa? Surely she must be home by now!

She opened her mouth to call Martin's name, but a roll of thunder so loud that it rattled the windows halted her before the words could leave her mouth.

For a moment, she leaned against the dining room table, staring down at the packages. She was feeling very odd, very disoriented, and why? A summer storm? She had experienced summer storms before. Because the house was quiet? Perhaps Melissa was napping, and, after all, Martin had said he would be working. Lily? Well, maybe she was busy in another part of the house.

Trying to smile at her own imaginings, Nina started toward the stairs. The rain was coming down in torrents now, as if the sky had been shattered by that last roll of thunder. Perhaps it would be cooler again, after the rain.

At the top of the stairs she paused, listening to the sound of the rain drops as they struck the roof and windows. It was a sound she had always loved.

Quickly then, she walked to Martin's study, and quietly opened the door. The light was on over his desk, and papers were spread out upon the desk top, but Martin was not there.

Her feeling of unease increased, and she pressed her fingertips against her temples to stop the growing pressure and pain there. Another headache coming on, and she had felt so well all day. Well, she might as well go into the bedroom and get out of the suit she had worn to town. Then she would look for Martin and Melissa.

As she was turning the knob of the bedroom door, she heard them, heard the sounds, but it was as if once started upon the task of opening the door, her fingers had a life of their own.

The doorknob continued turning, and the door opened, and Nina, only now really comprehending the meaning of those sounds, looked into the bedroom shared by Martin and her.

There, upon *her* bed, silhouetted against the large window, accompanied by the drumming of the rain, was the beast with two backs. Her husband, Martin, and the girl, Lily . . . limbs intertwined, moving, heaving, gasping. . . .

A flash of lightning ripped across the sky outside, and cruelly delineated the tableau for Nina—Lily's head thrown back, eyes closed, the heavy, glossy hair spilled across the clean whiteness of Nina's pillow, one plump breast—the nipple like a dark rosette—bouncing with the movement of Martin's thrusting body, Martin's face buried in that black hair—thank God, she couldn't see the expression upon *his* face—Lily's face, the sensous, somehow cruel smile, and then her eyes, opening, looking into Nina's eyes with an expression of knowledge and triumph.

Nina's scream, and the roll of thunder, tore through the room simultaneously.

FOURTEEN

Halley surveyed her clean, neat apartment and sighed. She had spent the morning cleaning, and now she was faced with several hours of unstructured time.

She debated the merits of reading versus shopping versus working on her macrame, which had lain untouched for weeks.

She had tried to call Isaaic Aschermann, but he had not answered his telephone; and then she remembered that he was probably at the university, with Nina and Dr. Allbright.

She was very curious about what was coming out at these sessions. Nina, who seemed to be better—more together and in control since the sessions began—had told her only that an amazing amount of information, that she had completely forgotten, was being uncovered.

Halley looked out of the living room window. The weather had been slowly growing warmer, but today was another gray day—not one of the pearly gray kind, but a dirty, yellow gray day—that looked unpleasant and depressing.

She really did need to talk to Isaaic. Earlier, she had gone downstairs and put a note in his mailbox. She realized that he must be very busy, but he was the only one she could talk to, the only one who would understand.

Things were better between her and Vince—not like they were before, but better—and now there was only one thing that she had to decide. The decision had to be made right away, before it was too late. Should she, or should she not, have an abortion?

"An abortion?" Isaaic was startled.

He sat opposite Halley, in her comfortable living room, holding the glass of brandy she had thoughtfully provided. He put the glass down, and sat back, feeling infinitely weary.

"How can I answer that, Halley? Something like that, only you can decide. Have you told Vince yet that you're pregnant?"

She shook her head. "Isaaic, after all that's happened, after what happened to me that afternoon, I just can't be certain that it's Vince's baby!"

He nodded. "I understand your problem. But even if the child is not Vince's, are you sure that you want to . . . well, to get rid of it?"

She drew back, and grabbed her upper arms with her hands, as if suddenly cold. "Isaaic, if it's not Vince's baby, then it's the baby of a demon, an incubus! How can I take the chance?"

Isaaic swallowed the last of his brandy. "All I can tell you is what I've told you before. Remember what you read in Patrick's book? Merlin, Luther, Romulus and Remus, none were noted for being particularly evil men, and yet they were all said to be the sons of incubi." He shrugged. "I'm sorry, Halley. I wish I could help; but there are some things that no one can help with. Some things only you can decide. I hope you won't think that I've failed you."

Halley tried to smile. "No. You're perfectly right. I've known it all along, but maybe I needed you to tell me. Thanks for bearing with me, listening to me."

Isaaic got up from the couch, moved forward, and gently touched her cheek. "You've become like a daughter to me, Halley; and if you were my daughter, I would have to say the same thing. Whatever you decide, I hope you rest easy with the decision."

She took his arm as he walked toward the door. "So do I," she said.

On the way to his apartment, Isaaic leaned tiredly against the wall of the elevator. Well, he had wanted to keep busy, wanted to be involved again. Hadn't someone once said that you should be careful of what you wish for because you might get it?

He sighed deeply, wondering about Halley and the baby. What would she decide? Well, that, at least, was out of his hands.

As the elevator doors opened to let him out at his floor, his mind turned to Nina Girard, and the information that she had given them during this afternoon's session, and a bit of energy returned to him. This afternoon he had felt that he had caught a glimpse of their quarry; that some of the pieces were beginning to fit together. The more Nina relived of that time in Italy, the clearer the pattern became. What he had heard today had moved and fascinated him. . . .

As Nina crouched upon the floor, the next few moments were a jumble of darkness and pain. She did not see Lily leave the room—the next thing she was aware of was Martin trying to help her up from the floor, and that she was hitting out at him with all of her strength. She could hear her own voice crying out, "Why? *Why?*"

Finally, despite her struggles, Martin got her to the edge of the bed, where she collapsed with great, wrenching sobs. Through the sounds of her own misery, she could hear him talking, but the words made no sense. The only real thing was the picture of him and Lily, on the bed. That was burned into her mind forever.

"Why? Why?" she cried again.

"I don't know, dammit! I don't know!" He did not try to touch her now. "I'd cut off my right arm before

I'd willingly hurt you, Nina; and yet, I obviously can't deny what you just saw. I don't *know* why, Nina. I wish to God I did. I love you, Nina!"

The words meant nothing. If he loved her, how could this have happened? If he loved her, how could he want Lily? If he loved her, how could he have hurt her so?

He tried to touch her again, but she pulled away in loathing and anger. "Get out, Martin. Just get out! Go away. Go away!"

"For God's sake, Nina, where? Look, I know how you feel, but we can work this out. We'll talk about it and . . ."

Talk about it? He thought they could talk about it, and it would all go away!

In a great surge of anger, she struck out at him with her fist, hitting his cheek. "Go to the Contessa's; you seem fond enough of her. Go to your whore, Lily! I don't care where you go, just *go*!"

Suddenly, through the heavy weight of pain and grief, she remembered Melissa. She took her hands from her face. She could barely make out the outline of Martin's body, through tear-swollen eyes. "Where's Melissa? What have you done with her?"

"Christ, Nina, do you think that I'm a complete animal?"

She sobbed. "Yes!"

"She's at the Contessa's. After you left this morning, the Contessa sent over a message asking Melissa to tea. There were going to be some other young people there, or something. So, when Melissa came back from Teressa's, I took her over to the Contessa and dropped her off. I was going back for her in . . ." His voice faded away.

"Well, go on and say it. You were going back for her after you'd finished fucking the maid! It certainly was convenient, wasn't it. Nobody home but you and she. Christ! What a fool I've been."

"Nina, Nina—it's not like you to talk like this."

"You're right. It isn't. Well, you don't have to stay and hear it. Just get out!"

She could feel the movement of the bed as he stood up.

"All right, Nina. If that's what you want."

"That's what I want."

"What about Melissa?"

"I'll go and pick her up myself. I don't want you near her."

"Look, we'll talk this over sensibly tomorrow. I'll call you."

"Don't bother. I don't think I'll ever want to talk to you again, except through our lawyers."

"All right. You're upset . . ."

"I'm upset—oh God! I'm upset! Sometimes you men are too funny for words."

"I was going to add, 'understandably so.' I just think that tomorrow, when you've slept on it, you'll be a little more . . ."

She looked at him through the swollen slits of her eyelids. "You actually think I'll sleep, don't you? You actually think that? Please, Martin, just go!"

"I'll go, Nina. But for the record, I *do* still love you. I don't know *why* this thing happened with Lily, and I *will* call you tomorrow. If you need me, I'll be at the Hilton, in Rome."

She lay huddled at the foot of the bed, her sobs finally slowing, as he moved about the room, tossing clothing into a suitcase. Then she heard the soft snick of the door latch, as he left the room. She scarcely noticed, for she felt numb now, with the shock that follows great injury.

The sound of the rain was heavy—a steady drumming on the roof and against the windows—and the room was growing very dark, as the hour grew later.

She had no idea of how long she lay there, but suddenly she remembered that she must get Melissa, that she must go to the Contessa's villa and bring her daughter home. Somehow the idea that Martin had let the child go alone to the Contessa was an additional breach of faith.

She got up from the bed with distaste. She had been sitting there, lying there, where *they* had been.

She shivered. She felt chilled through, heavy with cold.

She went to the winter-clothes chest and pulled out boots, wool pants, and a heavy sweater. Quickly, she pulled off her town suit and got into the warm clothes. Over all, she threw on a hooded rain cape. The clothes felt good upon her body, the layers of material bringing her a bit of security she sorely needed. Putting everything out of her mind except her daughter, she ran down to the car, still parked by the front door.

It was completely dark now, and the rain made visibility very difficult. The MG's energetic little windshield wipers flipped frantically, but could not dispell the downpour entirely.

Driving took all of Nina's concentration, and almost gratefully, she took off down the road toward the Contessa's villa.

Lights were on in some of the windows of the villa. Someone had to be there; why didn't anyone answer?

Nina again lifted the huge, brass doorknocker and let it slam against the door. She could hear the hollow sound it made even above the steady pounding of the rain.

She could also hear the light *pit-pit-pat* of the drops as they struck the hood of her rain cape. She could even feel them, like tiny blows.

Where were they? Where was Melissa?

Wildly, she hammered the door with her fists, screaming out her rage and terror. "Let me in, you bastards! Let me in!"

Again she lifted the doorknocker and let it slam, then kicked the base of the door with one booted foot.

At last she heard the protesting sound of a sliding

bolt, and felt the door move beneath her hands. Thank God! Now all she had to do was get Melissa, and make it home before the storm got any worse.

It seemed to take an age for the heavy door to swing open, and when it did, one of the Contessa's ubiquitous servants stood revealed, an elderly man with a stooped back, dressed in the Contesss's ornate livery. He peered at her with pink-rimmed eyes but did not move to let her in.

"I'm Mrs. Girard," she shouted at him. "I've come for my daughter, Melissa. She's visiting the Contessa!"

The wind blew a gust of rain into her face, and she wondered if he understood. "Melissa," she said again. "Melissa Girard. I've come for her."

"Sorry, not here," mumbled the old man, in almost incomprehensible English, and he started to close the heavy door.

Nina, angrier than she had ever been in her life, put both hands against the door, and pushed back. Her anger gave her strength, and the old man, caught unaware, fell back into the entry way.

Nina brushed past him in a flurry of rain and wind. The old man, eyeing her wonderingly, closed the door behind her as she stood dripping on the inlaid floor, and not caring that she did.

She felt much better now that she had taken physical action against one of her problems. Her heart was beating quickly, and she felt strong, elated with her success.

She turned to the old man and said firmly, "Where is my daughter?"

The old man seemed to shrink in upon himself. He rolled his eyes and shrugged his shoulders. "I do not understand," he complained in his rusty English. "I only came on duty at five o'clock. I saw no child."

Nina knew that he was lying. She could see it in the back of his rheumy, old eyes; but what could she do?

The old man shook his head. "The Contessa is not here. She has gone away for the weekend. If you wish to see the Contessa, you must come back on Monday." He reached toward the door as if to show Nina out.

Nina's elation at getting into the house was fading. How could she get through to this cretin? The Contessa was here, had to be here, because Martin had left Melissa with her, unless . . . Fanciful thoughts of abduction swirled through Nina's mind. No. That was ridiculous. The Contessa was eccentric, granted, but not mad; and she would have to be mad to kidnap the child of an important American businessman.

The sound of water dripping from her raincape brought Nina back to her immediate problem. Melissa *must* be here, and she intended to find her. She looked around the dimly lit entry hall. Where to start?

She turned back to the old man, intending to tell him that if he did not produce her daughter, or the Contessa, she intended to search the place herself—but he was gone. He had stolen away without a sound.

Made righteous by her anger, Nina stomped down the marble-floored hallway. Making no attempt to be quiet, she slammed open doors, and left them standing open behind her. One room after another, all empty, all dark. There was no sound save those which Nina herself made, and when she became conscious of this, her courage began to leave her bit by bit, to be replaced by a growing fear. What if the old man had been telling the truth? What if Melissa were not here? What if the Contessa had taken her somewhere else?

Her steps slowed, but she kept on, opening doors into silent rooms. My God, how many rooms were there in this place?

As she opened the door to one large room a sense of familiarity came over her, and she remembered the night of the fancy dress ball, when she had also gone through the hallways opening doors, looking for Melissa; but on that night there had been people present, hundreds of people—and then she heard the sound.

Voices, laughter, barely on the edge of audibility, but they *were* there. Nina almost sobbed with relief.

Now, where was the sound coming from? A rolling cannonade of thunder filled the room. As the reverberations slowly died away, she strained to hear the voices. There. A laugh. It was Melissa's laugh; she was sure. The sounds rose, then faded. Behind that door, there on the left.

Hurriedly, Nina ran to the door and flung it open. Another empty room, but this one was lighted by one lovely, crystal lamp. But she was going in the right direction. She could hear them clearly now—young voices. Hadn't Martin said that there would be other young people here?

Through the next door, and the next, always hearing the voices, but never getting any nearer. Why wasn't she getting closer? She stopped, her breath rasping in her chest. Perhaps it was the acoustics of the building. Old houses sometimes had strange acoustics, she knew.

She looked around and above her. Of course, upstairs. They were probably upstairs. But before she searched there, she would try one more room.

The door that she pushed open showed not the interior of a room, but a thick, red, velvet curtain, directly on the other side of the doorway. Instinct told her to move cautiously.

Carefully she moved the curtain aside, just enough to see into the room, and then had to choke back the sound that rose to clog her throat.

There in the dimly lit room, was a scene of incredible beauty, and, to Nina, incredible depravity.

A fire was flickering and glowing in the huge fireplace. The light from its flames danced over the nude body of Dion as he reclined upon a glowing Persian carpet in front of the blaze. The firelight moved over his body like hundreds of tiny fingers, delineating the beauty of his muscular, rounded limbs, and illuminating his male organ, which was lying upward along his flat belly, engorged and huge; and around him, touching him, fondling him, kissing him, were the children—all innocence and happiness—smiling, laughing in soft voices. . . .

Oh! My God! My God! What was going on here? Wildly, Nina looked around for Melissa, and then saw her, just coming into the room, her slender, pale, naked body shining in the soft light. Dion lifted his head and smiled at the child, and, as Nina struggled to cry out, Melissa seated herself by his head, moved closer, and took his dark head into her lap, where she began to stroke his curls. Dion reached out one brown arm and hand, and began to stroke her smooth, white, thigh.

The sound that had been stopping Nina's breath at last burst forth, shattering the scene in front of her, as a blow would shatter glass.

The children shrieked and leapt up from their places in front of the fire. Dion rose on one elbow, and Melissa rose to her knees.

Nina, fighting the heavy draperies, flung herself into the room, to stand before the young man and the girl. Feeling a rage so great that it could not be put into words, she stared at Dion in horror, then turned her eyes to Melissa, who looked startled, but unafraid. Why didn't she show fear, shame?

"Child molester!" Finally words burst forth from Nina's dry lips. "Perverted monster. And you, Melissa, you . . ."

Melissa, concern in her eyes, reached forward, as if to touch her mother.

"Now, now, my dear. There is nothing to be upset about. Why carry on so over a few harmless games?"

The voice was the Contessa's, and Nina whirled to see the older woman seated in the shadows, where she had evidently been all the time.

"You've been sitting there, watching them, while . . ."

The Contessa got up and moved into the light. She was wearing only a thin robe, unfastened down the front, which swung open as she walked. Her breasts, modest but shapely, and her flat stomach, looked like those of a young girl. Her legs, long and delicately shaped, ended in high-heeled velvet slippers. Even in this moment, Nina could not help but wonder about the woman's age; but how dare she, how dare she exhibit herself in front of these children like this? And how could she permit Dion to . . . to . . .

Her mind refused to complete the connection, to formulate just what it was that she supposed the young man and the children had been doing.

"How dare you?" She heard her own voice, shrill against the silence of the room. "*How dare you*?"

The Contessa smiled. "I dare anything I please, Mrs. Girard, and very many things please me. I like young people, children, around me; one can draw a sustenance of sorts from young people, and from their emotions. Is it not so?"

Nina resisted the impulse to back away. "You're mad!" she cried.

The Contessa shook her head. "No, not mad. Selfish, perhaps, but quite sane. Do you have any idea how old I am, Mrs. Girard? I am certain you don't, but take a guess. How old would you judge me? Forty? Thirty?"

Nina tore her gaze away from the Contess's black, glowing eyes, only to meet the eyes of Dion, thick-fringed, amused. He was, she noticed, lazily toying with himself as he watched her and the Contessa.

And Melissa, Melissa had not moved from her knees. Her clear eyes were fixed on Nina with a look of compassion. Of *compassion*?

"Can you make a guess? How old would you say I am?"

The Contessa touched Nina's shoulder with her hand, and Nina jumped back reflexively.

"I don't give a damn how old you are!" She spat the

words. "All I want is to get my daughter out of this crazy-house, and back to her own home. Now, get out of my way!"

"Dion!" The Contessa nodded, and Dion rose gracefully and walked toward Nina. She eyed him warily, trying to keep her gaze upon his face, away from the disturbing nakedness of his body.

"Now, Nina—I shall call you Nina—all in good time. You shall take your daughter home, but first, I would like to talk to you, just for a moment."

She moved her hand in a light gesture, and at that same moment, Dion stepped behind Nina, and pinioned her arms with his.

"Now, come and sit by the fire."

The Contessa moved languidly back to her seat in the shadows, and Dion, pushing Nina with his arms and his body, forced her down upon the Persian rug in front of the fire.

Nina was horribly conscious of his body next to hers, of his penis, still erect, against the lower part of her back. This was madness, all of it; a dream. Nothing in real life could be like this. The air in the room felt heavy and hot, and Nina was sweating beneath her warm clothing. There was a strange odor in the air, almost sickeningly sweet, rather like the scent of over-ripe oranges.

Melissa had mercifully moved to one side, where Nina could not see her. She was embarrassed that her daughter should see her like this, and yet angry at the girl for her apparent placidity, her acceptance of what was going on, and what had, presumably, gone on before.

"Now Nina, I am very sorry that you had to blunder in like this. I know you aren't ready for it yet. I know you find all this confusing in the extreme. Later, when Dion and Lily had done their work, I would have asked you to join us, to be a part of our little group, to join us in our little games."

"Games!" Nina hissed. "Games! You call what I just saw a game? You disgusting, old bitch! You . . ."

The Contessa sighed. "You see, I was right. You are not at all ready. And now you are angry and confused, and all because you came home a bit too early, and found your husband with Lily. It's too sad, really."

Nina gasped as if she had been hit with a pail of cold water. "How do you know? How could you know?"

The Contessa smiled. "Why from Lily, of course."

"You sent her to us," Nina whispered.

"Assuredly. Just as I sent Dion."

The youth's arms tightened around Nina, and he playfully touched her ear with his lips. Even as frightened and confused as she was, Nina felt an excitement begin in her body, and was disgusted with herself.

And then she looked up to see the Contessa bending over her, holding out a heavily carved silver goblet. "Here, drink this. You look unwell."

Nina shook her head and clamped her lips together. The Contessa leaned further forward, the robe falling away from her body, and Nina averted her eyes.

"Now, now, my little prude. I shan't poison you, if that is what you fear. I am going to let you take your precious daughter and go home. However, I fear that you will not have the strength to do this, unless you get something in your stomach. Here, now."

The Contessa extended the goblet, and Dion, lifting Nina's chin with one hand, squeezed her mouth open with the other. She felt the fluid, warm and spicy, flood into her mouth and down her throat.

For a few moments thereafter, Nina was confused; but then the warmth of the drink in her stomach seemed to revive her, and her mind cleared. The first thing she noticed was that the pressure on her arms was gone, and so was Dion.

She looked around for the Contessa, but saw only Melissa, fully clothed, sitting opposite her, on a chair.

As Nina looked up, Melissa rose from the chair, and

walked over to her. Nina got up unsteadily, and Melissa reached up and took her hand.

As Melissa led her through the apparently empty house, through the dimly lit rooms and down the shadowy hallway, Nina fought to create some kind of order out of the jumble of thoughts in her mind. Had it all happened? Could she have imagined the whole thing? Not possible. She had seen it. It was real; as real as Melissa's hand in hers. But where then was the Contessa? Where was Dion? And how was Melissa fully dressed, when Nina had, only moments before, seen her nude?

As Melissa struggled with the front door, Nina reached to help her. The storm blew in upon them with sobering chill, and, gratefully, Nina focused on the realities at hand: the storm, the need to get herself and Nina home, and the mechanics of driving, which required all of her concentration. Once they were safely home, in their villa, then she would think things through.

The road was now deep in water and mud washed down from the banks on either side of the pavement. The little M.G. rocked precariously, and visibility was almost zero; but at last, after what seemed like hours of driving, the lights of their own villa shone ahead, and Nina drove into the driveway.

During the drive, there had been no words exchanged between Nina and Melissa, and none were spoken now, as Nina herded her daughter into the warmth and safety of the house.

Nina was clinging as tightly as she could to the reality of the moment. She felt that her hold upon sanity was extremely tentative, that the slightest stress would send her mind plunging into chaos. The only bulwark against this eventuality was to follow regular procedures, regular rituals.

"You had better get upstairs and out of those wet things," she heard herself saying to Melissa. "And then, I want you to get right into bed. I'll bring you some hot milk as soon as I change my clothes."

"Yes, Mother." Melissa's voice was submissive and calm.

As Nina stripped off her clothing, wet through despite the raincape, she found her teeth chattering. All right, they were home. Now for the next step. They must get away from here, away from Italy as soon as possible. She knew this with a certainty that was rooted in her soul.

Wrapping herself in a terrycloth robe, she reached for the telephone beside her bed, then paused, hand outstretched. She had just enough of her reason left to realize that she could not possibly cope with the intricacies of plane reservations, packing, and all of the details necessary to such a trip. It seemed clear that there was only one thing to do. Carefully, she lifted the receiver and dialed information. When the operator answered, she asked for the number of the Hilton Hotel, in Rome.

FIFTEEN

"And so your husband, after hearing your story, gave up his job in Rome, and you returned to the United States," Isaaic said.

Nina nodded. "He sent us on ahead, and followed in less than a week."

"Surely, that must have proved to you that he *did* love you?" Sidney put the question gently.

She nodded. "Yes. And I understand now that he didn't *want* to have an affair with Lily; that it was some kind of, well, some kind of compulsion." She paused. "You know, it was so strange, hearing myself relive those days, remembering so much that I had forgotten. The whole thing is rather like a bad dream, one of those dreams where the memory won't go away even after you've awakened. Do you know what I mean?"

Isaaic and Sidney exchanged glances, and nodded. "Yes, I know very well," Isaaic said softly. "And now, now that you have remembered it all, now that it's out in the open, what do you think about it?"

Nina looked puzzled. "I'm not certain. I guess I have the feeling that the Contessa and Dion were some kind of perverts who molest children." She looked at Isaaic questioningly. "Do you think that was it?"

Isaaic shrugged. "And how do you think all that relates to what is happening now, to the fact that you hear a male voice in your daughter's room?"

Nina lowered her glance to the floor. "I don't know," she said in a whisper. "I only know that it makes me have the same feeling—the feeling that I'm caught up in some kind of bad dream, a feeling of unreality, of fear. But," she looked up, "what do *you* think about it? You're the doctors, the experts. What kind of sense do *you* make out of all this?"

Isaaic looked at Sidney, and the younger man nodded. Isaaic moved his chair so that he could put his hand upon Nina's shoulder. "Nina, I want you to listen carefully to what I am about to say—carefully, and with an open mind.

"Both Sidney and I agree that there would seem to be a possibility that Dion was, and is, an incubus, the kind of creature that I discussed at the tenant's meeting. We believe that Dion definitely had a connection with the Contessa, and that she sent him to your family deliberately, intending that at least one of you should be his victim, or lover, however you care to put it. We believe that he became attached to a member of your family, and that when you left Italy, he followed you, in order to be near his, well, his lover.

"After listening to you under hypnosis, it would seem to be clear that the person he is . . ." He bit his lower lip. "Nina, it can only be Melissa. I'm sorry, but . . ."

Nina's keening cry drowned out Isaaic's half-spoken words, as she buried her face in her hands, rocking her body back and forth. It was a painful scene to watch, and Isaaic and Sidney both looked away.

Then Isaaic again put his hand on Nina's shoulder. "It's all right. Let it out. Sidney, get her some brandy."

Sidney brought the brandy in a small glass, and both men helped her get some of it down.

"It's what you've been afraid of, isn't it?" Isaaic asked, when at last the tears had stopped.

She nodded dumbly. He gave her another swallow of the brandy.

"The scent of oranges," she said. "That night at the

Contessa's, the room smelled of ripe oranges, and the air was hot and sweet. But what can we do? What can we do?"

Isaaic stroked her bent head. "Now that we know what it is that plagues us, we will find something, some way to rid ourselves of this creature."

She looked at him through matted lashes. "But how?"

Sidney looked at him also. "Yes, Isaaic, how?"

Isaaic shrugged expressively. "I have always believed that if there is a problem, there must also be a solution. All we have to do now, is find the solution."

He looked thoughtfully at Nina. "Nina, does Melissa have anything that this young man, this Dion, gave her? A pendant, perhaps? A bracelet; some token?"

Nina raised her eyebrows. "Why, I don't know. That is, I don't think so. At least she never told me about anything. Why, is it important?"

He shook his head. "I don't really know. If he had given her something, it might have served as a bond, a talisman, something to guide him to her wherever she went."

Nina shivered. "That's a horrible thought." She was silent for a moment. "She does have this box of curios, art objects and things from the different countries that we've visited."

Her expression livened. "You know, she always has those things around her when I go into her room after I've heard the other voice there. She always has all of her treasures, as she calls them, spread out around her on her bed. It *is* rather strange, now that I think of it."

Sidney broke in. "But how are you going to find out which, if any, of these objects were given to her by the incubus?"

Isaaic smiled wryly. "I suppose that we'll have to get that information from the only one who knows, besides Dion: Melissa!"

* * *

Melissa sat curled up in the large, blue chair, and returned to Isaaic's gaze with clear, blue eyes.

They had decided that it would be best to talk to Melissa in familiar surroundings, and, since Nina was far too close to the matter to discuss it dispassionately, and Sidney was a stranger, that Isaaic should be the one to talk to the child.

Isaaic had given considerable thought to this conversation, going over words and phrases in his mind. Melissa's intelligence and sophistication would make the matter even more difficult, since she would be more likely to see through any ploy he might use, than would an ordinary child. Finally, he settled on honesty as the safest policy—honesty tempered slightly with evasion.

To put Melissa at ease, they had arranged it so it would seem that Isaaic was coming to visit with Nina, on a night when Martin Girard would be at a meeting; since at this point, Isaaic did not want to involve Martin.

After Isaaic arrived, Nina would invite Melissa to join them—a frequent occurrence when the family had guests—and, hopefully, Melissa would be at ease, thinking the visit an ordinary neighborly drop-in.

So far, all had gone according to schedule. After a brief exchange of pleasantries, Nina had left the room to prepare refreshments, asking Melissa to entertain Mr. Aschermann in her absence.

Melissa, polite, and always interested in adults, took over the duties of hostess with quiet aplomb. She really was a remarkable child, Isaaic thought.

He then began to steer the conversation into channels that he hoped would lead gracefully to the subject he wished to discuss.

It was not nearly so difficult as he was afraid it might be. He gently led the conversation into a discussion of works of art, and then told Melissa that he had heard that she had some lovely things, collected during her family's travels, and asked if he might see them.

Her eyes lit up. "Oh, yes. You know, I think I'll be an art collector when I grow up."

Isaaic smiled. "Indeed. A worthy goal."

She looked at him sharply. "Oh, I know that you have to have money to collect art. But you see, I mean to be a dealer. You know, an antique dealer. That way I can buy beautiful things, sell some of them, and keep the best for myself. Don't you think that's a good idea?"

Isaaic nodded. "I do, indeed. You are a very sensible young lady, as well as an art lover."

Melissa got up from the chair, and stretched like a small cat. "Well, it's really not all my idea. I borrowed it from a friend of Mommy's. She's been doing it for years. I'll get my things."

She walked sedately out of the room, and Isaaic, looking after her, shook his head. What a woman she was going to make.

In a few minutes, Melissa returned carrying a medium-sized cardboard box, which she placed at Isaaic's feet.

She then began to take items out of the box, one by one, presenting them proudly to Isaaic, for his inspection.

He took each item carefully, and held it in his hands, trying to make himself receptive, open to any vibrations that the objects might emit.

Although, so far, according to Melissa, the items he had seen had not come from Italy, he still gave each one a thorough perusal, on the chance that the contact might have been made at an earlier time, in another country; but so far, none of the objects had any special quality other than their beauty.

Then, Melissa took from the carton an intricately carved marble box, and Isaaic knew that this was it. He had only to see it to know that it was Greek in origin, and very old.

As she placed the cool weight of it into his hands, he experienced a strange sensation, as if a charge of electricity was going through his body. The air in the room suddenly seemed warm, and as he became aware of a pungent, spicy scent in the air, he was reminded of Nina's comment about "heat, and the scent of ripe oranges."

Carefully he looked down at Melissa, who was sitting at his feet. Her expression was open and pleased, the expression of a person sharing something she loved with an appreciative friend.

"It's very beautiful," he said sincerely. "And, I think, very rare. May I open it?"

Melissa nodded happily. "He said it was special."

Isaaic instantly caught the implication of her remark, but let it pass, not wanting to alarm her. His hands trembled as he opened the heavy, marble top. As he opened the box, the spicy odor became stronger, and the box itself seemed to grow warm under his fingers.

Inside the box was a small carving, also of marble. The piece glowed with an inner light, and the involvement of the carving made the object waver before his eyes. Oh, yes . . . this was it. There could be no doubt.

Gently, he closed the lid, not wanting, for some reason, to look too closely at the object inside.

"It's amazing," he told Melissa. "You must be very proud to own it."

"Oh, yes. It's the prize of my collection." She said the words very seriously, and at another time, Isaaic would have found her grown-up phrasing amusing, but now, there were other things on his mind.

"As one collector to another, would you mind telling me how you came by this?"

He noticed that she did not hesitate to answer. "It came from Italy. I got it when we lived in the pink palazzo. Do you know what a palazzo is?"

Isaaic, fighting the desire to hurry the child on, answered, "Yes, a palazzo is a small palace. So you lived in a palace. I've often wished that I might do that. And did you buy the box in Rome, or, in a nearby town?"

She shook her head, setting her pale curls bobbing. "Oh no—I didn't buy the box. Dion gave it to me."

Isaaic felt a great excitement mounting in him. Dion. Dion, the young gardener, described by Nina.

He handed the box back to Melissa—for some reason anxious to have it out of his hands. "He must have been a very good friend to give you something as lovely and valuable as this."

She smiled, as her fingers traced the carvings on the box. "Oh, yes. We were good friends. He used to tell me stories, and play games with me."

Trying to avoid the thoughts that the term "games" brought to his mind, Isaaic asked softly, "Do you miss him?"

Now the child's face turned secretive. "I think about him," she said cryptically. The open expression was gone now, and Isaaic knew that he would get little more from her; however it would seem that he and Sidney were right. Melissa was the focus of the incubus's interest, and the box was the talisman.

At that moment Nina came in with refreshments, and he nodded surreptitiously. Nina's face paled, but she carried off the rest of the visit with convincing naturalness, until it was the child's bedtime.

While Nina put Melissa to bed, Isaaic was thinking of how to verity the fact that Melissa was the focus of the incubus's interest. By the time Nina returned to the living room, he had formulated a plan that he believed would work.

Nina dropped into the chair across from Isaaic. Her face was pale, and her expression strained.

"So she is the one?"

He nodded sadly. "It would seem so. She has a box, a beautiful thing, very rare, that she says the boy gave to her. I held it in my hands, and the feeling . . . well, it's indescribable!"

"A box?" Nina looked puzzled. "I don't even remember her having a box, other than the carton she carries those things around in."

"A small chest really. It seems to be Greek. Very old. And you did not buy it for her?"

Nina shook her head. "No. I realize that I indulge Melissa, and buy her expensive things, but even I wouldn't give a child of ten an expensive antique."

"Well, she has one, and a strange one it is, indeed. It smells of something pungent and spicy, and gives off a strange heat."

Nina shivered. "That sounds too familiar for comfort. Well, what do we do now?"

"We must get the box away from Melissa; and we must get Melissa away from the Barkley Plaza, for at least a few days."

Nina sighed and rested her head against the cushioned chair back. "And how do we do that?"

Isaaic looked at her with a rueful smile. "Nina, I am afraid that you are going to become very ill, with a communicable disease."

She leaned forward. "What?"

He nodded. "Yes, it will be something particularly dangerous to children, and it will be necessary to have Melissa stay with friends for a few nights, until you are over the contageous period."

"Do you think she will believe that?"

"If you are a good enough actress."

"But what about Martin?"

"It will be a disease that he has already had, and to which he is now immune."

At the look of distress upon her face, he got up and moved to her side. Looking down at her, he said gently, "He will have to know the details, Nina. This is something that involves your whole family, and Martin is part of that family too. Can you tell him? Or would you rather that Sidney or I told him?"

She swallowed. "It might be better if Dr. Allbright talked to him first. Martin will believe him more readily—I mean, he won't be able to brush it off as hysterics, then, will he? After that, I'll talk to him too, and fill in the details."

Isaaic patted her hand. "That sounds very reasonable to me."

She cocked her head to one side. "But I do have a couple of questions."

"What are they?"

"Well, at this point, the only real friends I have in New York are right here in the Barkley, and you say that Melissa must get away from the Barkley. Where will she stay?"

He smiled widely. "Would I make a suggestion if I didn't already have a plan figured out? She will stay with friends of mine. A lovely family with several children near Melissa's age. The father is a musician with the New York Symphony. Melissa should love it."

"And what about the chest? How do you propose to get Melissa to leave her treasures behind when she goes on this visit?"

He shrugged. "Nothing that is not able to be scrubbed and sterilized will be let out of the apartment, because of the hightly contagious nature of your illness. Since we will tell her it is only going to be for a few days, I don't believe she will make too much of a fuss. The doctor will tell her she may only take a few clothes, and these only after they have been washed and boiled."

Nina put her hand to her forehead, "And just who is 'the doctor?' "

"Sidney Allbright, of course; whom she has never seen."

The corridor was long, with many branching hallways. The building that housed the corridor was very old; Isaaic could smell the mustiness of years.

The lighting was very poor, and Isaaic was having

trouble distinguishing reality from shadow; and yet he crept down the corridor, hand against the wall, following the boy who ran ahead.

It was difficult; for the boy, obviously, was able to see in the darkness. He was nimble, and young, and ran like a deer, in and out of the shadows, teasing, mocking.

And yet Isaaic kept on, stubbornly, slowly; for it was very important that he should not give up; that he should catch this mocking figure; for the boy knew something important. He held the answer, the key.

At that moment, the boy stopped, directly in the light, and held aloft the chest; and Isaaic ran forward, arms outstretched, afraid, yet determined, and as he reached toward the chest—

Isaaic awoke from the dream to find himself sweating, although the room was cool.

He pulled a handkerchief from his pocket and mopped his face, while waiting for the rapid beating of his heart to slow.

He had not meant to sleep, had taken a nap that afternoon to forestall just such a possibility. Another sign of age, he thought ruefully.

He looked across the room to where Sidney lay, snoring lightly, upon his bed. A fine guard he, Isaaic, was.

He swallowed, finding his throat dry, and reached for the carafe of water on the table beside him. Pouring a glassful, he drank it greedily, then sat back to listen.

The building was quiet. He opened his thoughts, his mind, hoping to sense out any presence other than the usual, and felt nothing.

He sighed, remembering the events of the day. Convincing Melissa of the seriousness of her mother's illness had not been difficult. Nina had looked appropriately pale and sick; and Sidney had played the medical doctor convincingly.

When they had told Melissa that she couldn't take any personal possessions with her, even her beloved box of treasures, she had protested; but Sidney had reasoned with her, and she was eventually resigned to the fact that she must leave them behind.

She had taken immediately to the Sheldons, dear friends of Isaaic, warm and loving people, and so all had gone according to Isaaic's plans—until the moment came when he was faced with the task of disposing of the chest.

This had been one of the most difficult things that Isaaic had ever done. His love of beauty, and his respect for antiquities were innate parts of his being, and to deliberately destroy an historical treasure was basically unthinkable.

He and Sidney and the Girards had discussed the matter at some length. Martin Girard, now fully aware of the story of his wife's experiences in Italy, and of the events that had transpired since, was cooperative, although Isaaic could tell he was having difficulty in accepting all that he had been told.

It was Martin who pointed out the fact that if the chest was crushed, or broken, the power might still remain within the shards. Isaaic agreed that this was probable.

Sidney, finally, came up with the plan that they used.

"Remember Jinns?" he asked.

"Jinns? You mean Genies? Like the one in *Aladdin's Lamp*?" asked Nina.

He nodded. "You couldn't destroy a Jinn, or a Genie, but you *could* seal them away so that they could not use their powers."

Martin looked at him and smiled. "If I hadn't heard those tapes, I'd think you were all mad. Now, we're discussing the *Arabian Nights*. Anyway, didn't it take a powerful magician to seal the Genie into the bottle?"

Sidney smiled. "Yes, but maybe we can improvise; use a little science, instead of magic."

Isaaic looked up quizically. "A little science? What do you mean?"

Sidney lifted his hands, palms up. "Well, I really haven't thought it through yet, but say, just off of the top of my head, that we try a little ritual, sort of an exorcism, over the chest—maybe wash it in holy water, something like that—then wrap it in . . . well, maybe wrap it in lead foil, and then drop it in the river?

"If lead keeps out radiation, maybe it will keep in the magical power, or whatever it is that makes that chest a focal point for the incubus. What do you think?"

Isaaic sat forward, his face breaking into a smile. "I think you have the beginning of a solution," he said. "I think it might work."

And that, substantially, was what they had done. The holy water was dispensed with, for although Isaaic had some faith in the magic of all religions, none of those present was Catholic, and so did not have the faith that might be necessary to make that particular bit of ritual work.

Instead, consulting his reference works on the occult, Isaaic annointed the box with a paste made of dried lupine, garlic, betony, and frankincense, mixed with tallow. After this was done, he wrapped the box in a soft cloth, tying it firmly with twine and sealing the knot with a large daub of black wax. While the wax was still warm, he carved into it a six-sided star, with small crosslike designs upon the points, and cryptic symbols in the center and to the left, explaining to the others that this was one of the Seals of Solomon—this particular one being used in binding spirits in the magic ceremony.

After the package was thus wrapped, Isaaic fumigated it over a special incense he had prepared, while he slowly spoke the words that would help to imprison and immobilize the power that the box contained.

While this procedure was going on, Isaaic was conscious of a terrible pressure in the room. He sensed vibrations of anger and hostility. Looking at the others, he could tell that they too sensed it, in varying degrees.

Nina looked sickly pale, and close to collapse; Sidney's forehead was beaded with sweat, and his jaw was clenched; Martin Girard looked uneasy, and kept glancing around, as if trying to find the source of his unease.

When the box lay before them, fragrant with the pungent balm and the fumigating incense, it seemed to glow with a strange, inner light that penetrated the cloth wrapping and illuminated the seal drawn into the wax.

Although they were now ready to wrap it in the heavy, leaded foil, none of them made a move to touch it, until Isaaic, fighting against a terrible inertia, reached toward the foil.

His arm felt heavy and ponderous. With great effort, he picked up the lead foil. "You'll have to help," he said, hissing the words out between locked jaws. "It will take all of us."

Slowly, the others began to move. Heavily, like deep sea divers compressed by the weight of water, they folded the foil around the box, wrapping it tightly.

As the last bit of the chest was covered, the pressure disappeared; leaving them all gasping and jerking, as if the weight against their limbs was suddenly released.

Isaaic exhaled noisily, and sat down on the nearest chair. "That proves it as far as I'm concerned. You all felt it, didn't you?"

The others nodded. Martin Girard's face was a study in shock. Isaaic was sure that the man had not really believed until now.

"Now, into the river with it," said Sidney, almost cheerfully.

"Wait!" Isaaic raised his hand. "One more thing. We'll wrap the whole thing with plastic. That way, the lead foil can't become undone, and also, the chest will be preserved."

Sidney shook his head. "Always the archaeologist, eh, Isaaic?"

Isaaic shrugged. "There is no use in destroying the chest; we already decided that. So why not preserve it safely? Perhaps, someday, in the far future, when our world is old and dead, archaeologists from another planet will find this in a dry river bed and open it, and see a thing of great and rare beauty. Maybe it will have lost its talismanic powers by then."

"And if it hasn't?"

Isaaic shrugged again. "So, maybe life from a different planet will be introduced to one of the old gods of our planet!"

And so it had been done. The package, finally wrapped in plastic over all, had been thrown into the Hudson River from the deck of a Staten Island ferry.

And now, with Melissa safely away from the Barkley, and the talisman at the bottom of the river, they waited, hoping that they were waiting for nothing.

Isaaic had gone to all of the tenants, telling them only that he was conducting an experiment to rid the building of the spirit, and that if they experienced anything out of the ordinary, anything frightening or unusual, to report it immediately to him in his apartment.

He impressed upon them the importance of coming to him with this information no matter what the hour of day or night. He and Sidney were going to sleep in shifts, so that one of them would be awake and alert at all times.

And now, he had fallen asleep at his watch—awake and alert indeed—but it seemed that no harm was done. The building was quiet, nothing seemed amiss.

He stretched mightily, heard his joints snap, and grimaced. A pot of tea would go good right now.

He started to rise from his chair, when a scream shattered the night quiet. Even inside the apartment, with the doors and windows closed, the sound was terrifyingly loud.

In an instant, he was on his feet, heart pumping frantically. Sidney was sitting bolt upright on the bed, his face wearing an expression of fear and confusion. "My God! What was that?"

The sound had come so suddenly that Isaaic had not been about to get a fix on its direction.

And then it came again, a raw shriek of pain and terror; and this time Isaaic could tell that it came from above, from the Girard's apartment.

SIXTEEN

"Upstairs!" Isaaic shouted, starting toward the door at an awkward run.

Outside, in the hall, Sidney passed him, not waiting for the elevator, but sprinting for the stairs. Isaaic followed him, but at a slower pace.

At the door to the Girard's apartment, their poundings and callings were in vain. The door was locked, and it was far too heavy for them to break down.

Isaaic leaned against the door jamb, panting. "Sidney, go back to my apartment, call Sal Bartlo. Tell him to bring his tools, and hurry!"

As Sidney ran toward the stairs; Isaaic pressed his ear to the door. There was no sound. Nothing. He felt terribly helpless and, yes, for the first time, afraid. His heart was beating too fast, and his chest hurt when he breathed. He was too old for all of this activity; too old. He resumed pounding on the door, and ringing the bell, but there was still no answer.

After what seemed like an hour but was, in reality, only a few minutes, Sidney returned with a pale-faced Sal Bartolo.

Sal was wearing an overcoat over his pajamas, and carrying his tool box in one hand. He looked at Isaaic worriedly. "Are you sure we should break in? If something's not wrong, we . . ."

Isaaic impatiently urged him toward the door. "Something *is* wrong! Trust me. Sidney and I both heard the screams."

Sal took a large bunch of keys from his overcoat pocket and, finding the master for the Girards' apartment, turned the tumblers in the lock. The deadbolt slid free, but still the door would not open more than an inch or so.

"They've got the chain on," said Sal.

"Get it off!" said Isaaic curtly. "We've got to get in there as soon as possible!"

Sal went to work with his tools, and Isaaic slumped against the wall. His eyes sought Sidney's. Sidney stared back, his drawn face looking older than his thirty years warranted.

They both turned at the sound of the elevator door opening. It was Ursula Bartolo and Tracy both in nightgowns and robes.

Ursula hurried toward Sal, but Sidney waved her back. "Let hin finish, please, Mrs. Bartolo. Someone in there may be in trouble."

She stopped where she stood. "What happened?" she asked, her dark eyes wide with apprehension.

"We heard screams from the Girard apartment, and no one answers the door."

"Oh, my God!" Ursula turned toward Tracy, who put a comforting arm around her shoulder.

Isaaic knew that Ursula was thinking of the murder in the Kauffmans' apartment, and he understood her fear, for he felt it must be something like his own.

"There it is!" Sal pushed open the apartment door. The living room on the other side was dark. For a moment they all stood silent.

Then the elevator hissed open again, and Halley and Vince McGuire were coming toward them. "I thought I heard a scream," Halley said. "We've been going to every floor. What's happened?"

Tracy turned toward her. "The screams came from up here. Isaaic and his friend heard them. Sal just got the door open."

Halley stepped forward toward the open door, her face anxious, but Isaaic moved to block the doorway.

"I think it would be better if Sidney and I went in alone. I know that you are all concerned, but believe me, a whole crowd of people won't help. If we meet anything we cannot handle, we'll call, loudly. All right?"

Halley nodded, and moved back into the protection of Vince's arm. The others, also, seemed to accept Isaaic's suggestion.

Before entering the room Isaaic switched on the lights by reaching around to the wall plate near the door. The large living room was beautiful and serene, as always.

He motioned to Sidney, who followed him into the room, carrying a pipe wrench that Sal had handed to him just as he started through the door.

As the others stared after them through the doorway, they walked carefully across the pale, beige rug, toward the doorway that led to the bedrooms and baths.

Gingerly, Isaaic opened the door to Melissa's room and gasped. The usually pin-neat room looked as if an earthquake had shaken it. The dresser was toppled face front onto the floor, and dolls, toys, and smaller pieces of furniture were flung about the room, as if a giant hand had picked up the contents and flung them down again.

He heard Sidney's muffled exclamation of surprise, and then his whisper. "My God, Isaaic. What caused this?"

Isaaic was afraid to answer. His very bowels felt cold with fear. He wanted nothing so much as to leave this room, this apartment, and go back to his own warm bed. Why had he gotten himself into this? He was too old. Too old!

The feeling of depression that followed these thoughts was massive and debilitating, and then he realized that the thoughts were coming from outside himself, that they were being forced upon his mind.

This knowledge gave him the strength to throw off

most of the effects of the depression. Up until now, he had kept his mind open, receptive to outside stimuli, but now, he closed it. He imagined a steel wall around his thoughts, his mind, an impenetrable shield, and as he did so, the influence waned, and some of his usual confidence returned.

He turned to leave the room, and saw that Sidney had been affected too. His face was ashen, and his forehead damp with sweat. "Sidney," he said, shaking the younger man by the shoulder. "Fight it! Close your mind! These thoughts aren't yours, they're *his*!"

Sidney, gulping air, nodded, and closed his eyes. In a few seconds his color began to come back, and his breathing had slowed.

"The parents' room," he said softly.

Slowly, they moved down the hall toward the door at the end. All of the apartments were laid out in the same pattern, and Isaaic knew that this was the location of the master bedroom.

The nearer they drew to the door, the more Isaaic had to fight the smothering feeling of fear and depression; but he held the wall around his mind, and Sidney seemed to be doing likewise—at least he was moving forward, just behind Isaaic.

At last they were at the door. Isaaic reached out and grasped the knob, then snatched his hand away. The doorknob was blistering hot—instantly raising angry red welts on his fingers.

Avoiding the knob, Isaaic pressed his ear to the wooden door. There were sounds, muffled and disturbing, and then the clear sound of a woman moaning.

Using the edge of his coat, Isaaic once more grasped the doorknob and turned it, Sidney close behind him.

The door opened inward with surprising force, and Isaaic and Sidney both stopped where they stood.

One light—a beautiful blue-green Tiffany floor-lamp, was lit, casting a soft, gentle glow upon a scene that was far from peaceful.

On the floor, on the side of the king-sized bed nearest the door, lay the prone figure of Martin Girard. He was not moving.

And upon the bed, among the tumbled covers, lay Nina Girard, writhing and tossing her body from side to side.

Her arms, outstretched, did not move, and Isaaic thought at first that she was bound; but as he cautiously came closer, he found that this was not true. There were no ropes or bindings holding her arms in that position, at least none that he could see.

The movements of her body were almost epileptic in intensity, and he feared that her slender arm bones would snap from the frantic tossing of her fragile body.

He looked at Sidney, who was approaching from the other side of the bed, and then back at Nina.

There was froth upon her lips, and her eyes were staring, wide and unblinking.

He reached forward to touch her, and was thrown back by a force sufficient to fling him against the wall.

Sidney, who had been reaching toward her from the other side, drew back his hand.

And then suddenly, without any kind of warning, her body went still. As Isaaic struggled to his feet, he heard her say something, two words, but he could not make them out. He limped toward the bed, as Sidney reached forward and put his hand upon Nina's arm. She showed no reaction. He looked at Isaaic with fear and consternation in his eyes. "She said, 'help me,'" he said.

Isaaic watched as the younger man took Nina's pulse, then checked her breathing. "She seems to be all right, although I don't see how she can be, after that."

Isaaic pulled a blanket over her body. Her gown

had been ripped by her body's violent contortions, and there was a long scratch down her stomach, between her breasts, probably made by her own fingernails during her convulsions—and then he remembered that her hands had not moved from their outflung position.

"We had better see to Martin," he said.

Both men went over to where Martin Girard lay, and Sidney gently palpated a large lump at the base of Martin's skull. "He's taken a terrific rap on the head. We'd best get him to a hospital as soon as possible."

Isaaic nodded. "You call. I'm not sure I'm up to it." He had dropped to the floor beside Martin, and now, he moved so that his back was against the side of the bed. "My Lord, I'm tired," he whispered.

He watched as Sidney reached for the telephone and began to dial, and then something hit him a sharp blow upon the temple. The next thing he knew, the entire contents of the room seemed to be in motion.

As he watched, the telephone was ripped from Sidney's hand, to smash against the wall. Bureaus toppled; pillows, cushions, dressing table equipment, all were airborne. Isaaic leaned forward and covered his head and face with his arms.

Besides the sound of objects striking the walls and floor, Isaaic was conscious of a roaring sound, like the sound of a high wind in a forest.

And then as abruptly as it had begun, the phenomenon stopped. Articles dropped to the floor and remained motionless. The roaring sound was gone.

Carefully, and with some pain, Isaaic got to his knees, and then, with the help of the bedpost, to his feet.

Sidney was still on the floor, sitting upright now, gingerly touching his thigh. "Something hit me a good one," he said, his voice expressing both anger and self pity. "What in the name of all that is holy, was *that*?"

Isaaic looked down at Nina before answering. Her

arms had fallen to her sides, and she seemed to be unhurt. If he had not known better, he would have assumed she was in a normal sleep.

"I think we have made someone angry," he said matter-of-factly. "I think we have just met a very angry incubus!"

Sidney got to his feet. "Well, I didn't care much for the introduction." He looked over to where Martin Girard lay on the floor. "Look, we'd better get him to the hospital."

Isaaic, not taking his eyes from Nina, nodded. "You go down to my apartment, and call for an ambulance. I'll go and see if the McGuires will go with him to the hospital."

Sidney gestured to Nina. "Should we have them take her too?"

Isaaic shook his head. "No, for her trouble, I don't think they have the cure. She will be better off with us."

Sidney came back into the room. "The ambulance is on its way."

At that moment, Nina sighed softly, and opened her eyes. Both men watched, as she yawned, and then lifted herself upon her elbows. Her eyes widened, and a look of confusion crossed her face as she caught sight of the two men.

"What?" Her voice was high. "Dr. Aschermann? Dr. Allbright? What are you doing here?" She looked around frantically. "Where's Martin? What's happened to this room?"

"She doesn't remember a thing," said Sidney wonderingly.

Isaaic walked quickly to Nina's side, and pulled the covers up over and around her shoulders. "Nina, something has happened. Martin's been hurt—but it's not serious. We've called an ambulance, and it should be here in a minute. I want you to lie back down, breathe evenly, and remain calm. We'll explain the whole thing to you when the ambulance crew is gone."

Nina lay back and gave him a shaky smile. She closed her eyes, and began to breathe deeply, as he pulled the covers over her.

The ambulance crew arrived then and, in a few efficient minutes, had Martin bundled aboard a stretcher and out of the room.

As the ambulance crew was leaving, Halley and Vince, followed by Tracy, Elva, and Ursula, came into the room, looking pale and determined.

Isaaic felt a flash of annoyance. His mind had caught hold of something—something he felt was important—and he did not want to be interrupted just then.

"I think it would be best if you all went back to your own apartments. Mr. Girard is injured, but it is probably no more than a concussion, and Mrs. Girard is all right. There is nothing you can do!"

Sidney leaned toward him, and whispered in his ear. "Didn't you want to ask the young couple to go with him to the hospital?"

As Sidney spoke, Isaaic felt a great rush of remorse. Halley looked hurt, and Ursula Bartolo's cheeks turned pink. They were his friends, and of course they were worried and anxious. He was treating them like strangers, and they were understandably upset.

"I'm sorry, friends," he said. "I guess all this has made me a bit edgy, but I shouldn't be taking it out on you. Halley and Vince, would you drive down to the hospital and stay with Mr. Girard, until you find out how he is?"

Halley opened her mouth to speak, but Isaaic raised his hand. "I promise I will tell you everything that happened, when you return. All right?"

"All right." Halley smiled suddenly, and running forward, kissed Isaaic on the cheek. "Come on, Vince. Let's get our clothes on."

Isaaic turned back to the others. "I'm sorry that I

was so brusque. I know you're concerned, and this involves you, as well as the Girards. I'll tell you what I can now, and later I will explain as much as I am able, without infringing upon the privacy of the Girards. Is that satisfactory?"

Tracy and Elva looked at one another, and Ursula Bartolo nodded. There was a murmur of assent.

"All right. As you can see, there has been some type of poltergeistic phenomenon here." He gestured at the room.

"I am reasonably certain that this activity was caused by our night visitor, and Dr. Allbright and I are going to attempt to control—and stop—its manifestations. Sidney and I will take turns sitting up with Mrs. Girard. I don't think the incubus will return tonight, but we will not take any chances. That is about all I can tell you right now."

Sal Bartolo put his arm around his wife. "Thanks, Professor. And I want you to know that Ursula and I really appreciate what you're doing. We feel . . ." He paused, and looked down at Ursula. "Well, we feel a lot better—more secure, you know—with you handling things. Isn't that right, Ursula?"

Ursula, pink-faced, murmured her assent.

"You want Ursula should bring you up some coffee, something to eat?"

Isaaic looked a question at Sidney, who smiled. "That sounds great!" His grin went a little askew. "You get awfully hungry fighting demons."

The remark was greeted by nervous laughter from the departing tenants, and a shake of the head from Isaaic. "So, are you a believer now, Sidney?"

Sidney sank down onto the one chair remaining upright, and sighed heavily. "Well, let's just say that I'm considerably less skeptical. Good Lord—Mrs. Girard!"

Both men turned toward the bed, where Nina Girard still lay quietly, breathing evenly.

Isaaic walked over to the bed. "Nina? Are you all right?"

She made a soft, mewling sound, and her eyelids fluttered, then opened. "I must have dozed off again. What did you say?"

Isaaic smiled. "That's all right. I guess you've answered the question anyway. Tell me, what do you remember?"

Her forehead wrinkled, and an expression of puzzlement crossed her face. "Not much, I'm afraid. I woke up and . . . and . . . you and Dr. Allbright were here in our room, and Martin . . ." She sat upright, quickly. "What happened to Martin? Where is he?"

"Martin's been taken to the hospital, but he is not badly hurt; they want to keep him a couple of days for observation." Quickly, Isaaic filled her in on the night's events, starting when he and Sidney heard her screams.

She looked at him silently, then shook her head gently. "Dr. Aschermann, if I didn't trust you two so implicitly, I'd have to think this whole thing was a figment of your imagination. It's difficult to believe that all of that happened, and I don't remember, or feel a thing." She winced. "Well, I do feel a scratch down my stomach." Her eyes widened. "But what does this mean, Doctor? If Melissa is the one the incubus is interested in, and if she is out of the building, and the talisman at the bottom of the river, why is the creature still here?"

Isaaic lowered his head, and then looked back at Nina. "Because it would appear that my theory was wrong," he said. "I guess I am not quite so clever as I had imagined."

An expression of joy crossed Nina's face, and her body relaxed. "Oh, thank God! I knew it couldn't be Melissa."

And then her expression grew thoughtful. "But what do we do now? How do we get rid of him now?"

Sidney leaned forward. "And why did he get so violent tonight? Maybe your theory isn't wrong, after all, Isaaic. Maybe the incubus is simply angry because you've taken away his . . . well, his love, the one he's most interested in, and because you've destroyed, for all practical purposes, his talisman, his link to that person."

Isaaic sighed. "Maybe, and maybe not. Oh, I'm sure the incubus is angry, we've annoyed him, no doubt of that; but maybe I put two and two together, and got five. But we'll talk about this later. Right now, I think we'd better get Nina back to bed. Nina, do you have any sleeping pills?"

She smiled thinly. "Do I ever. On the top shelf of the medicine cabinet."

Isaaic gave her two of the pills and a glass of water, and then he and Sidney straightened the bed.

Isaaic tucked her in like a child, and within a few minutes she was asleep again. This time, Isaaic hoped, peacefully, for the rest of the night.

"What do you mean you 'put two and two together, and got five?'" Sidney asked, speaking around a mouthful of roll.

He and Isaaic were seated comfortably in two upholstered chairs, in a small sitting room, just off of the master bedroom in the Girard apartment.

The small table between them was covered with food and two thermoses of coffee brought to them by Ursula Bartolo.

Isaaic swallowed some of the hot, sweet coffee, savoring the warmth that trickled slowly down into his belly.

"I mean that maybe I've been on the wrong track." He wiped his hands on a large, paper napkin. "Tell me, can a person lie, while under the effect of hypnosis? Or, will a person always tell the absolute truth?"

Sidney, licking mustard off of his fingers, looked thoughtful. "That's not as easy to answer as you might think. The answer depends upon several variables—how deep the subject is in the so-called 'trance'; how badly he, or she, wants to hide the truth. Let's just say that it is *possible* for a person to tell less than the full truth while under hypnosis."

Isaaic nodded. "I thought so. Sidney, I want you to put Nina Girard under again, very deeply under; and then I want you to go back again, over the same material, starting with the first day she met Dion, the young gardener."

Sidney looked at him speculatively. "You think Nina Girard didn't tell us everything?"

Isaaic lifted his hands, palms up. "Everything she *could*, perhaps. Now I am interested in hearing what she could *not* tell us. Maybe now, after tonight, something more will come out."

Sidney poured himself another cup of the steaming coffee. "That's fine with me. The only thing is, I can't guarantee that anything new will come out. Still, we can try."

Isaaic smiled. "That's all we can ever do—try. Now, I believe that it is my turn to sleep."

Nina lay supine upon her bed, her hands clasped just under her breasts. She watched Dr. Aschermann and Dr. Allbright as they plugged in the tape recorder, and inserted the cassette.

The bizarre occurrences of the night before had left her feeling only a little tired. She still did not remember anything that had occurred.

Her bedroom was tidy now, straightened by Mrs. Bartolo, but she could remember how it had looked earlier—a wild jumble of furniture and bric-a-brac, a frightening symbol of anger.

She shivered slightly—it was cool in the room—but she did not ask the men to turn up the heat.

She felt curiously relaxed and resigned. Relaxed, because it was not Melissa whom the incubus sought, and resigned, because now she *wanted* the truth, all of it, whatever it was, to come out. There would be peace in knowing; peace, in facing up to, and confronting, whatever had happened.

Martin was still in the hospital—they had kept him overnight for observation—and he was doing fine. He should be home by tomorrow if nothing further developed. And by that time, hopefully, they would know—she would know—the whole story of what had happened in Italy.

Sidney came over and stood by the bed. "All right, Nina, we're ready to start. Do you feel Okay?"

She nodded slightly. "Surprisingly, I do." She smiled. "Also, strangely enough, I feel ready to face anything now that I know the incubus isn't following Melissa."

Sidney frowned slightly. "You know, Nina, that the fact that the incubus is not seeking Melissa, may mean that your husband, or you yourself, is the focal point of its interest."

She turned her head toward him. "Yes, I realize that, and I'm prepared to face it, if necessary. I'm not afraid anymore, just terribly curious. I want to know what happened, *all* of what happened, and I want to be rid of this thing, and of my fear, forever!"

Sidney patted her shoulder. "Good girl. Now, this time, after I put you under, I'm going to turn the questioning over to Dr. Aschermann."

Isaaic approached the bed. "Are you ready, Nina?"

"As ready as I'll ever be, I guess."

"Very well, Sidney; let us begin."

Nina kept her eyes fixed upon the crystal at the end of the swinging chain. Rainbow sparks flickered and faded as the surface swung and turned. She could hear Dr. Allbright's voice in the background, telling her to relax, telling her that her eyes felt heavy, telling her that she was going to go deep, deeper, into the hypnotic state.

Now, her eyes were closed, but she could still see the prismatic flashes of color behind her lids. Dr. Allbright's voice changed, becoming deeper and softer, telling her to go back, back to the day when she had first met Dion. The rainbow colors wavered and thinned, to disclose a door. She knew that someone had just knocked; the sound was still fading away. She went toward the door and opened it.

SEVENTEEN

As she opened the door, she cried out, and her hand flew to her mouth. A young man was standing on the doorstep, hand raised, as if halted in the act of knocking.

"I'm sorry," said Nina. "You startled me!"

The young man smiled. "I am sorry too, signora. I would not have purposely startled you for the world," the young man answered in perfect, if heavily accented, English.

Nina realized that she was staring; but she could not stop. The boy's beauty was like a blow. Everything about him was dark, except for his slashing white smile and the whites of his large, heavily lashed eyes. Soft, black curls framed his smooth, brown face, and she could not keep her eyes from his mouth, which showed both sensuality and arrogance in the full, well-shaped lips.

His body was just as beautiful as his face, and his clothing was designed to show this fact. He was wearing a sleeveless jersey that displayed his smooth, muscular arms and shoulders to advantage, and skin-tight blue jeans that bulged imposingly at the crotch.

Nina, who had never before done such a thing, found her eyes irresistably drawn to this spot. She felt her face grow hot; but she could not look away. She found herself wondering what he looked like there, under his clothes, when he was unconfined and free; and a feeling of tension and excitement started and began to grow in her lower abdomen and between her legs.

Face flaming, she turned away so that he should not see her consternation, and walked a few steps back into the house.

As if this were a signal for him to follow, the young man came after her into the house. As he came toward her, his sly smile told her that her discomfiture had not gone unnoticed. His intimate, dark eyes slid slowly and acquisitively over her body, as he moistened his lips with his tongue. He made no effort to hide his interest; it was as if her perusal of him had given him the right to be bold.

She knew that she should say something, but no words would come to her mind or lips. Finally, she stammered out, "What was it you wanted?"

He smiled again, and took another step toward her, his eyes lingering on the tips of her breasts, which she suddenly felt were unduly exposed through the thin fabric of her summer dress.

"Why, I am Dion, signora. The Contessa sent me. I have come to work in your garden."

He spoke these last words in an intimate manner, never taking his eyes from hers. He might as well have said, "I have come to be your lover!"

Nina could feel her heart thudding uncomfortably in her chest. What was this boy doing to her, with his insinuating dark eyes and knowing smile?

At that moment, the sound of the piano stopped, and Nina could hear the patter of Melissa's running feet coming toward them across the tile.

Nina's eyes stared into the young man's eyes, and then Melissa burst into the entry way.

"Mother, I'm finished. It's been a whole hour. I'm going over to Annette's. Her daddy got her a pony!"

Nina's mind registered the words, but the focus of her attention was still on the boy.

"All right," she answered automatically. "Be home by lunch time."

"Okay." Melissa flung a bright, curious glance at Dion, and skipped past him out the door.

The young man's glance flicked toward the child, then returned again to Nina's face.

"Is your husband home?" he asked softly, his tone intimate.

Nina felt confused and off-balance. "Ah, I . . . no, he's not home. Why do you ask?"

The boy shrugged—a Continental gesture that was so much more expressive than an English or American shrug.

"I wanted to talk to him."

Again Nina could sense the laughter behind the words, as if they shared a common secret, as if he knew her thoughts. She flushed.

Again his eyes engaged hers, and for a few seconds she became dizzy and disoriented. She closed her eyes for a moment, trying to get a better hold upon her emotions. Then she felt a touch upon her arm, just above the elbow. The feeling was electric and devastating. Her eyes flew open and again stared into his, only slightly above her own.

She made no movement to stop him as he led her into the music room where the big fan circled slowly just under the ceiling.

His body close to hers, and his hand upon her upper arm, filled her with a frightening but sweet lassitude. Her will, her freedom of choice, seemed not to exist.

As he closed the door and locked it from the inside, the thought went through her mind that Maria, the maid, was in the village, shopping. She and the boy were alone in the house. The thought, instead of frightening her, excited her further. Her heart fluttered unevenly, and she breathed rapidly, as she watched him go from window to window, shutting out the bright morning sunlight until the room swam in a dusky haze through which his figure moved with incredible grace.

She made no move, no outcry, as he stepped close to her and took her in his arms. His lips upon hers were hot and demanding, and she did not, could not resist, as he pushed his tongue into her mouth and touched the tip of it to her tongue.

At this intimate contact, a wild sweetness pervaded her body, rushing along her nerves to every secret part of her. She felt her body spasm, then press against his, as his tongue made her mouth his own, while his hands gently made themselves familiar with her body.

And then, his lips were gone from hers, and he was leading her toward the low couch against the wall. As she lay back against the pillows the thought of what she was doing flickered briefly across her mind, but was immediately extinguished by such a surge of wanting, needing, that the small flame of reason stood no chance.

Without quite knowing how it happened, Nina found herself naked, and in the next instant, his hot, hard, young body was tight against hers, insistant and demanding. She moved against him, as eager as he, feeling greedy, hungry, wanting him inside her, wanting all of him.

Rubbing against him, feeling the hard maleness of him against her, she grew desperate for completion.

She pulled her mouth from his, and gasped against his throat, "Oh, take me! Please take me! Oh, do it now!"

He lifted his face above hers, and for an instant, she could see his quick, knowing smile. Staring down into her eyes, he lifted himself and entered her. The size of his organ made her gasp with pain and excitement. At first he moved slowly, lasciviously; and then as her passion grew, he moved faster and deeper, until flesh pounded against flesh, and she cried out her pleasure.

And then at last, when she had reached a pinnacle of feeling that she had never before known, when the pleasure was well nigh unbearable, the tension snapped, and her body jerked with spasms of climatic sensation.

For a short space of time she lay spent and utterly relaxed beneath his warm body. Then he lifted himself from her, and the sound of their damp flesh parting made a strange, intimate sound.

He stood looking down at her, his teeth a pale Cheshire smile in the golden darkness of his face, his expression still mocking. Then, in what seemed an instant, he had dressed himself and was gone.

She lay there a while longer, suspended in a dreamy, half-waking state; and then the knowledge came. She realized what she had done, how she had acted. She sat up suddenly and awkwardly, and looked down at her naked body still wet with his sweat and hers. My God! What had happened to her?

Quickly, full of shame and fear, she gathered her clothing and ran up the stairs to her bedroom. She still could not believe what she had done. It could not have happened. As she drew her bath water and stepped into the tub, she could feel the beginning of a terrible headache. After her bath she would take some aspirins and lie down. Maybe she would feel better after a good nap.

"And when did you next see the boy, Dion?"

"The next time he came to work in the garden, two days later."

"And did anything occur between you?"

"Yes, the same thing as before."

"And did this happen often?"

"Yes, often, every time he came to the house."

"And how did you feel about this?"

"Guilty, terribly guilty!"

"And how did you handle your guilt?"

"I hid it away. I hid it away in the back of my mind."

"Is there anything else that you have hidden away there? Anything other than the intimacy with Dion?"

"Yes, the . . ."

"The what, Nina?

"The Contessa. The Contessa's house, and. . ."

"Don't be afraid, Nina. Let it come out. You will feel better as you tell me. What do you mean, 'the Contessa's house?' "

"The night of the masked ball, and the day that I found Martin . . . the day that I found Martin and Lily together."

"What happened, Nina? Tell me what you hid away in the back of your mind. Can you do that?"

"Yes, I can do that."

"All right then, begin with the occasion of the masked ball. Tell me what you did not tell me before. Where are you now?"

"I am in the hallway. I am looking for Melissa."

As Nina went from room to room, several times she was certain that she heard the calling of childish voices. As she opened one large, empty room, she saw a door on the opposite side of the room just closing and caught a brief burst of childish laughter; but when she reached the door, it led only into another empty room. She could find no one.

Feeling depressed and weary, Nina crossed the large room, then suddenly realized that she did not know which door led back to the hallway. Fear followed this realization, although there was no reason for it. There were several doors, one of which had to be the one which led to the hall; it was only a matter of opening them one by one. Still, the chill feeling persisted, and Nina hesitated before a heavily carved gold-leafed door with a red glass knob; afraid to stay, and afraid to open the door.

Taking a deep breath to help hold down her fear, Nina reached for the knob and turned it. The room on the other side was lighted by a dim, rosy glow, and the room itself, unlike most of the villa rooms, was small and cozy.

Full of wonder, Nina pushed open the door and went inside. The walls and windows were heavily draped with expensive fabrics, and the room was made to seem even smaller by many pieces of furniture and ornamental bric-a-brac. But it was the pictures—portraits really—that caught and held Nina's eye. They were everywhere, on the walls and in standing frames on the mantlepiece, and the many ornamental tables. All the portraits were of women—seemingly related, for the features were very similar—in various styles of dress, representing many generations.

They were all quite attractive, in a bold, strong-looking way; and Nina, who had always been fascinated by family albums, was intrigued by the different hair styles and modes of clothing. There was something hauntingly familiar about those faces. And then she knew. They all resembled the Contessa; must be, in fact, the Contessa's ancestors.

Nina peered at the pictures with new interest, intrigued by the family line that had spawned such a woman. Most of the portraits seemed to have been done when the sitters were somewhat younger than the Contessa was now, and Nina thought that most of them had sweeter, kinder expressions, or perhaps that was only due to the artist's interpretations.

Why, she wondered, were the male members of the line not imortalized in paint and film; or was there yet another room, where the male members of the family were gathered in separate but equal spendor?

Piqued by this idea, Nina, her mood somewhat lightened, turned toward the door on the other side of the room, but as she moved toward it, it swung inward, toward her, startling her and causing her to cry out.

Hand to her mouth, she watched as a male figure entered the room; a young man, clad in a toga and wearing a full mask. It was Dion!

He came toward her, moving fluidly as a dancer,

until the gleaming mask was close to her face, and she could smell the musky scent of his body. With one hand he removed the mask, and with the other pulled her close to him. His lips against her throat seemed to throb in rhythm with her own pulse, and a hot, sweet fullness gathered in her lower belly.

She gasped, and called Martin's name; but Dion's lips moved to silence hers, and the grinding need that his touch engendered—the blind, mindless sexual seeking—pervaded her being. She expressed no protest as he pulled her down upon the rug and pushed her costume away from her breasts.

"And the other incident, the one that occurred on the day you found Martin with Lily, tell me about that. You are there now, and you are going to tell me what is happening, starting with the information that you did not tell me before. All right, where are you now?"

"I am kneeling in front of the fireplace. Dion is on the floor; he is naked. The Contessa is standing before me. She is holding a silver cup toward me. Dion is holding my arms."

"Very well, go on."

She looked up to see the Contessa standing over her, holding out a heavily carved silver goblet. "Here, drink this, you look unwell."

Nina shook her head and clamped her lips together. The Contessa bent down, and the robe fell away from her body. Nina averted her eyes.

"Now, now, my little prude. I shan't poison you, if that is what you fear. You shall take your precious daughter home; however, I fear that you will not have the strength to do so, unless you get something into your stomach. Here now."

The Contessa extended the goblet, and Dion, lifting Nina's chin with one hand, squeezed her mouth open with his fingers. She felt the fluid, warm and spicy, flood into her mouth and down her throat, making its way to her belly, where it gathered heat, spreading and warming her whole body.

She felt Dion's arms release her, but his hand was still on her arm. Her head felt fumey, and her thought processes blurred.

Then the Contessa grasped her hand, and pulled her to her feet, where she stood unsteadily until Dion, laughing, sprang up to help support her.

"Now," the Contessa said, "I shall show you something. Something that will make you wonder. Something that will shake your mind. Come!"

Nina felt herself propelled forward by Dion's strong arms. She could feel his breath, hot and moist against her ear, and although his hands took liberties with her body, she was hardly aware of it. Her muscles felt incapable of holding up her body, or of moving under their own volition.

The Contessa, preceding them, switched on a light as they entered a small, heavily draped room.

Nina gazed with blurred eyes at the rich furnishings and ornate ornamentation. Slowly, recognition came to her. She had seen this room before, on the night of the masked ball, when she had wandered through the house in search of Melissa, and found Dion. There, around her on the walls and tables, were the pictures—the cryptic, hauntingly familiar pictures.

She gazed drowsily at the one nearest to hand, a smallish, silver-framed photograph in sepia tone, of a slender-necked, high-coiffed young woman in wasp-waisted turn-of-the-century garb.

"Do you find her pretty?" The Contessa's voice sounded far-away and soft. Nina nodded, unable to keep from telling the truth.

"And the others, do you find them pretty also? Beautiful, perhaps?"

Nina nodded again, vaguely wondering why the Contessa wished to know how she, Nina, felt about the Contessa's ancestors' portraits.

"Have you noticed anything unusual about these pictures, my child? Have you noticed the remarkable resemblance?"

"They—" Nina's voice felt rusty. She cleared her throat. "They all seem to be related." Then she voiced the thought that had originally come to her when she had first seen the room, "Why no men? Why only women?"

The Contessa's sharp laughter cracked like breaking glass, and Dion tightened his possessive arm around Nina's waist and pulled her closer to his body.

The Contessa's face swam into view before Nina's eyes, shutting out the room and its contents. "Because, my sweet innocent, these pictures are all of one person. Me. The Contessa de Fiore; although I have had other names, many other names, in many other places. Do you believe me?"

Nina nodded silently. Suddenly it seemed perfectly natural. Off course the women all looked alike. They were the same woman. Why hadn't she thought of that? But then a thought struck her. "But they can't be," she said as firmly as she could, considering that her tongue would not seem to function normally. "They're wearing old-fashioned clothes, and their hair is in old fashioned styles."

Suddenly, into Nina's mind came the picture of Melissa that they had taken at an amusement park, a picture for which Melissa had posed wearing old fashioned garments, and an enormous hat with an ostrich feather; a picture made in sepia tone so that it would look like those photographs taken in an earlier age. "Oh," she giggled. "You had them made that way. It's a joke." She giggled again.

The Contessa slowly shook her head. At such close range her eyes looked enormous and her mouth seemed a giant, red slash. "No, Nina, it is no joke."

She moved away, and Nina, grateful that those cold eyes were no longer looking into hers, sagged in

Dion's arms. He used this excuse to pull her closer still, and cup his hands under her breasts.

"Here!" The Contessa pointed to a large, gold-framed oil of a woman in a crimson ballgown of the eighteenth century. "When that portrait was painted, I was called Catarina. I was courtesan to a king, who saw to it that I was well looked after in all ways, including the financial. Look at it closely. See the eyes, the cheekbones, the mouth?"

Dion pushed Nina forward, and she looked up at the portrait, and then back to the Contessa. Yes, they were the same, the eyes, the cheekbones, the mouth; although the woman looked much younger than the Contessa, she indeed might have been her daughter.

"It looks like you, but much younger," said Nina, hoping to hurt the other woman.

The Contessa's lips thinned. "Indeed, I was younger then; younger by two hundred years!"

Nina heard the words, but her mind had difficulty in registering them. She shook her head. The Contessa lifted Nina's chin with her hand.

"Look! Look again, my little prude. Could members of a family look so alike? You wondered youself why there are no pictures of men. No, all of these pictures are of one woman, myself!" She looked at Nina triumphantly, and suddenly, through the mind-mist engendered by the potent drink, Nina felt the cold touch of primitive fear.

"No one . . ." she whispered, "no one could live so long!"

The Contessa's smile was as cold and hard as a diamond. "No one *normal* you were going to say, and you were right. No one normal could live so long; but then, whoever said I was that dreary thing, normal? I am descended directly from a line of women so powerful that you can have no appreciation of their abilities. My ancestresses have been sibyls and priestesses for centuries. Through the compiled power of their skills—handed down from generation to generation—I will live several hundred years more. However, even my powers are limited. I have lived long. I will live longer; but I do age. I will grow old. Still, there are ways, methods, for staving off the decay of the flesh. I have the power to draw upon youth; to borrow from young lives a few precious moments, days, weeks of youth to barricade my face and body against the ravages of time. The young, they do not miss a few hours here, a week or a month there; they suffer no appreciable loss, and to me the collected hours mean the difference between spending my years as an old woman, or a young and vital one. That is all I want from the children, just a little time. The rest is just an amusement, a *divertissement*."

Nina, her head beginning to clear from the effect of the drink, felt her mind draw back in superstitious terror. She swallowed, as if to force back the trembling weakness that possessed her.

"And Dion, what about Dion?" she whispered.

The Contessa smiled cruely. "Ah yes, Dion, the pretty boy, the bold young man. Dion is, in a sense, my creature. He is not human, you know, not even as human as I!"

Nina's flesh quivered where Dion's hands touched her.

"Dion is an elemental being, an incubus, some call it. He is, in fact, not even male—or at least not only that." She leaned toward Nina. "For you see, Dion is also Lily!"

Nina drew back, as if slapped.

The Contressa seemed amused. "Yes, my little prude, you and your husband have shared the same lover. You are shocked, yes? Dion is Lily, and Lily is Dion. Did you not wonder why you never saw them together?"

"Lily told me . . ." Nina began.

"Ah, yes. Lily told you of the aged grandmother. A fine story. But you see, such spirits are neither male nor female; or perhaps I should say they are *both* male and female, creating an appropriate body when they wish to have union with a human lover. Dion could have appeared to you in the form of a large, black dog, if he had wished, and if he had thought this would please you."

The Contessa turned away, then turned back to fix Nina with a dark gaze, sharp as a dagger. "These spirits have a flaw—as least as far as their usefulness is concerned. Like their human counterparts, they sometimes become enamored of one individual—finding such pleasure with this one that they bind themselves to them with ties that are almost as strong as human love. And, to my displeasure, Dion has done this. He has become attached to you, my little Puritan!"

Nina felt her spirit flinch. Everything she had ever thought, everything she had ever believed in, all her moral standards and ideals were tottering and falling. "What do you mean, Dion is your 'creature'?"

The Contessa waved a long-nailed hand toward Dion. "I mean that I called him out of the darkness—called him up, if you prefer. A *strega* must have her familiar, her pet; and Dion was, and is, mine. I sent him to you and your family to lure you, seduce you, bring you closer to me; so that I might put you to use as I desired. I particularly wanted the child; and yet, with the vagary of fate, Dion became attached to you. You, the cold, New England Puritan, whose cool exterior covered a molten center of passion that he could sniff out, like a dog!"

Nina cringed. Oh, God! Was she really hearing this?

"Now, my wanton Puritan, I will offer you a chance to have this passion, this pleasure that Dion offers you, for many years to come. Stay here. Live in my villa. Be my friend and confidante—for mine is a lonely life, despite its attractions. I can give you many years of youth and ecstasy that you will never find with any human partner. Dion will never age, never tire. Being inhuman, he has no human limitations. Since he has attached himself to you, he is of little use to me, and I will give him to you willingly in exchange for . . ." Her eyes stared deeply into Nina's eyes, and Nina felt dizzy and sick. "in exchange for the company of your family, and your daughter."

"My daughter?"

The Contessa nodded. "I am the last of my line. I am sterile. All of the knowledge and power of my lineage will die with me unless I pass it on. I would like to pass it on to Melissa."

"No!" Nina's throat felt raw with the cry. "No!"

"She would have great power, great importance. Her life would not be circumscribed by the human limits of life and death. Like me she can live for centuries. Would you deprive her of this?"

Nina, sick with shock and fear, struggled vainly to pull her thoughts together. Melissa and she were in the hands of the Contessa. Would an outright "no" bring death or worse to both of them?

"Let me think," she pleaded. "I can't think it out now. I feel sick. Please!"

The Contessa motioned to Dion, and reluctantly the young man released Nina and let her stand alone.

"I will give you seven days. In seven days you must come to me with your answer. And remember this, if your answer is no, I will still take the child. It will be more difficult, and there will be the embarrassment of legal search and pursuit, but I am prepared to endure this to obtain the child. Now, you may take your daughter, and go. But remember, I must have your answer in seven days!"

Nina stood alone and trembling. Could the Contessa do this, or was it a bluff? Could she take Melissa by force, kidnapping, whatever? Or was she trying to make Nina think that she, the Contessa, was more powerful than she was?

"It's all right, Nina. You are all right. Come back now. Come away from this scene. You will relax. You

will feel relaxed and at ease. I am going to awaken you now. I will count backwards from three. When I reach one, you will awaken. You will feel relaxed and in good spirits. You will remember everything that has happened while you were under hypnosis. Three, two, one!"

EIGHTEEN

Isaaic watched as Nina's eyes blinked, then opened. She smiled at Isaaic and Sidney. "I feel wonderful," she said, and then her expression changed. "How can I feel wonderful, after what I've just been through?"

"Because I told you to," said Sidney cheerfully. "Post-hypnotic suggestion."

She turned toward Sidney. "I feel so strange, so relaxed. It's as though some kind of tension has snapped."

"It has. You've just gotten rid of a very big load of fear and guilt that you've been keeping hidden, as you put it, in the back of your mind. It takes tremendous energy to cover an experience that deeply, and keep it covered. Now that it is out in the open, it can't hurt you any longer."

She shivered. "I don't know about that. You know, I remember it all, everything I said. I thought that a person always forgot everything that happened while they were under hypnosis."

"Not unless the hypnotist tells her to. You weren't really asleep, you know."

"But how could I have forgotten all that? How could I have just put it out of my mind?"

Sidney put his hand over hers. "Because it was simply too painful to face. Those headaches you had, they were a part of the process. If you will think back on it, you will see that the headaches always came after you had been with Dion, or at the Contessa's, didn't they?"

She flushed pink. "What must you both think of me! You must think I'm some kind of . . ." She turned her head away.

Isaaic took her other hand. "Nonsense! You mustn't undo Sidney's good work, fill yourself with guilt again. This thing, these events, are not your fault. You did not willingly harm anyone. You did not initiate these experiences."

She hung her head. "But I . . . I participated! I didn't stop him!"

Isaaic loosed her hand, and shook her gently by the shoulder. "Nonsense! In Dion, you were up against a specialist in his field, a being with perhaps a thousand years of experience in seduction. Do you think you could stand up against that? Perhaps you were a bit more vulnerable than most, because of your upbringing, because of your repressed sexuality; but believe me, there are few who could have withstood his siege, for he, or it, has a way of knowing just where all of us are vulnerable. So you must not torment yourself. You must simply face what happened, and in your own way, deal with it."

She blinked and swallowed. "Thank you, Isaaic. Thank you both. I think I'm strong enough to face this and pull myself together; but what do we do now? We know what happened, and in a sense, how, but he's still here. How do I get rid of him?"

"How do *we* get rid of him," said Isaaic. "You may have been the primary victim, but we are all involved now, and we will find a way. But first, we must figure out the rest of it. You did not see the Contessa again?"

She shook her head. "We were out of Italy before the seven days were up." She shivered. "Do you suppose that she sent him after me? Or, maybe after Melissa, to bring her back?"

Isaaic frowned. "I don't think so. From what you have told me, I should not think she had that much power, despite her threats. I believe that her statement that she would take your daughter by force was probably a ploy, that she needed your consent, else why should she have taken the time to woo you, to persuade you? No, I think that Dion came of his own volition. Traditionally, it is not unusual for an incubus to follow the object of his desire; and, as the Contessa admitted, he had formed a strong attachment for you.

"When he learned that you were leaving, he gave the marble chest to Melissa, knowing that *you* would not accept it. He might have been able to find you without it, but such a talisman could act as a beacon, something like a radio receiver sending out signals, thus making it much easier for him to follow your trail."

Sidney cleared his throat. "But why, when he got here, did he cause so much trouble? Why did he molest the other tenants in the building? That is, considering your hypothesis as valid."

Isaaic raised his eyebrows. "Very simple. Because he was angry."

"But why? Because Nina left Italy?"

"No, because Nina was no longer receptive to him. Although she had locked away the memory of all that had happened in her unconscious, that last scene with the Contessa must have frightened her so much that she had put up a wall against Dion, and he could no longer get through to her. Imagine his rage, after following her across the world, to find that she was closed to him."

Nina sighed deeply. "Thank God! I've been wondering whether or not I'd been . . . whether he and I . . ."

"No!" said Isaaic. "I'm sure you had no contact with Dion after you left Italy. If you had, he would not have been angry. But as it was, with you closed to him, he had to find other outlets, other ways to get through to you."

"And I wondered why I always felt so tired."

"You were fighting a continual battle. Also, if Dion had made contact with you, I'm sure it would have come out during this last session. Isn't that true, Sidney?"

"Yes. That's true. But assuming you're right, we're still left with the problem of getting rid of the incubus. Just what, Dr. Aschermann, my friend, do we do now?"

Isaaic put his fingertips together and looked at Sidney over the tops of his glasses. "And well you might ask, my young colleague. I should imagine that the only course open to us now would be exorcism of some kind."

"Exorcism?"

"Yes, exorcism. Bell, Book, and Candle; prayers; ritual against evil."

Sidney scratched his head. "Now look, Isaaic. Have you got any idea of how difficult it is to get the Catholic Church to agree to perform an exorcism? Why, the whole thing takes months, maybe years. First they have to examine the circumstances, to decide whether or not an exorcism is in order, then . . ."

Isaaic raised his hand. "Wait a minute there. Slow down. Who said anything about a *Catholic* exorcism?"

Sidney looked chagrined. "Well, as far as I know, the Catholics are the only ones who deal in such matters. I've never even heard of a Protestant exorcism."

Isaaic smiled. "My boy, there are rituals older than either the Protestant or the Catholic rituals. Nina, would you have any objection to a Jewish exorcism?"

"Of course not. If you think there's a chance it might work, I'll try anything."

Isaaic smiled slightly. "Well, I do have a copy of a Tartar exorcism, but it calls for at least one horse and a suit of princely clothing, and I really don't think it would be practicable."

Sidney laughed. "I have just one question. This demon of ours, this Dion, is either Roman or Greek in origin. Will a Jewish exorcism be effective against a nonJewish spirit?"

Isaaic made a temple of his fingertips. "First of all, who really knows the origin of a spirit? Just because Greek or Roman mythology had a name for a certain entity does not mean that this entity was not known by another name, in another culture. It is difficult for me to believe that spirits are ethnic or racial. I believe that spirits are simply spirits, and that each race and culture labels them in its own tongue. Any way, what about that picture—the one that caused such a sensation, where the girl was possessed by a demon? In that picture—which they tell me was based on fact—the girl was freed from the demon by a Catholic priest. And yet the demon, an ugly fellow, Pazuzu, I think it was, the demon of the south wind, is supposedly Babylonian in origin."

"That makes sense," Nina said. "It seems to me that if good has the power to abolish evil, this power should be universal."

"Exactly! Over many years of reading and studying, I have come to the conclusion that it does not matter which religious ceremony is used in an exorcism, for the ceremony is only a device, a ritual to focus the powers of the exorcist. What it comes down to is a fight between good and evil—or if you like, call it order and chaos.

"In this case, I don't believe that our spirit is evil by intent, merely by the nature of his being alien to us and to our frame of reference."

Nina got to her feet and began to pace back and forth nervously. "Do you think that will make it easier? For you, I mean?"

Isaaic gave his questioning shrug. "I can only hope so, although my studies have led me to believe that it is not always easy to exorcise an incubus. Some authorities say that this is *because* he is not evil in the accepted sense, as are other demons. On the other hand, there are many records of cases where incubi *have* been driven out. At any rate, we must try.

"I will use a Jewish ritual simply because I am Jewish. It will be easier for me to believe, easier for me to focus whatever power I have. And easier for me to draw upon the power of the supreme being, or beings. Now, we must get down to business. Sidney, can you get me some black candles? I'll need seven large ones. From Rabbi David I will obtain a *shofur*," he dipped his head toward Nina, "or ram's horn, and he will be able to provide me with a *loulaf*, or palm frond.

"We will meet here, Nina, at eight tonight."

"All right, Nina. I want you to relax as much as possible."

Nina half-lay back against the arm of the large sofa, with her legs stretched out in front of her.

"Now, Nina, I am going to turn off the lights, and light the candles. While I am doing this, I want you to call upon Dion, with your mind. Open yourself to him."

Nina stirred anxiously. "I hope I'm strong enough for this."

"You will be. You are stronger than you know. You have already proved that."

On the long coffee table in front of the couch lay the *shofar*, the *loulaf*, and two tall, black candles in brass holders. Other black candles, five in number, were placed strategically around the room, one of them above Isaaic's shoulder, on the mantlepiece.

Isaaic did not feel nervous, but looking down, he could see that his fingers were busily worrying the edges of the worn, leatherbound book he was holding. Consciously he stopped the movement, and smiled at Sidney and Nina reassuringly. He had to be strong, if the exorcism was to work. He *must* be strong, and he must be sure; sure enough to call upon the greater powers that he would need to do this thing.

In most respects, he knew, he filled the traditional requirements necessary for an exorcist. He was of mature age, humble, of blameless life, courageous of experience, and of well-attested prudence. He was a man of scholarship and learning, and well versed in the latest trends and developments of psychological science.

During the day he had prepared for the encounter by fasting and prayer. He was as ready as he would ever be. He took a belly-deep breath, and turned to Sidney.

"All right, Sidney, we might as well get on with it. Light the candles for me, and then retire to the other room. If I should need you, I will call. If I do not call, under no circumstances should you come into this room. No matter what you hear or see. Agreed?"

Sidney looked troubled. "Are you sure you don't want me to stay here with you?"

Isaaic shook his head. "No, it would be dangerous for you, and distracting for me. Thank you, my friend, but go."

Sidney moved forward and took the older man's hand. "I'll do as you ask, but I just want you to know that I think you're a hell of a fellow, Isaaic; and whatever happens . . . well, I'll keep my thoughts with you. If there's anything to all of this mumbo-jumbo, it can't hurt to have another mind working on your frequency . . . if you know what I mean."

"I know what you mean. And thank you."

Isaaic watched as Sidney lit the seven black candles, then turned off the room lights.

It took a moment for Isaaic's eyes to become used to the dim light. Nina, her eyes closed, her face illuminated by the flame from the candle on one end of the coffee table, looked pale and eerie, the light making shadow-pools of her eye sockets and nostrils, so that her face looked vaguely skull-like.

"Are you all right?" he whispered.

She opened her eyes and nodded slightly.

"Then we shall begin. You must call him. Keep your mind open. Call his name and his presence with your mind. We must have him here, if we are to exorcise him."

"I'm trying." Nina's voice was strained.

"I know it is hard, Nina. Think of him with desire. Think of being with him. He will come."

Nina moved her head against the cluster of small pillows and folded her hands beneath her breasts. Isaaic saw her bite her lower lip, take a deep breath, and then, seemingly, relax.

The room was very quiet. Isaaic could hear the wind rising outside, and the candle flames danced lightly in a sourceless draft.

At first he felt nothing, except perhaps that this whole thing might be a waste of time, a foolish fancy; and then he became aware of something, a pressure, a presence in the room.

The sensation of pressure grew, until Isaaic could feel it against his ears. He found it difficult to breathe; he was smothering, being crushed.

Fighting against the feeling, his eyes searched the room, looking for something, anything, that would indicate the presence of the incubus.

Eyes straining, he fought for breath. Nina moved slightly, and moaned, but she seemed generally unaffected by the pressure in the room. As Isaaic looked at her, he became aware that the darkness behind her was deeper than the darkness in the rest of the room. As he watched, this darkness thickened and drew in upon itself, condensing, coalescing into a form.

As this form grew clearer, the feeling of pressure lessened. Isaaic, his eyes fixed upon the spot where the darkness moved, experienced a feeling of elation. The incubus was coming! He was here!

Nina moaned again, and rolled her head from side to side. Isaaic's gaze moved to her face, and when he looked back at the dark form, a shock of pure awe and fear coursed through his body. For the form was a man now, a young man, beautiful and terrifying in the candlelight.

Smoothly, with the lightness of smoke, the figure moved around to stand by Nina's head.

Isaaic literally held his breath, as the boy leaned forward and pressed his lips to Nina's. The candlelight illuminated his strong cheekbones and thick, glossy hair, and danced down the musculature of one strong, brown arm.

For the duration of a heartbeat, Isaaic hesitated. It was unbelievable! The young man was as real, as solid, as Nina herself, and achingly beautiful.

For the duration of a heartbeat, Isaaic hesitated. It almost seemed a sacrilege to destroy something of such beauty. He had to remind himself that the beauty was only a construct, a form created by the spirit, and not the spirit itself; and that he would only be banishing, not destroying, the spirit that created the form.

Keeping his eyes upon the book in his hands, he lifted it nearer to the light, and slowly began to speak the words written upon the yellowed page before him:

"In the name of the forty-two letters of the God with long sight which has indeed no end, in the name of the lesser and greater celestial families . . ."

As Isaaic spoke the word "families" he was staggered by a blow to his right side. Confused, he looked down and saw at his feet a small bowl, which had been on a side table.

He looked toward the couch, where the incubus still bent over his mistress, but now the dark eyes were turned toward Isaaic, and as the young man's gaze met his own, Isaaic felt a shock that set him trembling. Trying to ignore his physical symptoms, he noted that the incubus's eyes were as clear and as unfathomable as a wild animal's; and then he felt the heat, waves of it, as if someone had opened a huge, oven door. A heavy scent accompanied the heat—the smell of over-ripe oranges, nauseating in its intensity.

Nina lay quietly, as if asleep, seemingly untroubled by the heat and smell.

With an effort of will, Isaaic tore his gaze from the incubus and looked down at his book.

"In the nane of the chiefs of the bodyguard: Uriel, Akatriel, and Usiel . . ."

As Isaaic pronounced the name "Uriel" the room came alive with flying objects. Isaaic threw up his arms to protect his face from a sharp crystal ashtray, and felt something heavy strike his back. A dull, roaring sound, such as he had heard the night before in the Girard bedroom, accompanied the phenomenon. Strangely enough, although the room was criss-crossed by flying objects, few of them struck Isaaic, and the candles—although their flames flickered perilously—remained upright, unharmed. Through this noise and confusion Isaaic could glimpse the figures of the incubus and Nina. Nina was still quiet as death; but the incubus was crouched now, and an expression of anger and fear turned his beautiful face into a frightening mask.

Greatly encouraged by the fact that the candles—symbols of power—remained inviolate, and that he himself was not really hurt, Isaaic, keeping one hand raised, continued to read:

"In the name of the potent Matateron, surrounded with strength . . ."

Abruptly the room quieted, as objects fell to the floor with dull thuds, the sound softened by the heavy carpet. Isaaic lowered his arm. The incubus was gone! There was only Nina, half reclining upon the couch.

He swallowed painfully—his throat was raw and dry. Could it be? Was it going to be this easy? Was the creature really gone?

He stood quietly for a moment as the candle flame

flickered gently, and the air in the room grew cool. Relaxing a bit, he tentatively opened his mind, reaching out with psychic fingers, attempting to sense the incubus's presence, or lack of it. He felt nothing. Nothing except the beginning of unease. Something was wrong, he was certain. It could not be over so quickly.

Nina gave a soft, mewling sigh, and lifted her head. "It's over, isn't it?" she asked softly. Her face looked golden in the candlelight, and her robe had slipped from one pale shoulder, half exposing one small, but well-formed breast.

Isaaic's feeling of unease grew. "I'm not certain," he said. "Please don't move."

Ignoring his request, Nina sat up, stretching, causing her robe to slip further away from her body. Then, in one sensuous movement she stood up. "Oh, don't be tiresome, Isaaic. You're too cautious. We can relax now. It's all over."

With measured steps she came toward him, around the coffee table, moving slowly and suggestively, her pelvis thrust forward. Isaaic felt the unease grow into fear.

"I shall have to thank you properly, Isaaic, for all you've done for me." She was very close now, and Isaaic stood frozen, his mind jammed like a faulty computer.

"You're not an old man, Isaaic. You're still young enough to know what a woman needs. I can make you happy, Isaaic. It's been a long time since you've had a woman, hasn't it, Isaaic? Do you remember how it was; how a woman's body felt against yours? I can bring it all back for you, Isaaic."

Her arms were reaching toward him, and Isaaic took a step backward. She smiled as he did so, and he knew that the incubus had won a small victory. Sweat beaded his brow as he felt the swelling of his genitals. Oh, yes, he remembered, and it had been far too long.

Nina's face, the expression gentle and yearning, looked up into his. The air felt thick in his throat, and a tremendous sexual longing filled him with a force that he had not known for years. His very body was turning into a traitor, even though his mind coolly told him that this could not be Nina, in her own mind, offering herself to him, but the incubus, inhabiting her body.

Limbs rigid, body burning, Isaaic turned his eyes back to the book:

"In the name of the potent Matateron, surrounded with strength, awe inspiring, vouchsafing salvation or damnation, I adjure thee, abject spirit, to reply to my words, and obey all my commands!"

As Isaaic spoke these words, the room grew very still with a pregnant silence that was worse, in a way, than the prior violence. He reached for the *shofar* with his right hand, trying to keep his eyes from the figure of Nina, who still stood before him.

And then he heard the sobbing. Low and heavy, as if her heart would break—was breaking. Sobbing that came from the very depths of a woman's being.

Slowly, holding the horn in his hand, he stood erect and looked at the woman before him.

It was not Nina. This woman—girl rather—was small and dark, with pale, translucent skin, and heavy, dark hair hanging in two plaits that reached to her waist. Her head was covered with a dark kerchief, and her clothing was of another time and place. Her body was slender, but ripely formed, with high breasts that rounded out the dark material of her dress.

She raised her head and looked at him with brimming, mournful, dark eyes of unusual size and brightness.

Isaaic literally felt his heart leap in his chest. The hand holding the *shofar* trembled. "Rebecca!" he whispered hoarsely. "Rebecca!"

She reached toward him with small, helpless looking hands, the hands of a child, with long, tapering fingers. Oh, how well he remembered those hands; remembered how they had once touched him with love.

"Isaaic! Oh, Isaaic! It has been so long. I thought you would never come for me."

Isaaic swallowed frantically. He could feel his pulse pounding frantically in his temples. Only the knowledge that Rebecca had died more than thirty years ago in Auschwitz prevented him from believing she was real.

As if reading his mind, she smiled, and wiped the tears from her pale cheeks. "I am real, Isaaic. As real as I ever was, and I am here, Isaaic. Don't make me go. Don't drive me away. You loved me once, Isaaic, and you love me still!

"We can be together, Isaaic, the way we never were in the past. I can come to you every night. I can come to you, and we can make love . . ." She began to unbutton the neck of her dress, and the sight of her smooth, white throat affected Isaaic as the sight of no other woman ever could.

She smiled shyly. "There has been no one else, Isaaic. I have saved myself for you. See, my body has not been spoiled."

She pulled the sides of her bodice apart, showing her pearly, pink-nippled breasts. Her flesh gleamed like fine ivory, against the dark dress material, and Isaaic's heart seemed about to beat its way out of his chest.

Frozen, unable to move, to stop her, Isaaic stared, as the girl he had once loved lifted the worn dress over her head and stepped out of it. Beneath, she wore only a coarse petticoat tied around her waist.

"You see, Isaaic, I am even prettier than you remembered. You never saw me like this, Isaaic. We did not have time, but we have time now, Isaaic. You will be able to touch me, to hold me. We can have all of the years that were taken away from us. I can give you all this, if you do not drive me away."

Panting and sweating, dizzy with his lust and remembered love, Isaaic swayed, staring at the girl's tender body. Beneath the pearly breasts, her body tapered quickly to a small, delicate waist, then flared out into rounded hips, and a slightly convex belly upon which a line of soft, dark hair was barely visible, making its way downward to the point where it met the secret of her sex.

Smiling tenderly, she untied the petticoat and let it fall. She reached toward him, slender arms glowing in the candlelight. "Come to me, Isaaic. Come to me!"

For the longest, most painful moment of his life, Isaaic struggled with himself, trembling in a nonexistent wind, tortured by desire and pity. Then, slowly, as if his head were a tremendous weight and his neck an iron rod, he bent his head, looked at the page before him, and grated out the word: *"Tekiah!"*

Awkwardly, he raised the *shofar* to his lips and blew. A clear but shaky blast came from the horn.

As the sound filled the room, the girl before him cried out like a soul in torment. He could not help but look at her, and could not help but cry out himself when he saw the wound between her breasts; the bright blood worming its way down her white stomach and abdomen. "Isaaic. Do not do this to me!" she cried in a voice of such terror and pain that Isaaic came near to swooning.

Again he lifted the horn. *"Teruah!"* he cried, then put the horn to his lips. Again the horn's sound shattered the silence of the room, and again the girl cried out.

Isaaic was breathing very rapidly now. He felt that unconsciousness was close upon and, and although he knew that he must finish this thing, he could not help but look again at the girl. A shudder ran through his body like a palsy. There was another wound now, above the left breast, over her heart; and the blood was pouring down over the ivory breasts, droping in dark drops to the rug. He suppressed a cry as her eyes, pleading, frightened, met his.

"Shevarim!" With what felt like his last breath, he blew three blasts upon the horn in rapid succession.

Falling back against the mantelpiece, he stared at the girl. His heart beat was erratic now, and a heavy pain was beginning just below his breastbone.

The figure of Rebecca was melting, changing. For a moment, the face of Dion, twisted with fear and fury, hung in a swirling matrix, which slowly resolved again into the figure of Rebecca. As Isaaic watched, she drew back, as a low, animal-like ululation poured from her open mouth. As she moved backward, she fell against the couch behind her, her body arching like a bow, while the terrible howl continued to flow from her in a river of sound.

Staggering slightly, Isaaic moved forward, and picked up the *loulaf* from the table. With what force he could muster, he began to strike the girl's recumbent form. With each blow, the girl's body twisted and jerked.

With tears streaming down his face, he whispered hoarsely the final words: "Rise up, O Lord, and let Thine enemies be scattered before Thee; as smoke is dispersed so let them be scattered. Oh, obstinate spirit, with the power of the Almighty God, I do with these words rend asunder every cord that binds you to this woman and this place!"

The girl's body began to jerk spastically, and a howling wind appeared out of nowhere to roar around the room like a living thing.

Isaaic felt the pressure blossoming in his chest, growing, pressing, like the opening of some huge, painful flower. He staggered back, pushed by the force of the wind. The book fell from his hands, and he clutched at his chest.

Through dimming eyes, he saw the girl's body rise from the couch, until it hung suspended at least a foot above the cushions, then fall back onto the couch, as another figure seemed to separate, split off, from hers. Made dizzy by the pain, Isaaic could see that the form upon the couch was now that of Nina Girard.

As another, even greater spasm of pain struck him, he whirled rapidly, losing his balance and grabbing at the mantlepiece for support. As he did so, his hand struck a gilt clock, which came crashing to the floor.

A high, sorrowful wail, like that of a lost child, echoed in the room, seeming to come from nowhere and everywhere. Isaaic, his hand slipping from the mantle, pitched forward onto his face, not even feeling the shock of his body striking the floor, opening his eyes just once to stare straight ahead. The last thing he saw was the broken clock face with the narrow black hands pointed straight up, as if they were praying.

There was light, very faint and far away. Gradually it grew, expanded, and then there was sound—the rattle of paper, the murmur of voices.

Isaaic came toward consciousness as a swimmer toward the surface of the water, slowly, hindered by pressure.

His eyelids flickered, then lifted. A pale oval, a face, blurred before his eyes, and he closed his eyes and tried to make some kind of order out of the data his senses were recording.

As he came nearer to the surface of consciousness, he became aware of the feel of crisp sheets, and the smell of rubbing alcohol.

Again, he opened his eyes and, this time, was able to focus on the space around him—a room, a hospital room, and beside him, her features slowly resolving out of the blur, was Halley.

His lips and throat felt terribly dry. He managed a small smile, and an abortive gesture toward the water bottle, which he could see on the stand beside his bed.

Halley's face lighted in a wide smile. "Thank God!" she said, quickly pouring him a glass of water, and inserting the flexible straw between his lips.

Gratefully he sucked the cool water into his throat. "How long. . . ?" His voice felt rusty and alien.

"Seven days. A week. You had a heart attack. We weren't sure you would make it." She bit her lip, and tears shone in her eyes.

"I'm a tough old buzzard. How is. . . ?" He hesitated, almost afraid to ask if all that he had gone through had been for nothing. "How is Nina, and her family?"

Halley pushed a vagrant lock of hair out of her eyes. Her face was worn and tired. She reached down and took his hand in both of hers.

"They're fine, Isaaic. All fine. Martin and Melissa are both home, and there has been no further sign of the incubus. The building is just as quiet and peaceful as it used to be. You *did* it, Isaaic. He's gone!"

He let out a long sigh, unaware that he had been holding his breath.

Halley squeezed his hand. "Nina has been helping me sit with you. So have the others—Steven, Ursula, and at night, Martin Girard. We're so grateful to you, Isaaic. We. . . well, we felt pretty guilty after Sidney found you on the floor like that. I mean, we thought you might die, and in a way, it would have been because of us."

Isaaic made an effort, and found that his fingers could still move. He squeezed her hand back. "Nonsense. I was doing it for myself too. There was no need to feel guilty. You say that there has been no further sign of our night visitor?"

She shook her head. "Absolutely none. You should feel like a hero!"

He turned his head against the pillow, remembering Rebecca's face as it faded into darkness and chaos, remembering the lonely, childlike cry. "I'm not certain quite how I feel," he said slowly. "In a way, I feel like a man who has been offered paradise and turned it down because of moral principles, not certain whether he made the correct decision."

She stared at him, her eyes very clear. "What do you mean, Isaaic?"

He closed his eyes. "Nothing, child; nothing. Just an old man's maunderings."

She shifted her hand on his. "Isaaic, what happened in that room? What was it like; can you tell me?"

He turned his head away. "No Halley. I can't tell you. I will never tell anyone. Just be content that it worked. All right?"

"Sure, of course, if that's what you want. Hey, I have some other news for you. I decided that I'm going ahead and having my baby. I've told Vince that I'm pregnant, and he's fantastically happy. I . . . I still don't know whether or not I made the right decision, but it's the only one I could make. We've put a down payment on a little place about twenty miles from the city, and we'll be moving at the end of the month. A kid should have a yard and grass to play on and, well, I really don't want to stay in the apartment, after all that's happened."

She squeezed his hand again. "I feel pretty good about it, except for leaving you. You've been just like family to me, and well, I'll really miss you." She leaned forward and kissed him gently upon the cheek. He could see that there were really tears in her eyes now. Her voice began to choke up. "You'll come and see us won't you? The doctor says that if you just follow a few simple rules you'll be fine—probably live forever. You'll be able to come and visit in no time."

He smiled at her, feeling his own eyes and nose beginning to congest. He would miss this girl, miss having her nearby; but he would keep in touch, would visit them, and would—it went without saying—keep an eye on the child that she was to bear. In the meantime, he would comfort himself with the fact that he had helped her; helped them all; and that he had been instrumental in saving Nina Girard from madness, or worse. Yes, he had done the right thing. Hadn't he?

As he closed his eyes, he could see Rebecca's pleading face against his eyelids.

DATELINE ROME, ITALY. A mysterious explosion last night virtually destroyed the beautiful Villa de Fiore, just outside of Rome. The villa was occupied by the Contessa de Fiore, her guests, and her servants; all of whom were believed to have been in residence when the explosion occured. The Contessa de Fiore was well known in the social circles of Rome, and her untimely demise has caused considerable shock among her many friends and acquaintances. The police report that as yet they have no evidence as to the cause of the explosion. The only information so far available is that the tragedy struck at exactly twelve o'clock, midnight, according to the testimony of Mrs. Elena Cardoni, who saw the flash and resulting fire from her window, while attending her sick child.

EPILOGUE

THE BARTOLOS

The Bartolos still manage the Barkley Plaza, and have successfully put the peculiar incidents that occurred there pretty much out of their minds.

Once in a while, Ursula Bartolo will have a bad dream, but she does not have it too often. The dream is always the same: she enters the Kauffman apartment, after a call from Mrs. Kauffman, to find the woman drenched in blood, vacant-eyed, and withdrawn, holding in her hand a blood-splattered statue, which still bears tufts of hair and brains.

Then, Ursula looks down upon the body of Ernest Kauffman on the floor. His pants are around his ankles, and the hairs on his legs are dark and gross-looking upon his dead, white flesh.

On the bed, above Kauffman's body, lies Helga, smiling in the face of horror and death, playing with her own body.

Here the dream speeds up, like a silent movie, as Ursula struggles, holding back her vomit, to arrange Mr. Kauffman's clothes, and to get Helga dressed and out of the room. This part of the dream goes on and on, until she wakes in a sweat, and turns for comfort into her husbands arms, with the knowledge that she did it all for the honor of the Barkley Plaza.

TRACY CUMMINGS AND ELVA MILLER

Tracy and Elva split up just about a month after Isaaic got out of the hospital, and Tracy moved out of the apartment. She is now engaged to marry a young man from her office and has given up all interest in, and practice of, the occult.

Already her lesbian interlude seems like something she imagined, and she seldom thinks of those months she spent at the Barkley Plaza.

Elva was very unhappy for a while after Tracy left, but she finally got over Tracy, and now has a new roommate, a young dancer from an off-Broadway ballet company. She will not discuss with anyone the unusual happenings at the Barkley, and although she is polite to Isaaic Aschermann if they chance to meet, she avoids him as much as possible.

THE KAUFFMANS

Getrude Kauffman is still in a mental institution. The doctors say that it is doubtful that she will ever be well enough to stand trial.

Helga Kauffman is in the care of a sheltered workshop, and is doing well within her limitations. She no longer exhibits the great preoccupation with sex, which marked her behavior during that period at the Barkley, and has adjusted well to her new environment.

She seems to have forgotten her mother and father, but late at night she will sometimes call out a name, which the medical attendants cannot make out, and search her small room with outstretched hands, as if she is looking for someone.

STEVEN STREET

Steven no longer has visions from which to draw inspiration for his paintings; but the experience in the Barkley has opened him up. He is continuing to paint, in the same bold style, subjects other than the sexual, and is having considerable success. He is seeing Wilma King regularly, and is still living in the Barkley.

HALLEY AND VINCE McGUIRE

Halley and Vince moved from the Barkley Plaza and are now living in a charming house on Long Island. Although Halley never mentions it, things have never been quite the same sexually between them. Despite the fact that it has been many months, she has not been entirely able to forget that strange afternoon, and the phantom lover who came to her.

She and Vince are very devoted to their six-month-old son, Daniel—named after Vince's father. He is a beautiful child, dark-haired and olive-skinned, like his father. At first Halley watched him closely for any signs of the unusual, but he seems a perfectly normal child, although slightly precocious, a trait Vince insists comes from his side of the family.

ISAAIC ASCHERMANN

Professor Aschermann is still at the Barkley Plaza. He says he is too old to change his residence, and there is no need for it now, for all is peaceful there once again.

He is well recovered from his heart attack and, considering his age, is in excellent condition.

He keeps in close touch with Halley and Vince McGuire, and was asked to be the godfather to their son, Daniel. He is very fond of the child, and takes a great interest in his development.

Only one thing mars his quiet existence at this time: he has again begun to dream of Rebecca—a thing he has not done for years.

THE GIRARDS

The Girards have moved to a house in New Jersey. Martin's job is going well, and he commutes to work in New York.

Nina, now able to face her own sexuality, has been able to put the past into its proper perspective. She has begun to have an interest in the occult, and when Martin asks her about the sprigs of herbs that she has hung over the windows, she tells him that it is an old custom, to freshen the air.

Melissa has outgrown some of her prettiness, but still shows signs of becoming a beauty when she grows up. She no longer seems to care about her "treasures" but has started collecting Shaun Cassidy records and flirting with boys.

Nina is learning to be less protective of her daughter, and their relationship is good. Nina sometimes wonders that her lovely child seems to be totally unmarked by what she experienced, while she, Nina, will bear the marks the rest of her life.